THE MARCELLA II

VAMPIRES AND GODS, BOOK ONE

Eva Pohler

Eva Pohler Books
20011 Park Ranch
San Antonio, Texas 78259
www.evapohler.com

Publisher's Note: This is a work of fiction. Names, characters, places, and incidents are a product of the author's imagination. Locales and public names are sometimes used for atmospheric purposes. Any resemblance to actual people, living or dead, or to businesses, companies, events, institutions, or locales is completely coincidental.

Book Layout ©2017 BookDesignTemplates.com

Book Cover Design by B Rose Designz

The Marcella II/ Eva Pohler. -- 1st ed.
Paperback ISBN 978-1-958390-48-1

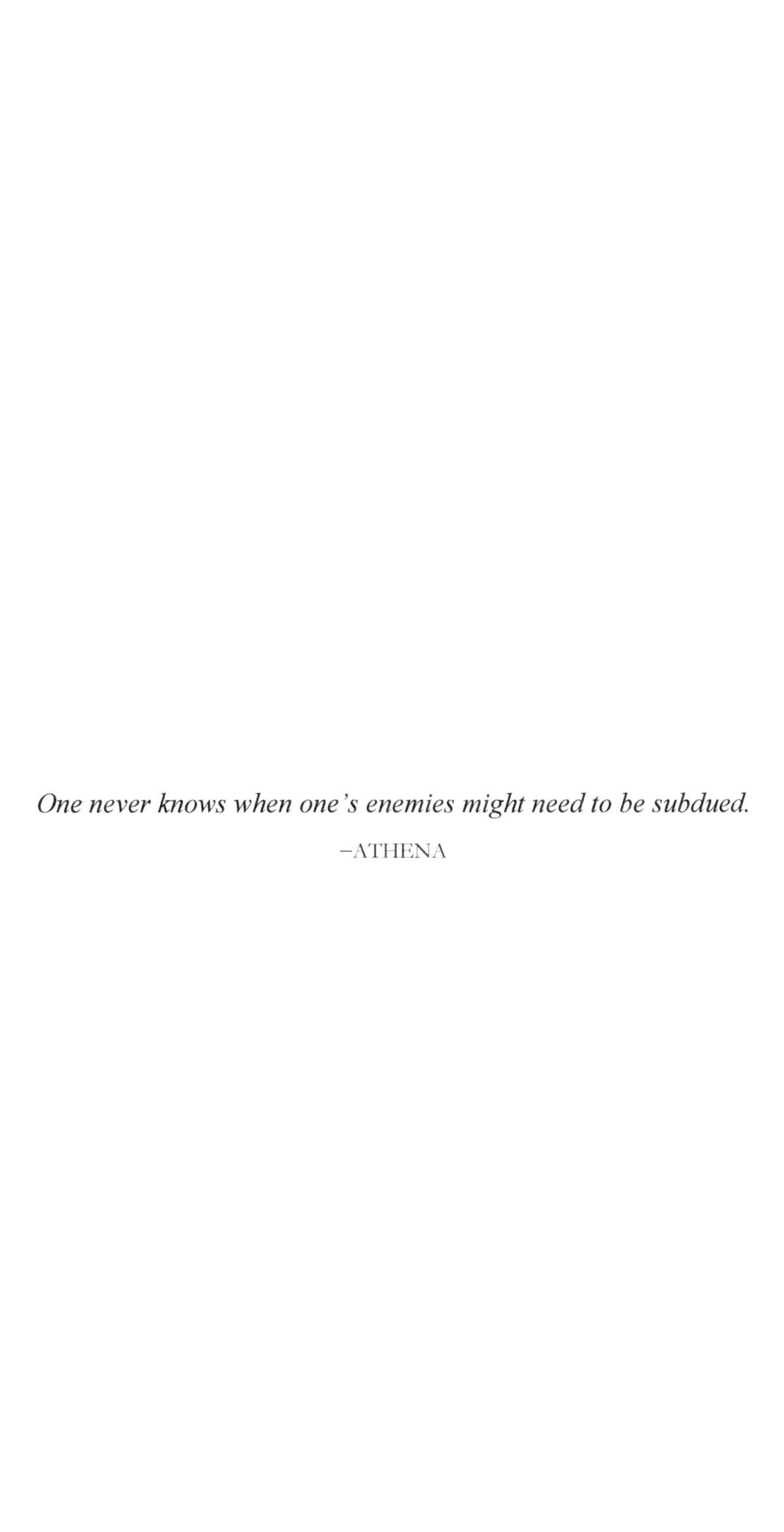

One never knows when one's enemies might need to be subdued.

—ATHENA

Contents

For my children.

CHAPTER ONE

A Rare Find

Hestie took a deep bite of the warm September air before she dove from the deck of the *Marvella II* into the Arabian Sea. She'd swum hundreds of feet on the heels of Poros when it dawned on her that she could breathe underwater.

"I'm a goddess," she reminded herself. "I'm the goddess of languages and international relations."

And, because she could, she said those words—though they were a mouthful—in seventy-five other languages as she descended.

Poros, son of Zeus and lord of the sky, led her down—nearly ten thousand feet toward the ocean floor.

Even though it had been four weeks since she and her brother, Hermie, had become the newest gods in the pantheon, she still hadn't grown used to the liberty of not having to wear a wet suit, diving gear, or mask. The weighted belt and flippers were the only accessories she and Poros needed, besides their swimming suits and the netted cross-body bags they wore to carry their finds.

They soon reached the uneven floor and picked through sand, rocks, and seashells. Unlike the last place they'd searched a few weeks ago, this place was desolate—not a living thing in sight.

After a while, Hestie approached a boulder the size of a Volkswagen Beetle. Poros swam up behind her just as she gave it a shove, revealing the mouth of a cave.

Did you know about this? she asked him telepathically.

Poros shook his head. His hair swished in the water like the short tentacles of a yellow sea anemone. *I've never searched this spot before.*

Together they peered into the darkness. Hestie was glad for the benefit of god-sight, which enabled her to see without a dot of light.

Within a few feet of the opening, the cave veered sharply to the left. It was impossible to know where it led or what it contained without entering it.

Should we go for it? Hestie asked.

We should stay on task. Jinsoo and Captain will be here any minute and will wonder where we've gone.

She rolled her eyes. Sometimes Poros could be too much like her brother.

You stay, she said. *I'm going in.*

Her job was to look for treasure, not to explore caves, and it was unlikely that any of the treasure from the *Camille*—a ship of Prometheus's which had sunk in the Arabian Sea in the 1970's—would have made it past the giant boulder and into this small cave. Nevertheless, she swam inside to have a look around.

She wasn't surprised when Poros followed.

The opening was only a few feet in diameter. Hestie propelled herself through the tunnel by pulling on the rocky floor beneath her. This helped her to avoid scraping her back along the top of the cave as it veered right.

Bracing herself for what might be waiting just around the bend, Hestie expected to find an eel, octopus, or other sea creature hiding in the crevices of the rock, but, as she veered left and right again, she found the cave to be as desolate as the rest of the area.

It came to a dead-end in a chamber not much bigger than her bathroom on the *Marcella II*.

This would make a great hiding place, she said to Poros.

For lovers? he asked with his brows lifted.

She smirked. *For treasure.*

She swam into his arms and gave him a kiss. It wasn't easy to do underwater, but, when he cupped her cheeks and kissed her again, she tightened the embrace and enjoyed the feel of his warm body against hers.

We better go look for Jinsoo and Captain, he said.

Mood killer.

Poros laughed.

As she was about to follow him from the cave, she noticed a small wooden box—no bigger than a shoe—tucked into a crevice.

What's this? she said.

She pulled it free.

Poros returned to her side as she opened it.

She gasped, nearly choking on the sudden intake of water.

The box was filled with gold coins.

Hermie sat beside Mina on the flybridge of the *Marcella II* and grinned at the look she was giving him.

"Let's just try it," he said. "If we ruin Jinsoo's kimchi, Captain will have no choice but to take us to shore for more food. And you know what that means."

She arched a brow. "Mr. Burger?"

"Or its equivalent," he said.

"I don't know. Captain might make us starve."

"He wouldn't."

"I thought you don't need as much food, now that you a god," she said in her broken English.

Hermie sighed. "I may not need it, but a burger sure sounds good. Doesn't it? Besides, I think that kimchi is expired."

"Kimchi don't expire for a long, long time."

Hermie cocked his head to the side. "I think that's more of an ideology than a fact."

Chidori chirped, "Hilarious! Hilarious!" from where she perched on the helm.

Mina giggled, even though, being mortal, she couldn't understand the language of animals. To her, the yellow canary's sounds were nothing more than tweets.

"In orphanage, one batch of kimchi last two month," Mina said.

"You're used to it," he said. "But I'm used to hamburgers and French fries and nachos and just about anything that isn't kimchi."

Mina climbed to her feet. "Okay. Let's do it."

"Really?" Hermie hadn't thought she would agree, and, now that she had, he was having second thoughts. He didn't want to make Prometheus angry. "I don't know. Maybe it's not such a good idea."

She sank back into her chair. "No. It bad idea. Captain will be mad. He don't like waste."

"You're right," Hermie said. "How long do you think they'll be gone?"

"Two hour. Three hour." She shrugged.

"That long?"

"Why? You want to watch *Naruto*?"

"We've seen every episode."

"So?"

"Not again!" Chidori chirped.

Hermie said to Mina, "You could have gone with the others."

"I want to stay with you!"

Becoming a god hadn't changed his dislike of swimming. He'd rather avoid encounters with slimy, creepy, and sharp-toothed creatures if there were other people willing to dive in his place. He was the god of technology, after all, and he preferred to be in front of a computer screen than almost anywhere else.

He gave Mina a once-over. She looked cute in her skimpy bathing suit with her black hair tied in pigtails. She had claimed to be working on her tan, but he sensed she enjoyed showing off.

"You want to play a game?" she asked. "I can get Jinsoo's *Yu-Gi-Oh* cards. Or we could play *Urban Fighter.*"

He had a better idea but was too shy to say it.

"You want to kiss me?" she asked.

He laughed. "You read my mind. Want to sit on my lap?"

"Oooh. In Captain's chair? That funny. We make out in Captain's chair."

"Chidori, why don't you keep watch for Jinsoo and the others on the lower deck?"

"Fine," she chirped before flying away.

Hermie folded Mina onto his lap and pressed his lips to hers.

"You taste like kimchi," he said with a frown.

"Oh, stop saying kimchi and kiss me."

Unable to get past the sour taste in her mouth, he moved his lips to her neck.

"I like that," she said.

He chuckled. Every time they made out, Mina gave him a play-by-play of her feelings.

"That spot there," she said when he kissed her shoulder. "You make me crazy, Hermie!"

"But you're glad I brought you back from the dead?" he teased.

"Not again!" she said, chuckling. "How many time you want me to thank you?"

"I'm sorry. Never again."

"You said that yesterday!"

The sound of fluttering wings too large to be Chidori's made Hermie lift his head in time to see a gray owl land on the center mast.

He cleared his throat before saying, "Hello, Athena."

The owl flew from the mast to the bridge and morphed into the goddess of wisdom, her long black hair blowing away from her face as she turned her bright gray eyes on him.

"Sorry to interrupt," she said with a smile. "I have something for Poros."

She didn't look very sorry to Hermie as Mina jumped from his lap and returned to her own seat.

"He's not here," Hermie said of Athena's brother. "He's out diving."

"Is Prometheus diving, too?" Athena asked.

Hermie smiled. It wasn't the first time Athena had used her brother as an excuse to see Prometheus.

Mina nodded. "With Jinsoo. They be back in two hour or so."

"They're here! They're here!" Chidori chirped.

Just then, Prometheus emerged from the sea near the lower deck at the back of the boat, his dark curly hair and beard flattened by the water, until he shook it out like a dog, and the curls returned. Three other heads popped up with him.

Mina jumped to her feet. "They back already? That was fast!"

Athena flew to the lower deck to meet the divers. Hermie and Mina followed on foot.

"We found something!" Hestie cried as she climbed aboard.

"Oh, hi, Athena," Poros said, as he flew from the water to the lower deck.

"Hey, little brother."

Prometheus followed. "Hello, Athena. Welcome aboard."

As soon as Jinsoo climbed from the water and onto the deck, Chidori perched onto his shoulder.

Jinsoo grinned. "Hi, Chidori! Miss me?"

Chidori gave him a playful tweet.

"What did you find?" Athena asked.

Hestie took a small box from her bag and opened it.

Hermie and the others huddled close to get a view of its contents.

"Are we rich?" Mina asked.

"Those are ancient Persian darics," Athena said.

Prometheus took one from the box and turned it over in his hand. "That's exactly right. And each coin is worth over three thousand euros."

"How many coins are in there?" Jinsoo asked. "Fifty? A hundred?"

"Let's count and find out," Hestie suggested as Prometheus returned the coin to the box.

They followed Hestie up to the salon and into a u-shaped booth with windows overlooking the main deck on the bow. The teens sat around the table to help her count. Chidori remained on Jinsoo's shoulder, as usual.

While the others counted, Hermie listened to Prometheus and Athena, who were speaking together in the food prep space by the refrigerator—what to the other members of the crew was the *galley* but would always be a *kitchen* to Hermie.

"What brings you here?" Prometheus asked. "Not that you need an excuse for a visit."

"I found something else of my father's that I want Poros to have." Athena opened her palms to reveal a pair of what looked like silver cuffs. "I thought he might like these."

"Indeed." Prometheus took one of the cuffs and turned it over in his hand. "Fine white gold, is it?"

Athena shook her head. "It's adamantine. The strongest element there is—the only one that gods can't break."

"I've seen these cuffs before—on my own wrists, I believe."

"My father warded them, to prevent the wearer from conjuring weapons or from…"

"God travel. Yes, I know. Did you find his adamantine chains as well?" Prometheus asked with a frown. "The ones he used to chain me to a rock as his eagle ate my liver each day?"

"I kept those for myself, along with two other sets of cuffs just like these," she said.

"I don't think Poros will find them of any value—except sentimental, perhaps."

Athena furrowed her brows. "One never knows when one's enemies might need to be subdued."

"Your brother has no enemies."

"Don't be naïve," Athena said.

When Prometheus glanced his way, Hermie averted his eyes, back to the table and to the coin counting.

But Hermie listened as Athena added, "He's the lord of the sky and the most powerful of the Olympians. You don't think that warrants him a few enemies, especially now, while we're adjusting to the new order?"

Before Prometheus could reply, Hestie and the other teens cried out, "Sixty-seven!"

"How much is that worth, Captain?" Hestie asked.

Prometheus stepped out from behind a counter to give the coins a closer look. "I know a collector on the island of Malta who would give us a half a million euros for these coins."

"Wow!" Jinsoo cried. "That a lot, right?"

"Right," Poros said with a laugh.

"Wait a minute," Mina said. "If you are gods, why can't you *make* money? Why you dive for treasure and sell it?"

"I'm pretty sure Captain has already answered that question," Hermie said.

"Not for Mina and Jinsoo, I haven't," Prometheus said. "You see, Mina, if I create money out of nothing, the value of all money goes down."

"It's called inflation," Hermie added.

"So?" Mina said. "Who cares? More money is more money!"

"Would you rather have a hundred silver US dollars or a hundred pennies?" Hermie asked her.

"Dollars, of course!" Mina said.

"If gods make more money out of nothing, then the dollars will become pennies. They won't be worth dollars anymore. All money will go down in value."

"Oh!" she said. "I see! I see!"

"These coins will buy a lot of medical supplies and technology for communities in need," Prometheus said. "Good work, Hestie."

Hestie beamed.

"When you make me and Mina gods, Poros?" Jinsoo asked in his broken English. "It not fair, you know? My sister and I work so hard. Everything easy for you."

"Remember what I said?" Poros asked. "If you still want to become immortal on your fifteenth birthday, I'll do it then."

"That three more months," Jinsoo said.

"It's a big decision," Prometheus added.

"Are you sure that's a good idea?" Athena asked her brother. "You can't keep turning mortals into gods, Poros. There's a balance that must be maintained, and there are existing gods who will feel threatened when it's upset."

Poros's cheeks turned red. Hermie felt the blood rush to his own cheeks, too. Did Athena resent Poros for turning Hermie and Hestie into gods?

"Just these two," Poros said of Mina and Jinsoo. "No more after that. We couldn't have won against Zeus without them."

"They've got a point," Prometheus agreed.

"I suppose you can take it up with the council," Athena said. "You'll need the support of other gods to make it happen."

Poros shrugged.

"So, now what?" Athena asked. "Is the *Marcella II* heading for Malta?"

"Indeed, it is!" Prometheus smiled from ear to ear. Then he said, "Poros, pull up the anchor!"

"Yes, Captain!" Poros left for the lower deck.

"Mina and Jinsoo, prepare to hoist the mains!" Prometheus cried.

"On it, Captain!" Mina said as she followed her brother to the main deck.

"Hermie and Hestie, coil and stow the lines!"

"Yes, Captain!" Hestie said with a chuckle as she and Hermie followed the others.

As the teens prepared to sail, Prometheus and Athena flew to the flybridge.

Once they were travel-ready, Prometheus cried, "To Malta!"

CHAPTER TWO

The Best Laid Plans

High school was nothing compared to this," Gertie said to her best friend, Nikita, over coffee at the student center at the Athens Conservatoire.

"Tell me about it," Nikita said before taking a sip of her latte.

"At least you've had some *success*," Gertie pointed out. "Who gets cast in a musical during their first year? Nikita Angelis, ladies and gentlemen!"

"Oh, stop. It was beginner's luck. I *look* the part: dark hair, dark eyes, small, female."

"I think you just described over thirty percent of the student body."

"It's not a big part," Nikita said.

"Well, I'm flunking photography. Who flunks *photography*?" In a muttered voice she said, "Gertrude Morgan, ladies and gentlemen."

"You aren't flunking. It's only our third week. Quit being so dramatic."

"Maybe I should have auditioned for the musical," Gertie said.

They both laughed.

"Maybe not," Nikita said in between giggles.

"Seriously," Gertie said. "I don't think I can do this. I can't produce on demand. I can only do it when the muse strikes me. All these assignments and deadlines—they're ruining my mojo."

"Don't give up so soon. You just started. You'll get your groove."

Gertie took a sip of her latte. "I don't know. I was such a good student when it came to memorizing facts. Maybe I should go back to my plan of becoming a librarian."

"That wouldn't be the worst thing, since you love books."

"True. I think I would love it, actually."

Nikita's phone, which was sitting beside her cup on the table, vibrated.

"It's Lajos. Hold on." Into the phone, Nikita said, "Hey, babe!" After a beat, she frowned. "Oh, no. Okay. I'll tell her. Keep me posted, and I'll do the same."

"What's wrong?" Gertie asked.

"It's Hector. He got kicked out of the police academy and took off in his car. He wouldn't tell Klaus or Lajos where he was going. Lajos said he didn't go home."

"Oh, no." She called his number. When Hector's recorded voice played on her phone, she said, "It went straight to voice mail."

Gertie had known that Hector was struggling in the academy. They'd commiserated in the evenings together over their shortcomings in their respective fields. She'd pointed out that, as the son of Hephaestus, Hector should consider a craft. Or, since his mother was a daughter of Apollo, maybe he should go into medicine. Gertie suspected that Hector had chosen the police academy because that's what Klaus and Lajos were doing.

Maybe she had chosen the conservatoire for the same reason: to be with her friend.

She really *would* rather be a librarian. What was she doing at the Athens Conservatoire?

Gertie sent Hector a text: *Please call.*

"Do you have any idea where he might have gone?" Nikita asked her.

"Yes," Gertie said. "Let's go."

Gertie drove her new Porsche—a high school graduation gift from her parents—across town toward the acropolis. She didn't go to the acropolis proper, but along another road that led to her favorite bookstore.

"Hector's not much of a reader," Nikita said as Gertie parked the car. "Why would he come here?"

"He wouldn't." Gertie climbed from her seat. "Come on."

"Are we going to the Music Factory?"

"No. Hephaestus's Temple."

"Ah, yes. That makes sense."

The two friends hurried along the road uphill to where Hector sat on a ledge overlooking the ruins of the ancient agora—what was once the town square of Athens.

"Hey," he said as they reached him.

"Hey," the girls replied as they sat on either side of him.

"You didn't answer your phone," Gertie said.

"It died. My car charger doesn't work."

"Oh," Gertie said.

Hector glanced at Nikita. "I guess you heard."

Nikita nodded. "I'm sorry."

Gertie took his hand. "Are you okay?"

"I screwed up. I can't believe I screwed up so badly."

"What happened?" Nikita asked. "You should have been at the top of your class."

"You're right. I thought I had it in the bag. I guess I should have tried harder."

"Can't you talk to your captain?" Gertie asked.

"I did. I begged him to give me another chance."

"What did he say?" Nikita asked.

"I can try again next year."

"Oh, well, that's not so bad, then," Nikita said.

"I'd rather not waste a whole year," he said. "I've been a warrior for this city since I was twelve years old. I'm stronger and faster than any other demigod in Athens. How could I have let this happen? My mom's probably turning over in her grave."

"She's in the Elysian Fields," Gertie said.

Hector shrugged. "It's just an expression."

"It was a hard lesson," Nikita said. "But you've learned it. Now quit being a baby and move on. Where do you go from here?"

Hector shrugged again. "That's why I came up here. I was hoping for some inspiration from my father."

Gertie squeezed Hector's hand and closed her eyes to pray to any god who would listen.

They sat together in silence for many minutes as the sun prepared to set. Gertie wondered if Helios could see them sitting there, looking up at him.

Their silence was broken by a howl in the distance. On closer inspection, Gertie noticed a golden wolf bounding toward them through the ruins in the ancient agora.

Hector jumped to his feet. "Is that Apollo?"

Gertie and Nikita stood up beside Hector.

"I think so," Gertie said.

Twenty meters below them, the wolf came to a halt and transformed into a beautiful god with light brown hair—just a shade darker than Hector's and Gertie's but lighter than Nikita's—and emerald eyes that sparkled in the afternoon sunlight. He wore a quiver full of silver arrows and a bow across his back.

"I've had a vision," Apollo said. "Soon you'll be called to sea for an important cause. Be ready, Hector and Gertrude."

Then the god returned to his wolf form and barreled away.

That evening, the teens met up at Hector's house, as usual.

"Are you sure you want to do this?" Hector asked Gertie, where they sat around on couches in the living room.

Gertie held the last bottle of wine she had from Dionysus. Any wine would increase her powers, but the wine from her father gave her the special power of foresight.

"If Apollo took the trouble to tell us about his vision, it must be important," she said just before she took three gulps of the wine.

Within seconds, the room spun, and Gertie fell back against the couch cushions. Then everything around her became as black as pitch, except for one tiny spot of light across the room. She stared at the light, her entire body trembling. Her ears filled with the buzzing of bees.

As the light moved closer to her, it expanded, blocking out everything else in the room. She saw herself floating near the ceiling. Someone with long, coarse, dark curly hair was leaning over her. Gertie felt a sting at her throat before she was awash with euphoria. She watched herself across the room, floating near the ceiling, as the curly-haired person turned to look at Gertie where she lay across the couch cushions.

The curly-haired person was a girl—a vampire—with fangs dripping with Gertie's blood.

Gertie gasped.

The vision left her and was replaced by the worried faces of her friends.

"Are you okay?" Hector asked.

Gertie blinked. "Um, yeah. I think so."

"Did you see anything?" Klaus, Nikita's older brother, asked.

"Yes. I saw a vampire drinking my blood."

Gertie noticed Klaus shiver.

"I haven't seen a vampire since the uprising," Nikita said. "Aren't they serving Hades as reapers or something?"

Lajos nodded. "Most are, I think. Not all. Not all wanted that lifestyle."

"Which makes no sense," Klaus said. "They're guaranteed blood from a fresh corpse just before they deliver the soul to Charon. What vampire wouldn't want that? It's better than living in caves and tricking unsuspecting mortals, like in the old days."

"Or preying on mortals who become addicted to their powers," Nikita added.

Gertie felt the blood leave her face. That had been her just over a year ago. She'd loved the feeling that the vampire virus gave her during the six hours it was in her system after being bitten. She'd been addicted to the powers of flight, invisibility, strength, and mind control. Specifically, she'd been addicted to Jeno, though, at the time, she thought it was love.

She still wondered if it might have been both.

"We all agreed that forced servitude would be wrong," Hector reminded them. "So, naturally, a few outliers will go their own way. There's still at least a dozen vampires who hang out in the streets of downtown Athens at night and sleep in caves beneath the acropolis during the day."

Gertie shivered at memories of Jeno and his sister, Calandra.

Nikita leaned closer to Gertie. "Do you think your vision is related to Apollo's?"

"I don't know," she said.

"You saw nothing related to the sea?" Klaus asked.

Gertie shook her head.

Nikita turned to Lajos. "Hey, babe. Do you think your mom might know anything?"

"I suppose it's possible," Lajos said. "I'm supposed to visit her next month, but I could go sooner."

"That would be great," Nikita said. "Can we all go? All five of us?"

A few days later, on Saturday afternoon, Gertie drove her friends from Athens to Parga. Along the way, she told them bits and pieces she had learned about Alecto since the last time she had seen her.

"According to Hesiod," Gertie said to her friends from behind the wheel, "Alecto is a fan of snakes. So, I thought she might enjoy this pair of earrings I found at a boutique near the acropolis."

"Cool!" Nikita said.

"That was nice of you," Lajos said. "But I can tell you what you want to know about my mother. You don't have to conduct research."

"Do you know me at all?" Gertie said with a laugh.

"Obviously not," Hector said from the passenger's seat. "Let her do her research. She gets irritable if she can't be the expert in all things."

Gertie punched Hector playfully on the shoulder. "Not true."

"Yeah, right," Nikita said laughing.

"Are you guys saying I'm a know-it-all?" Gertie asked.

"Your words, not mine," Hector said before he kissed her cheek.

They stopped for dinner around five o'clock in Agrinio and arrived at dusk at the marina, where they rented a boat.

This was the first time Gertie had returned since her friend Jeno had died. As they reached the end of the dock, where their rental was waiting, she wiped a tear from her cheek.

"You okay?" Hector asked as he helped her onto the boat.

She nodded and sat on the bench behind the captain's chair. Nikita sat between her and Lajos. Klaus took the swivel seat at the front of the boat, and Hector, who had the most experience operating boats, took the captain's chair, where he brought the engine to life.

"This is supposed to be a fun adventure," Nikita said beside her. "Lighten up."

Gertie shrugged. "I don't have a good feeling about this."

It took them half an hour to reach the place where the Acheron met the Cocytus River near the ruins of the Necromanteion—an ancient temple devoted to Hades and Persephone. Darkness had fallen, along with a chill that made Gertie shiver as they docked the boat and climbed ashore. Using the flashlight app on their phones to guide them, the five teens followed the lonely path to the ruins.

Lajos, whose vibrant red hair seemed brighter in the moonlight, led them to an underground tunnel. Below them was an uneven path, but above them were beautiful stone arches evenly spaced like something one would find in an ancient castle. They followed the tunnel until it came to a cave glistening with moonlight that shone through cracks above them onto a pool of water at their feet.

They stopped at the edge of the pool.

"I'll call my mom," Lajos said as he closed his eyes and lifted his palms.

Gertie and Nikita exchanged glances. Gertie knew Nikita was nervous, as she should be. Alecto the Unceasing was a terrifying Fury who punished the souls of evildoers in Tartarus. They'd met Lajos's mother a year ago during the vampire uprising. The meeting hadn't been long, but it had been long enough. Gertie wondered if Lajos planned to introduce Nikita as his girlfriend.

"Here," Gertie said as she handed the earrings to Nikita. "You should give them to her."

"Thanks." Nikita forced a smile, though she was clearly scared to death.

From across the pool, a set of twinkling lights, like fireflies, appeared and floated toward them. Once they were less than twenty feet away, the goddess appeared. Her golden eyes were fierce, and her red hair was spiked. Her face was pale and beautiful, like an artfully chiseled statue. A thick snake curled around her neck, poised to strike.

Gertie wondered where her wings were. The last time Alecto had appeared to them, she'd worn pale green wings, shaped like the wings of a bat.

"Mother," Lajos said. "Thank you for coming."

"I'm glad to see you, Lajos," the Fury said. "But I'm alarmed. You're early. Is something wrong?"

"Apollo appeared to Gertie, Hector, and Nikita," Lajos said. "You met them last year, remember?"

"Indeed," the goddess said.

Gertie wasn't sure if she should say hello or keep quiet, so she gave the goddess a nod as Lajos continued.

"Apollo said that he'd had a vision in which Hector and Gertie were called to sea for an important mission. Do you know anything about this?"

"No, I'm afraid not. I can ask around. Hecate might know. She has visions, too."

Gertie sighed, hiding her disappointment.

"Thank you," Lajos said.

The Fury moved closer and put a hand on her son's shoulder. "It's so good to see you. I worry about you, with your father gone. Would you be terribly frightened if I came to visit you now and then?"

"Frightened? I'd be happy, Mother. I'm always happy to see you." Lajos kissed her cheek.

The goddess smiled at Lajos and then turned to Hector. "Thank you for being a friend and for inviting him to share your home."

Hector bowed as he said, "It's my pleasure, goddess."

Then she turned to Nikita. "And you, my dear."

Nikita gave the Fury a hopeful smile.

"If you break my son's heart, I'll break your neck."

Nikita's mouth and eyes became wide.

Then Alecto laughed. It sounded like a cackle. "I'm only joking."

Gertie chuckled but Nikita's face remained pale.

"For you, goddess," Nikita said as she held out the earrings.

"How beautiful. Thank you." Alecto took the gift and turned to his son. "Are you still enjoying the police academy?"

"I love it. It feels like it's what I was meant to do."

Gertie wanted to give Hector's hand a reassuring squeeze but thought her pity would make him feel worse, so she didn't.

"I'm glad to hear that," Alecto said. "You'll make a fine officer."

"How are things in Tartarus?" Lajos asked.

"Busy." Alecto laughed.

Gertie and her friends laughed, too.

"Do more people end up there than in the Elysian Fields?" Nikita asked.

"No, but many people start there," Alecto said. "Before they move on to the fields, they need to be purged of their guilt and regret."

"Does that take a long time?" Klaus asked.

"More for some than others," Alecto said with a grin.

Then Klaus said, "Would it be possible for us to see the form you take in Tartarus?"

"Be careful what you ask for," Alecto said.

"Please?" Gertie asked.

Alecto combed her fingers through her spiky, red hair. "I'd hate to make my son afraid of me."

"That would never happen," Lajos said.

"Okay, then," Alecto said. "You asked for it."

Her spiky hair transformed into dozens of red snakes, with red eyes, fangs, and slithering tongues. Alecto's eyes were equally red, with blood dripping from them. Green wings, as thin as paper, emerged from her back. Each wing had a green claw on its tip. Her hands also became claws, and when she opened her mouth, it was filled with sharp teeth.

Gertie and her friends took several steps back from the horrifying sight. It was only a few seconds before Alecto returned to her beautiful form, but it had been long enough to leave a lasting feeling of terror in Gertie's chest. From the expressions on her friends' faces, she suspected they felt the same.

Even Lajos was no longer smiling.

"I warned you," Alecto said. "But don't forget how important my work is. People who do bad things would never find peace if it weren't for me and my sisters."

"I know that, Mom," Lajos said. "It was just a shock, that's all."

"I thought you looked sexy as hell," Klaus said with a smile.

"Klaus!" Nikita punched her brother's shoulder.

Alecto laughed. "I need to get back to work."

"Thanks for meeting me." Lajos took Nikita's hand as his mother turned to go.

"I'll come to you if I learn anything about Apollo's prophecy," the Fury said before she vanished into a collection of sparkling lights.

"Sorry, guys," Lajos said, once they were alone in the quiet cave. "I guess this was a waste of time for you."

"Are you kidding?" Klaus said. "It's never a waste of time to see a goddess, especially one as badass as your mother."

"It wasn't a waste," Hector agreed as they followed the tunnel in the direction from which they had come. "Your mom will ask around for us, and maybe she'll learn something."

CHAPTER THREE

Trouble at Sea

I'm literally about to die of starvation," Hermie said from where he stood on the upper deck beside Mina on the *Marcella II*.

Hestie threw her head back and laughed at her brother. "That saying was so much more dramatic when we were mortals. Now, it just sounds silly."

"Technically, I can still starve to death," Hermie insisted. "I just won't stay dead."

"Come on, Captain," Mina said. "We stop soon. Yes?"

Helios, the sun god, was already dropping in the west, causing the temperature to drop along with him.

"Yes," Prometheus said. "We're nearly there."

"And where is *there*?" Poros asked.

"Port Said," Prometheus replied.

"Yes!" Poros clapped his hands and then high-fived Jinsoo. "That means Dallas Burger!"

"Yippee ki yay, Rubber Ducky!" Jinsoo said.

Hestie giggled at Jinsoo, but the expression on her brother's face soon had her in stitches. He looked like someone who'd just been told he'd won the lottery.

"Did you say *burger*?" Hermie asked with tears in his eyes.

"Yes!" Mina cried. "Dallas Burger almost as good as Mr. Burger!"

"Almost?" Hestie asked.

"I'll take it!" Hermie said as he did a little dance on the deck.

Chidori whistled at him, making everyone laugh.

Less than an hour later, just before dusk, they docked at the Egyptian port and walked the short distance to the hamburger joint. It felt strange to Hestie to walk on solid land after spending so many days at sea. It reminded her of the feeling of walking after being on ice skates for many hours.

She liked that Poros held her hand as they walked to the restaurant. They hadn't really talked about their relationship, and sometimes she wasn't sure if they were on the same page. On the boat, they always sat together, like Hermie and Mina. And they stole kisses from one another when the others weren't looking. They'd even made out a few times while the others were busy with other things. But Hestie wasn't sure if Poros liked her as much as she liked him.

"Why is Athena not coming?" Jinsoo asked Captain.

"I don't think Dallas Burger is her style," Prometheus said.

Poros grinned. "She doesn't know what she's missing."

When they reached the counter, Hermie asked, "Can I order *two* burgers, Captain?"

"Get whatever you want," he said. "I'm not the food Nazi."

"They have nachos," Poros said to Hestie. "Want to share a platter?"

"Do you have to ask?"

They found a table near a window overlooking the marina. Hestie watched in disbelief as her brother gulped down his burgers.

"Are those tears in your eyes?" she asked him.

"No. Maybe. I plead the fifth, on the grounds that answering may incriminate me."

"He hasn't eaten *at all*," Mina said.

"Nothing?" Poros asked. "For three weeks?"

"He hate kimchi," Mina explained.

"No offense," Hermie quickly said to Jinsoo, who was the one who'd prepared it.

Jinsoo waved his hand. "It not for everybody."

"Can we buy some snacks for Hermie?" Mina asked.

"For me, too," Jinsoo said. "Believe it or not, I'm tired of kimchi."

"We'll buy more supplies in Malta," the captain said.

Hestie saw a familiar figure across the room. Although he had a baseball cap pulled down low on his brow, she'd recognize those turquoise eyes and that sun-bleached beard and hair anywhere. She blinked and rubbed her eyes. Then she leaned across the table and said to Prometheus, "Am I seeing things, or is that Poseidon sitting over there with a group of sailors?"

Prometheus turned to look. Then he muttered, "Well, well, well. What do we have here?"

Poseidon noticed them and lifted his brows with surprise. Hestie tried not to stare but found herself glancing over at him throughout her meal. She was disappointed when he left without coming over to say hello, but she decided not to ask him about it telepathically, since he was probably busy.

"I wonder why he didn't come over," Poros said.

"I'm sure he didn't want to draw attention to himself," Prometheus said.

They finished their meal and headed back to the boat, stopping on the way to buy sunflower seeds for Chidori. When they reached the *Marcella II*, they found Poseidon waiting for them on the upper deck—what the others called the flybridge. He looked like a beacon beneath the moonlight, shining nearly as bright as the moon itself.

Hestie glanced around. The neighboring docks were empty of people.

Always cautious of blending in among mortals, Prometheus climbed onto the boat, rather than fly. Hestie and the other gods did the same. Mina and Jinsoo followed.

When they reached the upper deck, Prometheus said, "Hello, Poseidon."

"Hello, Prometheus. I can't tell you how glad I am to have crossed paths with you."

Poseidon acknowledged Hestie and the other teens with a nod of his head but said nothing by way of greeting.

"That's an exceptional compliment, coming from you," Prometheus said.

"If truth be told, I need your help."

"How can I be of service?" the captain asked.

"Those sailors you saw me sitting with…they didn't know who I was. I came to them because they and others like them have been praying to me nonstop for months on end about the same pirate ship, and I was fishing for information."

"Pirates are common in these waters," Poros pointed out.

"Indeed, they are," Prometheus said.

"Quite right," the god of the sea agreed. "However, this particular vessel has eluded me and my warriors time and time again. It's known as the *Tarantula*."

"That's a strange name for a ship," Hestie muttered.

"It really is," her brother said. "Tarantulas are nocturnal carnivores who literally live in dirt."

"This vessel may not live in dirt," Poseidon said, "but it appears to be nocturnal—only attacks at night. That's one of the reasons it's been so hard to stop."

"*One* of the reasons?" Prometheus asked. "What are the others?"

"The sailors say the pirates are monsters with superhuman strength," Poseidon said.

"That can't be true, can it?" Poros asked.

"Sailors and their legends," Prometheus said with a shake of his head. "They're more dramatic than teenagers." Then, glancing at his crew, he added, "No offense."

Hestie smiled and rolled her eyes.

"You're right to say that sailors love their stories," Poseidon conceded, "but I haven't heard prayers like these in many years."

"You think there's some truth about the pirates being monsters, then?" Poros asked.

"I've never heard of such a thing before," Poseidon said. "At any rate, I'd be grateful to you if you'd keep an eye out for the *Tarantula*."

"Where was it last seen?" Prometheus asked.

"A boat was attacked last week not far from the island of Crete. The prayers of the victims align with others I've heard—monster pirates with super-human strength and speed."

"We're headed in that direction," Poros said.

"We'll look for the *Tarantula* and let you know if we spot her," Prometheus added.

"You have my thanks," Poseidon said before he disappeared.

Hestie turned to Prometheus. "What do you think, Captain?"

"I think a story has a way of taking on a life of its own. There's a kernel of truth that sets things in motion, but I doubt this talk of monsters with superhuman strength looks anything like that original kernel."

Hestie glanced at Hermie, who shrugged and said, "I agree with Captain. It's highly unlikely that there are monsters on these waters that the god of the sea doesn't know about."

Jinsoo took a handful of sunflower seeds from the bag and fed Chidori, who chirped her thanks.

"Why wait for morning?" Prometheus said. "Let's set sail tonight. Unless Mina and Jinsoo are too tired?"

"Not at all, Captain!" Mina said.

"Let's do it, mother trucker!" Jinsoo cried.

The crew got to work preparing the ship.

While Poros hoisted the mainsail of the center mast, Hestie coiled the line. She caught him checking her out as she bent over the line.

"Like what you see?" she teased.

"It's the best view on the seven seas."

She busted out laughing. "I think you ate too much cheese with those nachos, Poros."

Once the *Marcella II* was underway in the open sea, Hermie, Mina, and Jinsoo went below deck to Hermie's room to play *Urban Fighter* on the three personal computers he'd set up for that purpose. Hermie sat between his friends at the wooden desk that ran the length of his cabin below a portal to the sea. At night, the portal was nothing more than a circle of darkness to mortal eyes, but, with his god vision, Hermie saw all manner of life writhing, eating, defecating, or being eaten. He preferred his computer screen.

It was a tight squeeze in the small cabin, with his twin-size bed taking up the bulk of the room, but he was proud of how he'd set everything up, and Mina and Jinsoo seemed to like it, too.

"I'm getting good with this dash jump," Hermie warned them.

"I will beat you anyway," Mina said.

"She probably will," Jinsoo complained.

They'd been playing for over an hour when something massive caught Hermie's attention through the portal.

"What the hell is that?" he asked.

The twins looked up from their computer screens.

"What?" Jinsoo asked. "I don't see anything."

"Me either," Mina said. "What do you see?"

It was the hull of a huge vessel sitting idle. The *Marcella II* sailed right past it—a little too close for Hermie's comfort. What had Prometheus been thinking?

Hermie half-ran, half-flew to the flybridge, where Prometheus was playing dominoes with Poros, Hestie, and Athena.

"Captain!" Hermie cried, pointing to the enormous craft not fifty yards away from them.

"My gods, I didn't even notice her! Why doesn't she have her lights on?" Prometheus flew to the helm and looked over his readings. "How strange. There's nothing on the sonar."

As the others turned to look, Hermie blinked and squinted. Painted on the bow was *Tarantula*.

Mina and Jinsoo caught up to Hermie.

"What happen?" Mina asked.

Hermie pointed to the ship in the distance. "That's what."

Hermie gasped when he made eye contact with someone aboard. She had long, black, curly hair and dark skin and wore a silver scabbard at her waist. Her mouth fell open the instant his did.

"I don't see anything," Jinsoo said.

"You kids don't see that vessel?" Prometheus asked.

Mina and Jinsoo shook their heads.

"How can it be invisible to mortals?" Athena said. "A god must be involved."

"With pirates?" Poros asked.

Hestie folded her arms. "How else?"

Hermie continued to stare at the girl as the distance widened between them, and she continued to stare at him.

"What should we do, Captain?" Poros asked.

"Notify Poseidon," he said. "I'm praying to him now."

"I'll go and speak with him in person," Athena said. "I'll bring him back, to this exact spot."

"Keep us informed," Prometheus said, just before the goddess disappeared.

"What god would help pirates?" Hestie asked the captain after Athena had gone.

"I haven't been in touch with most of them for centuries," he said. "Athena would know better than I."

"Maybe Circe the witch escaped the pit," Hermie said.

"Can we turn around and investigate?" Hestie asked.

"We should leave it to Poseidon," Prometheus said. "Now, Mina and Jinsoo, you need your sleep. We'll be in Malta by dawn, and it will be a long day."

"Yes, Captain," the twins said.

Mina gave Hermie a peck on his cheek. "Good night."

"Good night, Mina. See you in the morning, Jinsoo."

"You're lucky the game was cut short," Jinsoo said. "I almost had you."

"In your dreams," Hermie said with a laugh.

Chidori, who, as usual, was perched on Jinsoo's shoulder, chirped her laugh, too.

"Thanks a lot, Chidori," Jinsoo said. "I thought you believed in me."

Just before daybreak, the *Marcella II* docked at a marina in Malta. As he helped to secure the ship, Hermie continued to think about the girl who had stared at him from the bow of the *Tarantula*. She'd appeared to be his age—around seventeen, maybe older. With dark skin, dark eyes, and full pink lips, she had been perhaps the most beautiful girl he'd ever seen—not that he'd ever admit that to anyone. It wasn't her striking appearance, though, that haunted him so much as the shock she'd worn on her face.

He'd been shocked to see a girl on a pirate ship that had been purported to be run by monsters. But why had *she* been shocked to see *him*? Who was she, and why was she with pirates? He wondered if Athena and Poseidon had already done something about the *Tarantula*—though what that would be, Hermie didn't know.

By the time Helios had made his appearance in the sky, the captain and his crew were eating the best breakfast of Hermie's life at a restaurant overlooking the harbor. Then, with their stomachs full, they walked a few blocks to a supermarket to buy supplies and to pass the time before their meeting with the coin collector, who, according to the captain, was a professor at Malta University and lived in a grand house not far from the institution.

Hestie couldn't stop laughing at how excited her brother was to be in a supermarket surrounded by food. As Poros pushed the cart, Hermie lifted things from the shelves and asked, "Can we get this?" just like when they were kids.

"Milk spoils too quickly," the captain said when Hermie held up a box of Captain Crunch.

"I can eat it without milk," Hermie said.

"Almond milk lasts forever," Hestie pointed out.

"Fine," the captain said.

"Hestie, look!" Mina pointed across the store to a clothing and cosmetic section.

"Oh, my gods!" Hestie cried. "Captain! Can Mina and I go shopping for clothes and makeup?"

"I want to go, too!" Jinsoo said.

"As long as you don't get carried away," Prometheus replied.

"What snacks do you want?" Poros asked.

"Hermie knows what I like," Hestie said.

"I need chocolate," Mina said.

"And I want bananas," Jinsoo added.

"Oh, and I need more tampons," Mina said.

"Too much information," Hermie said with a frown.

Mina giggled and skipped away with Hestie and Jinsoo.

Hestie was thrilled to find one of the cutest outfits she'd ever seen. The top was a turquoise tank with a cute pullover, crocheted with a white and turquoise pattern. It was short-waisted and short-sleeved, and it was paired with white shorts that had one-inch fringe all around the hemline. She put it on and came out of the dressing room to show Jinsoo and Mina.

"Fabulous!" Mina said.

Hestie pulled out her phone. "I think it's time for another edition of *Hestie's Style.*"

"Oh, yes!" Mina clapped her hands. "I'm sure your fans wonder what happen, where you been."

"You put something on, too, guys, and you can be in the video with me."

"How about this?" Jinsoo showed them a pair of skinny jeans and a button-down peach linen top. He found a denim baseball cap, too.

"Gorgeous!" Hestie said.

"What about this bikini?" Mina said. "Hermie like it, yes?"

"You already have too many bikinis," Hestie said. "What about this short skirt and fringe t-shirt?"

The t-shirt was cut into long fringe beginning just below the bust.

"Okay. I try it on."

Hestie went to the cosmetic counter and bought a lip gloss while the others put on the new clothes. When they emerged from the dressing room, Hestie lifted her fists in the air. "Yes! We look totally fab!"

She pulled out her phone and held it out in front of them before pushing record.

"Hey there, besties!" She said hello in twenty-five languages before she continued in English. "I'm sorry I've been away. I've been sailing the seas, diving for treasure, and delivering medical supplies to remote areas in need. Today I'm on the island of Malta with two of my besties, Mina and Jinsoo." She quickly repeated her words in Spanish, French, German, Italian, Portuguese, Russian, Greek, Arabic, Hindi, Persian, Filipino, Chinese, Japanese, Vietnamese, and Korean. Then, in English, she said, "Say hello!"

Mina and Jinsoo waved and said, "Yeoboseyo!"

"Don't we look amazing in our new threads?" Hestie asked. "Who knew the supermarket in Malta had such style?"

Hestie repeated herself in at least twenty more languages before waving goodbye and promising to upload another video soon. Then she published the recording to Youtube.

"Let's wear our new clothes—want to?" Hestie asked her friends.

"Yes!" Mina and Jinsoo said together.

They met up with the others at the checkout.

"Nice," Poros said as he gave Hestie a once-over.

She beamed at him. "Thanks."

"Do you like my outfit, Hermie?" Mina asked.

"Yes. It looks good," he said. "Yours, too, Jinsoo." Then he added, "Look what I found for Chidori."

"A swing!" Jinsoo said. "She will love it!"

"Oh, Hermie!" Hestie said. "Chidori will be so pleased!"

After Prometheus paid the bill, they carried their supplies along the three blocks to the marina. When they reached the *Marcella II*, they were horrified by what they saw.

Lifejackets and other supplies were strewn about the deck. Even worse, the salon and galley had been ransacked—with broken dishes, utensils, and other supplies covering the floor. The ship had been trashed. But why?

"Who would do such a thing?" Hestie said as she looked at the mess in disbelief.

"Chidori?" Jinsoo called. "Where are you?"

Jinsoo ran out onto the flybridge. The others followed.

"Chidori?" Hermie cried.

Everyone called for the bird, but she was nowhere to be found.

With her heart beating fast and her hands trembling, Hestie leapt into the air to go looking for her bird. Chidori had been a part of her life since she and Hermie were six years old. She loved Chidori and would be crushed if anything had happened to her.

Poros and Hermie were soon searching with her in the sky, too. The captain remained on deck with Mina and Jinsoo.

After an hour of searching, the three young gods returned to the *Marcella II*. Hermie and Hestie were in tears. They found Jinsoo in the same condition.

Poros put an arm around Hestie as she asked Prometheus, "What do you think happened?"

"While you were gone, I asked around. The captain on our right arrived at dawn and neither saw nor heard anything unusual. The captain on our left was here all night. He heard a banging sound just before daybreak, and when he looked over, he saw a small tornado directly over my ship. He said it only lasted a few minutes."

"A tornado?" Hermie repeated. "Were any of the other boats affected?"

"Looks like ours was the only one hit," Prometheus said.

"That seems highly unlikely," Hermie said.

"Yeah," Poros said.

Hestie noticed the seat to the bench around the kitchen table had been pulled loose, exposing the storage bin beneath it. She hurried to it and searched the bin. Her stomach felt sick when she didn't find what she was looking for.

"The coins," she said. "Did you move them, captain?"

"No. Why?"

She pointed to the empty bin. "This is where I put them, and they're gone."

"What happened here?" Athena asked, after she and Poseidon appeared.

"We don't know yet," Poros said.

"The captain next to us said it was a tornado," Prometheus said.

"But the ancient daric coins are missing," Poros said.

"Along with our bird, Chidori," Hermie added.

Poseidon crossed his arms. "So is the *Tarantula*."

"What?" Hestie couldn't believe it. "That was fast."

"How far could she have gotten in eight or nine hours?" Hermie asked.

"We searched for miles in every direction," Athena said. "There was no sign of her."

Poseidon rubbed his chin. "Something's amiss."

"And a god *must* be behind it," Athena added. "Sea monsters don't have powers of invisibility."

"Do you think what happened here is connected to the disappearance of the *Tarantula*?" Poros asked.

"It's not likely that the two are unrelated," Hermie said.

"So, what do we do, Captain?" Jinsoo asked. "We need to find Chidori."

"We should look at night," Mina said. "You only see the boat at night, yes?"

"The mortal makes a good point," Poseidon said. "We'll scour the seas tonight."

CHAPTER FOUR

Morpheus

Gertie lay in bed, curled up with her e-reader, re-reading one of her favorites: *Interview with a Vampire*. Revisiting the Necromanteion had filled Gertie with nostalgia for her friend, Jeno. She'd been reading *Interview with a Vampire* the day she'd met him.

But she found it hard to focus on the novel, because she couldn't stop thinking about her vision at Hector's house. Why had she seen a *vampire*? Did the vampire have anything to do with Apollo's message to Hector?

She groaned and tried to focus. It had been months since she had picked up a book to read for pleasure. Everything else in her life seemed to take priority over her favorite pastime.

When she was too sleepy to keep trying, she turned off her e-reader and said a prayer to her favorite gods—Hephaestus, Apollo, Aphrodite, Hades, and, of course, Gaia.

To each of them, she said, "If Hector is to be called on a quest at sea, please keep him safe."

To the Fates, she added, "Please help me to better understand my vision with the vampire."

Then, she rolled onto her side and tried her best to go to sleep.

When Gertie next opened her eyes, she found herself floating on the wide blue sea beneath the bright sun in a raft the size of a laundry basket. The hull of an enormous ship towered over her, spraying cold water on her after the tumultuous waves slammed against it. Wearing nothing but a t-shirt and shorts, she shivered from the cold and gripped the handles of the raft as the sea swelled and lifted her toward the bright sky.

"What the hell?" she muttered.

The wave carried her over the bow, and she and her raft landed on an abandoned deck. She stepped from her raft, grabbed ahold of the main mast, and held on for dear life, to keep from being washed overboard as another wave crashed against her.

When she saw the monster Charybdis swirling with her wide, open mouth in the giant waves, Gertie prayed to Poseidon for help. That's when she realized she was dreaming.

She held onto the mast until the raging sea died down and Charybdis had receded to her cave. Then the water became still like glass. The sun bore down, drying her clothes and everything on deck. She walked on wobbly legs to investigate.

Seeing no one in sight, she went below deck. Although it was a dream, she was frightened. She'd once read that if a person dies in their dream, they die in real life. As much as she'd like to see Jeno in the Elysian Fields, she wasn't ready to die. She wanted to do something with her life first—something worthwhile.

The hull appeared to be one large space. It was dark, damp, and dreary and smelled like sweaty feet. Once her eyes adjusted to the darkness, she found it to be filled with chests and crates stacked along the perimeter of the space, and, in the center, there were over a dozen coffins lying side by side in three rows. She shivered at the prospect of vampires sleeping inside them.

She held her breath and froze when a snake appeared from behind a box. She watched in terror as it lifted its emerald-green head, flicked its tongue, and glared at her. Then it slithered on the floorboards away from Gertie. Surprised, she followed it.

The deeper into the hull she went, the more she trembled with fear, wondering if she should turn back and wait out the dream above deck in the light of day. But something in the pit of her stomach—maybe nothing more than curiosity—compelled her forward.

She had crept across half the length of the vessel when she spotted a cage tucked against the stern. At first, she thought it was an animal cage, but as she moved closer, she heard the whimpers of people. The snake stopped near the cage and coiled on the floor beside it.

Hiding behind one of the coffins, Gertie studied the cage, trying to get a better look. Someone inside shifted, and Gertie made out the figure of a girl, sitting on her bottom, her long red hair falling like a curtain over her face.

A boy whispered, "I just can't believe it."

"Me either, Hermie," the girl said. "I keep hoping to wake up and this will have all been a nightmare."

Gertie crept closer and saw that *two* boys sat in the cage with the girl. One boy was blond and the other had dark hair.

"Me, too," the blond boy said. "I've been praying to Morpheus, begging him to let this be a dream."

"It's my fault," the girl said.

"Not true," the blond one said. "I should have made them gods when they asked."

"You couldn't have known, Poros," the girl said.

Gertie suddenly recognized the girl from *Hestie's Style*, a Youtube channel that was widely popular all over the world. Gertie wasn't a fan. While Hestie seemed nice in the videos, she also seemed shallow and materialistic. Gertie wondered why the Youtuber was making an appearance in her dream.

"I doubt I can get her back a second time," Hermie said. "Maybe Jinsoo, but not Mina."

"I doubt you could get either of them back," the boy named Poros said.

"Maybe this is why the Fates let Mina return from the dead in the first place," Hermie said sourly. "They knew it wouldn't be for long."

Gertie lifted her brows. This dream was getting even weirder. She knew better than anyone than it was impossible to bring someone back from the dead.

"It's so unfair," Hestie said before breaking out into tears again.

Gertie wanted to tell them that it *was* a dream. Maybe telling them would help her to wake up. She inched closer to the cage.

"Poor Chidori," Hermie said through more tears. "If we ever find her—"

"*When* we find her," Hestie interrupted.

"*When* we find her," Hermie repeated, "she'll be so heartbroken. I think she loved Jinsoo more than she loved anyone else."

Hestie straightened her back and turned in the direction of Gertie. "Is someone there?"

Gertie stood up and revealed herself, but the people in the cage didn't seem to be able to see her.

"I sense someone, too," Poros said.

"Maybe they're wearing the helm of invisibility," Hermie suggested.

"If anyone's there," Hestie said, "please tell Poseidon where we are. This cage is made of adamantine, and it's warded, we think."

They wanted her to contact Poseidon? What a strange dream.

"Help us," Hermie said. "Please."

Gertie inched closer to the cage. "Can't you see me?"

The teens in the cage gasped.

"We can hear you!" Poros said. "Who are you?"

"Gertrude Morgan. I'm a demigod, and this is my dream."

Hestie climbed to her knees and grabbed the bars of her cage. "Help us, Gertrude. Tell Poseidon where we are."

Gertie heard a loud *clack* behind her. She turned to see one of the lids on the coffins had opened on its hinge. Gertie backed away, upsetting the snake. It hissed and slithered away. Then a figure sat up in the coffin and glared at Gertie with red eyes.

It was the vampire from her vision.

Gertie flinched and fell back. When she opened her eyes, she found herself in bed at home. She sat up, smoothed her hair with her fingers, and tried to remember her dream.

"That was intense," said a figure who'd appeared in the corner of her room.

His bright, silver wings were folded behind him. Silver-rimmed black eyes peered from a lustrous, bronze face. He wore white trousers but no shirt, and his bare chest was ripped like that of a bodybuilder.

Gertie pulled her covers up to her neck and pressed her back against the headboard of her bed, to put as much distance between her and the figure as possible. "Who are you?"

"Morpheus, the god of dreams. No need to be afraid."

"Why are you here?"

"To discuss that freaky dream of yours."

"You saw it?" Gertie wondered if he had caused it, too.

"Only the last bit."

"Why do you want to discuss it?"

"It came through the gates of horn."

Gertie's stomach formed a knot. "Then it was a *true* dream, right? And it came from the Fates?"

Of all the prophetic dreams Gertie had ever had, this one had to be the weirdest.

Morpheus nodded. "I didn't catch everything, so, before I go and warn my cousins—"

"Your *cousins*? Hestie from *Hestie's Style* is your cousin?"

"Yeah. And her brother, Hermie. They were born demigods but recently became gods."

"Oh." Gertie would never have pegged Hestie for a demigod. Her Youtube channel seemed like such a waste of whatever gift she'd inherited.

"Have you had prophetic dreams before?" Morpheus asked.

Gertie nodded. "Dionysus is my father. When I drink his wine, I get visions. I've had a few prophetic dreams, too. What do you think this one means?"

"I need you to fill in some of the details," he said. "I didn't enter your dream until the end, when I heard you talking to the figments."

"The what?"

"Figments—you know, the characters in your dream."

Gertie straightened her back. "So, those weren't your cousins, then?"

"No. They were figments that took the form of my cousins. What you experienced hasn't happened yet."

"So, there's time to warn them?"

"Yes. But tell me everything that happened first."

Gertie told him what she could remember. "There were wooden crates and coffins. A snake hissed at me and then crawled away. I heard your cousins talking and crying in the cage."

"Crying?"

"I think two of their friends had died. Gosh, what were their names?" She struggled to recall the details. "Mina. Mina was one. I can't remember the other."

"Jinsoo?"

"Yes! That was it! Mina and Jinsoo had just been killed, and someone else had gone missing. I think her name was Chidori."

"Oh, man. This is bad news. Mina and Jinsoo killed? Chidori missing? I gotta go."

"But—"

Morpheus vanished as quickly as he had come.

Hestie swept up the rubble left behind on the main deck of the *Marcella II* by the thieves. Mina held the dustpan and collected the waste in an old barrel. They'd been cleaning for hours.

It was hot, and the water in the marina was calm. Hestie was anxious for nightfall, so they could go looking for the *Tarantula*. She felt personally violated by the theft. *She* had found those coins. Those pirates had no right to take them.

Mina asked Hestie, "Why can't you use magic to clean up?"

Prometheus, who was helping Jinsoo to mend the sails, said, "Because then I wouldn't know where everything was."

"Then can you do it, Captain?" Mina asked.

"I'll remember where things are better if we clean up the old-fashioned way."

"I don't like the old-fashion way," Mina complained.

The captain added, "I don't like drawing attention to myself. One never knows when mortal eyes are watching. The old-fashioned way is best at port."

Hermie, who was helping Jinsoo and Poros to clean up the kitchen and salon, cried out, "Morpheus is here!"

Hestie glanced across the deck at Prometheus.

"Let's go see what he has to say," the captain said.

Mina, Jinsoo, and Hestie followed the captain into the salon.

Hestie gave her cousin a hug. "Hey, Morpheus! What brings you here? Is everything okay at home?"

Hestie knew that Morpheus would know that by "home" she meant the Underworld.

"Are our parents okay?" Hermie asked.

"Uncle Than and Aunt Therese are fine."

"And *your* parents?" Hestie asked.

"Everybody's good," Morpheus said.

Hestie sighed with relief.

"You missed us, then," Hermie said. "Admit it, bro. You're here for some cousin time."

"How's married life?" Poros asked. "You and Iris still like each other?"

"Iris is great. Marriage is great." Then Morpheus said, "Dudes, I really wish I was here for a visit, but I've got something important to tell you."

Hermie frowned. He hoped it wasn't bad news about Chidori. If she'd died, Hermie's dad would know, since he was the god of death. Hermie closed his eyes and prayed to his father: *Please don't let Chidori be dead.*

"What's going on?" Prometheus asked.

Morpheus glanced at Mina and Jinsoo before turning back to Prometheus. "Can I talk to you in private?"

"Of course," the captain said.

Then Morpheus said, "Actually, I need to talk to you, you, you, and you." He pointed to everyone but Mina and Jinsoo.

Jinsoo said, "Hey, if you need to have a god chat, just say so!"

"We need to have a god chat," Hermie said.

"Come on," Jinsoo said to Mina. "Let's play *Urban Fighter.*"

"It better than cleaning," Mina said before handing the dustpan to Hestie.

"Later, gators," Jinsoo said.

Once the mortals had gone below deck, Morpheus said, "Maybe you should sit down."

"Sit down for what?" Hermie's father, who'd suddenly appeared, asked.

"Dad!" Hestie cried just before she gave him a hug.

"Hello, Thanatos," the captain said.

"Uncle Than?" Morpheus said with surprise. "Did someone die?"

"Please tell me Chidori isn't dead," Hermie said.

"I haven't seen her. When did she go missing?"

They took seats in the salon while Hermie and the others caught the new arrivals up to speed.

"It only gets worse," Morpheus said. "A demigod with the gift of prophecy had a dream from the gates of horn that you should know about."

A cold chill crept up Hermie's spine as he listened to his cousin relay the nightmare that someone named Gertrude living in Athens had dreamed the night before.

"I should have found Mina and Jinsoo jobs on another ship weeks ago," Prometheus said. "It's my fault their lives are in danger."

"You *have* to turn them into gods *now*," Hermie said to Poros. "It's the best way to prevent this from happening."

"Immortality isn't for everyone," Hermie's father said.

"This is a no-brainer, Dad," Hestie insisted. "They *should* be gods."

"And if they don't figure out a purpose within three months?" their father asked. "They'll not only lose their immortality, but they'll be even more vulnerable to enemies than they are right now."

Poros added, "I don't even know how I did it before. It just sort of happened."

"But you've already offered to change them," Hermie pointed out. "Why would you offer, if you don't know how?"

"I thought I'd have time to figure it out."

"What do *Mina and Jinsoo* want?" Morpheus asked as he crossed one leg over the other.

"They want to be gods," Hestie said.

Prometheus scratched his beard. "But they don't really know what that means."

"Poros can't do it *here*, anyway," Hermie's father said.

"I don't understand," Hestie said.

Hermie's father clapped Hermie on the shoulder. "When Poros turned you and Hestie, he was in the Underworld surrounded by powerful gods who supported him."

"Your father's right," Prometheus said. "Apotheosis can only happen at Mount Olympus, Poseidon's Palace, or the Underworld. And it can only be done by the most powerful god, with the cooperation of other gods."

"We're not far from Poseidon's Palace," Morpheus pointed out.

"We need to get away from the sea," Hermie said. "Can't we go to Mount Olympus?"

"We'd have the least support there," Prometheus said.

"I agree," Poros said. "My own sister is against this."

Hermie's father turned to leave. "I'll check with Hades. The Underworld is your best chance. I'll let you know as soon as I have an answer."

Hermie's chest felt heavy, like someone was stepping on it. The thought of losing Mina and Jinsoo filled him with dread. "I don't think we should tell Mina and Jinsoo about the dream."

"Yeah, no," Morpheus said. "Don't tell them."

"I should have gotten them jobs on another ship," Prometheus said again. "I've done this for centuries—taken on orphans, trained them to be sailors, gotten them jobs on reputable ships. I usually don't keep them for more than a year."

"It's not your fault, Captain," Poros said.

"I need to get back," Morpheus said. "See you guys later."

"Bye, Morpheus," Hermie said.

Hestie and Poros waved as Morpheus flew away, his bright silver wings sparkling in the fading light.

"I hope Dad has an answer for us before nightfall," Hestie said. "I feel like we're sitting ducks."

"Me, too," Hermie said.

CHAPTER FIVE

The Tarantula

When dusk arrived, Hestie turned from where she'd been organizing the kitchen supplies and said to Poros, who was helping, "I think we should look for the *Tarantula.*"

"I doubt Captain will allow it."

"Do we need his permission?" she asked in a lowered voice. She wondered if Prometheus could hear her from the upper deck. "You're the strongest god…"

"He's the *captain,*" Poros interrupted. "To go against him would be mutiny."

"Surely the rules don't apply to *this* ship. Aren't we special?"

"Rules are rules," he said.

"We can't just sit here, doing nothing," she argued. "What if they attack us?"

"Now that we know something's coming, we're ready for it."

"Are we, *really*?" she said. "We don't even know what we're up against. You and I could go and get a better idea of what these supposed monsters are. They can't be *actual* monsters. Can they? Do vampires really exist?"

"We were so upset about what had happened to Mina and Jinsoo in the dream, that we forgot to ask about the vampires."

"The dream came through the gates of horn," Hestie said. "Does that mean vampires are real? Or are they symbolic of something else?"

"We should ask Captain."

"I bet you and I could solve the mystery on our own."

"I don't know."

"Please? What's the point of being gods if we don't do anything with our powers?"

"Those pirates could be anywhere," Poros said.

"But they're more likely to be nearby, don't you think? Since they just robbed us this morning?"

Poros sighed. "You're going to wear me down until I say yes, aren't you?"

She smiled.

"We can't go far," he said, "in case they attack. We have to protect Mina and Jinsoo at all costs."

"Of course," she said as a thrill coursed through her. After a day of cleaning and organizing, Hestie was ready for an adventure.

"Fine, then," Poros said as he snapped the overhead cabinet closed. "But we have to tell Captain what we're up to."

Hestie shook her head. "You're such a goodie-two-shoes."

"What does that mean?"

She laughed. "Never mind."

"Good," Hermie said to Jinsoo from where he stood on the main deck.

Hermie had hung a burlap sack from the center mast. The bag was stuffed with organic garbage. It swayed with the wind and with the movements of the ship like a pinata. After teaching Mina and Jinsoo about grip, stance, and footwork, Hermie used the burlap bag as a target as he demonstrated various attacks with the sword—maneuvers his parents had taught him throughout his childhood.

If they were going to be stuck at port, they may as well do some training.

Captain watched from the flybridge, where he sat at the helm, waiting for Hermie's father to return with news from Hades.

"How was that?" Jinsoo called up to Prometheus.

"Better!" the captain said. "Keep your center of gravity low."

Jinsoo turned to Hermie. "What did he say?"

"Your center of gravity," Hermie said. "Bend your knees and take a wider stance."

Jinsoo and Mina did as he said.

"Now *you* try the attack," Hermie handed his sword to Mina.

"Why we doing this, Hermie?" Mina asked. "I'm tired from cleaning all day."

"It's fun," Jinsoo said.

"You just afraid to play me at *Urban Fighter*," Mina complained. "Since I beat you so bad."

"I am not."

"Poros said he's going to change you into gods *soon*," Hermie said. "He's not waiting for your birthday. I want you to be ready."

"Can't we do this tomorrow?" Mina asked. "I'm so tired."

Hermie took back his sword. "I thought you'd be happy."

They went into the salon, got cups of water, and sat down to drink and rest.

"Aren't you excited by my news?" Hermie asked the twins.

"Yes," Jinsoo said. "I can't wait to fly!"

"I don't know," Mina said.

"What?" Hermie was taken aback. "It's all you talk about!"

"I'm scared."

"But you won't be scared once you're a god," Hermie argued.

Mina put her hands on her narrow hips. "*You* are."

Blood rushed to Hermie's cheeks. "True."

"Don't you want to live forever?" Jinsoo asked her.

"That long time," she said.

"Has Athena said something to you?" Hermie asked.

Mina shook her head. After a pause, she said, "Before Captain get Jinsoo and me from orphanage, I thought I want to die…to be with my mother and father. I still think about that sometime. I remember them."

"I remember them, too," Jinsoo said. "Only a little. Maybe we can see them, when we're gods."

Mina studied Hermie's face.

"I don't know," he said, even though he knew it to be impossible. Even if the twins saw them in the Elysian Fields, their parents would have no memory of their children. "Maybe."

Mina and Jinsoo's eyes filled with tears.

"How did they die?" Hermie asked.

"They were murdered by thieves," Jinsoo said.

"Jinsoo saw it happen," Mina added. "I was asleep in my room."

"Give me the sword," Jinsoo said. "I want to practice."

Hestie flew beside Poros in the evening sky as Helios descended in the west and dusk covered the horizon like a weighted blanket.

"I can still see the *Marcella II*," she said to reassure Poros that she respected the captain's condition. "But I see no sign of the *Tarantula*. You?"

"No. But what's that?"

She followed his finger to a cluster of clouds swirling above them in the darkened sky.

She gasped. "It looks like a…"

"Tornado," he said.

As she observed the swirling clouds more carefully, she recognized a huge vessel at its center. "Is that the *Tarantula*?"

"It is," Poros said as he stopped her in mid-air.

"But how?"

She studied the spinning ship and was shocked to see more than a dozen people holding onto the center mast as their legs flew out behind them. Four clung to the top of the mast, four more clung to the middle, and five clung to the base. They wore boots or sneakers, trousers made of denim or leather, and, in a few cases, long coats.

"Those people," she said. "Are they in trouble? Do they need our help? Or could they be…vampires?"

"I've never seen anything like this."

"Captain said he'd heard stories about vampires but had never encountered one," Hestie said. "He's been around forever. If they're real, he should have seen one, don't you think?"

"I don't know *what* to think."

Hestie and Poros inched closer to the wind tunnel, trying to make out the expressions on the faces of the people, to determine whether they were victims of some mystical force or the cause of it. Hestie was surprised by how young and beautiful they were. Could they really be vampires?

Then she watched in awe as the ship lowered toward the sea like a helicopter and stopped spinning before gently landing—with not so much as a *plop*—amid the gentle waves. The people who had been clinging to the mast landed on their feet and began talking amongst themselves.

"You're in invisibility mode, right?" Poros asked her when one of the sailors below looked up into the sky.

"Yes, you?"

"Yes."

"What if they're gods?" she asked.

"They would have sensed us by now. And we would have heard of them."

"Then a god must be working with them," Hestie said. "Unless they're vampires."

"I wonder if Boreas, or one of his brother winds, is involved."

"That's a good guess. Or maybe Aeolus, their keeper."

"Wait, what are they doing now?" he asked.

Hestie covered her mouth and gasped. "Are they…flying?"

"Maybe a wind god is carrying them."

"Where are they going?"

All thirteen of them lifted into the air in one massive herd and flew away, in the opposite direction.

"This is our chance," Hestie said. "Let's go look for Chidori."

"There could be more of them below deck."

Hestie used her god-sight to see through the hull. "I don't see anyone, do you?"

"No."

"Let's just make a quick sweep. Come on!"

"Be ready to god-travel back to the *Marcella II*," Poros warned.

Hermie looked up into the darkening sky from where he'd been training Mina and Jinsoo on the main deck. A tornado appeared in the distance from out of nowhere. He and the twins sought protection in the salon.

"In here," Jinsoo called from inside the pantry.

Mina dropped Hermie's sword and joined her brother.

"Come on, Hermie!" she cried.

Hermie hesitated, worried about the others. "Hold on."

He peered through the windows to take a better look at the tornado. In the center of the wind tunnel, he saw a herd of creatures—people—descending toward him.

To the twins, he yelled, "Stay where you are, guys! Don't come out!"

He scooped up his sword and rushed out to the main deck. Above him, on the flybridge, Prometheus fought with six or more of the strangers. Another six landed on the deck and surrounded Hermie.

One of them was the girl he'd seen the previous night aboard the *Tarantula*.

With his sword ready, he asked, "Who are you, and what do you want?"

"That's what *I* want to know," the girl said. "You're working with Poseidon against us. Why?"

Someone behind him scuffled toward him. Hermie turned to defend himself just before the sharp sting of a blade cut through the skin on his back. He turned and swung, only to clash blades with the girl. She opened her mouth and hissed before she sank her fangs into his wrist.

Hermie couldn't believe his eyes. Was she an actual vampire?

She stopped and stumbled back. "Don't drink! He's a god!"

"So is the captain!" someone shouted from above.

"I wouldn't worry about him!" another shouted. "He's lost his head."

"Bring the boy!" another said. "We'll let our lord decide what to do with him!"

The pack of strangers attacked Hermie and disarmed him before lifting him into the sky.

He looked down to see Prometheus beheaded on the flybridge.

In the next moment, Mina emerged from the salon. She saw him being carried away. She scooped up his sword and cried, "Hermie!"

The girl who'd bit him was still recovering on the main deck. She climbed to her feet and whipped her blade through the air.

"No!" Hermie screamed just as the girl's blade cut across Mina's neck.

Hestie hovered in the air beside Poros near the top of the *Tarantula's* center mast, scouring the ship for signs of life. The vessel seemed ancient and old fashioned and lacking in all the modern conveniences of the *Marcella II.*

"There's no one there. I don't see Chidori. Not a single soul," Hestie said again.

"Unless a god is hiding beneath the helm of invisibility," Poros pointed out.

"Without Hades's knowledge?" Hestie asked.

Poros shrugged.

"What about the coins?" she asked.

"Let's be quick."

First, they checked out the enormous salon. It was more of a dining hall with tables and chairs and what at one time must have been fancy chandeliers. Along the back, near an old bookcase were chests. Hestie lifted one of the lids. It was filled with what appeared to be valuable artifacts.

"Let's look below deck," Hestie said, hoping to find Chidori and the coins.

There, they saw thirteen wooden boxes shaped like coffins lying side by side on the floor in three rows.

"This is what Gertrude described in her dream," Poros said.

At that moment, Hestie heard a desperate prayer from her brother. Poros must have heard it, too, because his eyes widened as she glanced up at him with fear.

"Let's go," he said.

As they turned to leave, they were met with the same herd of strangers that had flown away in the opposite direction not fifteen minutes ago. The strangers swarmed the two young gods and held them with super-human strength.

"Who are you?" Poros asked, as he and Hestie struggled against their captors. "What do you want?"

Hestie repeated Poros's question in multiple languages, but the strangers ignored her. Who were these people that they were able to overpower the most powerful god alive? Were they really vampires?

The strangers dragged Poros and Hestie down deeper into the dark and musty hull, where the two gods were thrown into a cage.

"Who are you?" Poros asked again. "Why are you doing this?"

Hestie was horrified when her brother was shoved into the cage with her and Poros. He was bleeding and sobbing his eyes out.

She rushed to his side. "Hermie? Hermie, are you okay?"

"No," he said. "And I'll never be okay again."

C H A P T E R   S I X

The Marcella II

Gertie paced around Hector's bedroom while he sat at his desk and Googled nautical terms on the Internet. It was late and nearly time for her to leave. As much as she loved research, this wasn't how she'd planned on spending her evening with him.

She studied the drawings he had lying around on his desk and dresser. They were mostly of her, but he'd also sketched his mother, Hephaestus as a white crane, the temple of Hephaestus, and Athena as an owl. His most recent sketch was of Apollo, both as a golden wolf and as a god.

Then she looked over his shoulder at the screen of his laptop, where he was reading about knots, wenches, and jibs.

"Do you really think that's going to help?" she asked.

"Apollo told us to be ready," Hector reminded her. "Any better ideas?"

"Well, according to my research, vampires could be a symbol of…"

Just then, the hair on the back of Gertie's neck stood on end. Across the room, Morpheus appeared.

Hector jumped to his feet and stood between the winged god and Gertie.

"Who are you?" Hector demanded.

"It's okay," Gertie said. "This is Morpheus, the god of dreams. Morpheus, this is Hector."

"Hey, Hector," Morpheus said. "Sorry to just show up like this, but it's kind of urgent."

"Has something happened?"

"Are you here about my dream?" Gertie clasped her hands together. "Please tell me it didn't come true."

Morpheus looked down at his feet when he said, "Not completely, but yeah."

"What does that mean?" Hector asked.

"Grab your phones and a change of clothes. I'll explain on the way."

"I don't have a change of clothes," Gertie said with her heart beating fast and her mouth hanging open. "Not here, anyway."

Hector found a duffle bag in his closet. "You can use something of mine, Gertie."

She grabbed his toothbrush, toothpaste, and deodorant from his bathroom and added them to his bag, all the while trembling with fear and excitement.

"What about my parents?" she asked Morpheus. "I should be home already."

"You can text them on the way," he said. "Let's go."

Morpheus held them each by the arm and god-traveled with them from the room.

Gertie hadn't god-traveled in over a year. She'd forgotten the pressure and the strange feeling of disorientation one felt just before landing in a completely different location.

When she opened her eyes, she found herself on a boat moored to a crowded dock in a marina. The lights from the dock sparkled on the dark sea, like the stars in the night sky.

"Where are we?" Hector asked.

"The island of Malta," Morpheus said. "This is the *Marcella II*. Its captain is Prometheus."

"The titan?" Gertie asked.

"That's right."

Gertie filled with excitement over the prospect of meeting the god who gave humans fire and had his liver eaten out by Zeus's eagle as punishment for it.

"Where is he?" Hector asked, glancing around the abandoned upper deck.

"Recovering in his quarters," Morpheus replied. "You better sit down."

Morpheus motioned to an L-shaped couch that was bolted to the upper deck, along with an oval table, behind two swivel seats near a control board and steering wheel.

Setting his duffle bag on the table, Hector slid onto the couch and made room for Gertie, who slid in beside him.

She didn't have a good feeling about this.

Morpheus sat in one of the swivel seats. His knee bounced nervously up and down. "Hades asked me to bring you here, because you have experience with vampires."

"Morpheus, what's happened?" Hector asked.

"This ship was attacked about an hour ago," the winged god said. "Prometheus and a mortal girl named Mina were beheaded."

Gertie gasped. "The girl they talked about in my dream?"

Morpheus nodded. "My father, Hypnos, and my uncle, Thanatos, and I buried her at sea just before I came to you."

"What about the other one—Jinsoo?" Gertie asked.

"He's in the deep boon of sleep below deck, in his quarters. My father is with him. Hypnos would be here to greet you but…"

"He'd put us to sleep," Hector finished.

"Exactly," Morpheus said.

"Thank Gaia he's alive! Will he live?" Gertie asked.

"Jinsoo is unharmed. But Prometheus may take a week or two to recover. To make matters worse, my cousins, Hermie and Hestie, along with Poros, the son of Zeus, were taken."

Gertie covered her mouth. She wondered if they were in the cage she saw in her dream.

"And you think vampires did this?" Hector asked.

"Poseidon has been investigating a pirate ship known as the *Tarantula*, because of prayers from sailors claiming to have been robbed by monsters from that ship," Morpheus explained. "Hades spoke with Prometheus's soul in Tartarus, and he confirmed that the monsters are vampires."

"Vampire pirates?" Gertie asked. She wanted to punch something. "There's no excuse for this. They were offered sanctuary and purpose with Hades over a year ago. Why would they choose to live this kind of life?"

"For the thrill of it," Hector said. "I'll wager they aren't very nice."

"We need to find them and rescue Poros and my cousins," Morpheus said.

"And you can't communicate with them through prayer?" Hector asked.

"No. Something's in the way."

"I wonder why the gods can't handle this themselves," Gertie said. "Not that I'm not thrilled to be here."

"Well, the pantheon is in chaos over this," Morpheus said. "Poseidon and Athena want to destroy the vampires. Dionysus has threatened war against any god who touches the vampires. And Hades wants to recruit them, which is why he asked me to get your help. He says you've done this kind of thing before."

"Could my father be helping the vampire pirates?" Gertie wondered out loud.

"He was their leader for centuries—before the uprising," Hector said.

Gertie nodded. "Maybe he resents losing that role to Hades and has organized a rogue coven to cause trouble."

"That sounds like a good possibility," Hector said.

"He may be holding Hermie, Hestie, and Poros for ransom in exchange for cooperation," Morpheus said. "That's Iris's theory. She's my wife, and she hates Dionysus—no offense."

"None taken." Gertie wondered if the god of dreams knew that she was the one who'd released Iris from her servitude to Hera, during the vampire uprising.

"So, what's the plan?" Hector asked.

"We need to find the *Tarantula*," Morpheus said. "Poseidon has been searching for months, with no luck."

Gertie sighed. "How are we supposed to find it if Poseidon can't?"

"He's still looking. Other gods are, too, including me and Iris. Meanwhile, Hades wants the *Marcella II* out at sea, hoping to draw the vampires out."

So, Hades meant to use them as bait.

"We know nothing about sailing a craft of this size," Hector pointed out.

"What kind of ship is this, anyway?" Gertie asked. "It's bigger than my father's yacht."

"According to Prometheus, it's a sailing yacht hybrid with caravel features," Morpheus said. "He likes to do things the old-fashioned way—hence the three masts and sails. But the cabins and furniture are modern."

"Not too shabby," Hector said with a smile.

"I can help you get her underway until Prometheus is rejoined with his body in another week or so."

"You don't think we should wait for him to heal before setting sail?" Gertie asked.

"There's no time to lose," Morpheus said. "But if you don't think you can do it…"

"We can do it," Hector said.

Morpheus turned to Gertie, who nodded.

"We won't be alone," Morpheus assured them. "Prometheus's mother, Clymene, is an Oceanid and will follow for added protection."

That made Gertie feel much better. "I've read a great deal about Clymene! She's the wife of Iapetus and the mother of Prometheus, Epimetheus, Atlas, and Menoetius. She's also one of the three thousand daughters of Oceanus and Tethys and the goddess of fame, right? And, if I remember correctly, she had a son with Helios named Phaeton."

"You know more than I," Morpheus said with a grin.

"When do we set sail?" Hector asked.

"Tonight," Morpheus said. "As soon as possible."

A lump formed in Gertie's throat. How would they navigate this enormous ship through dark waters? She could tell Hector was wondering the same thing.

"Let's wake up Jinsoo," Morpheus said, leading the way from the upper deck. "We're hoping that making him the temporary captain will help take his mind off his loss."

Gertie worried the boy might be too overwhelmed with grief to be much use to them, but she wasn't about to complain to Morpheus.

"I know enough to help you prepare to set sail, but not much more," Morpheus added as he led them through an enclosed area with couches, a tiny kitchen, and an eating area.

Through the windows near the table, Gertie spotted the deck of the ship, where two of three masts towered without sails toward the sky.

"Isn't there anyone else who can captain us?" Gertie asked.

"Not on short notice," the winged god said. "Besides, this is a chance for Jinsoo to prove he's got what it takes to become a god."

"I don't understand," Hector said.

"Poros, son of Zeus, plans to grant Jinsoo immortality, but he needs the support of other gods."

Gertie wondered if Poros would consider making her and Hector gods, too.

She followed Morpheus and Hector down another set of steps below deck into a narrow corridor. It was a tight squeeze. They came to a stop beside one of six doors. Across from it was an impressive laundry facility and storage bins.

Morpheus opened the door to a cramped chamber consisting of a bed, a small desk and chair, and overhead bins. There was a television mounted to the exterior wall beside a portal to the sea that showed nothing but darkness. An Asian boy lay sleeping on the bed, and a beautiful, young-looking god, with deep blue eyes and light-brown hair, stood over him.

"Hey, Pops," Morpheus said to the god.

"Hey, son. Hello, Gertie and Hector. Thanks for coming."

The god of sleep looked nothing like the god of dreams, and he was almost as youthful looking.

"It's our pleasure," Hector said to Hypnos.

"Thanks," Hypnos said. "Hades appreciates your service."

Gertie yawned. "Is it true that you're the son of Nyx and Chaos?"

"Hades and Persephone are my parents," the god said.

"The books are wrong?" she said with another yawn.

"Not always," Hypnos said with a wink.

Hector fell to the floor and began to snore.

"That's your cue, Pops," Morpheus said.

"When the mortal wakes up, he'll still be in shock," Hypnos said. "Let him work through his feelings on his own time, okay?"

Gertie closed her eyes and nodded.

"Call me if you need anything," Hypnos said. "Everyone calls me Hip." Then to Morpheus he added, "Later, son."

"Later, Pops."

Hypnos vanished.

Gertie flinched. It was unsettling when a god entered and exited a room. She wondered if she would ever get used to it.

Hector awoke as she gazed down at the Asian boy named Jinsoo. She wished he hadn't lost his sister, especially in such a cruel and violent way. Gertie had never had a sibling, but Nikita, Klaus, and their little sister Phoebe had been the next best thing, and she couldn't imagine how she would cope if she were to lose any one of them.

"How long before he wakes?" Hector asked.

"Any minute now," the god of dreams replied. "I'm helping him in the Dreamworld to work through some stuff. He's nearly ready."

"You're here with us *and* in the Dreamworld?" Gertie asked.

"It's a special gift," Morpheus said.

"That's so cool," Gertie said. To Hector, she said, "Remind me to research more about the Dreamworld. Maybe it will help me with my prophetic dreams."

"Look," Hector said. "He's stirring."

Jinsoo opened his eyes and stared at his visitors with wide eyes. Then he asked, "Where's Mina?"

Hermie huddled in the corner of the cage in the hull of the *Tarantula* barely able to breathe. He was angry—angrier than he could ever recall feeling. He wanted to punch something—or someone.

Even when he closed his eyes, the only thing he could see was the blade of the vampire's sword slicing across Mina's neck and the shocked look on Mina's sweet face as her head fell from her severed body onto the deck.

"Hermie, please," his sister said again, stroking his arm. "Tell us what happened."

He didn't want to be touched right now. "Back off, Hestie! Can I have a minute? Just give me a minute, will you?"

It had all happened so fast. Hermie closed his eyes and sucked in his lips, wishing he could go back in time and do everything differently.

How could this have happened? Had it really happened? Was Mina really gone, for good?

Worried he might throw up, he held his belly and tried to clear his mind, but a prayer to his father seemed to rise up of its own accord: *Is she really dead? Is there anything I can do to bring her back? Dad? Dad, answer me.*

Hermie opened his eyes and studied his cage. He gripped the bars and pulled, to no avail.

"What's this thing made of?" he asked.

"Adamantine," Poros said from where he stood in the opposite corner. "I think it's warded. I can't make contact with anyone, and we can't god-travel out."

"Hermie, please tell us what happened to you," Hestie said, standing over him but not touching him.

"To me?" the anger throbbed in his head, in his throat. "Nothing happened to me. Didn't you see them before the vampires brought you here?"

"See who?" Poros asked.

"Prometheus and…Mina." Hermie's voice caught on her name.

"No," Hestie said.

"Hermie, what happened to Prometheus and Mina?" Poros demanded.

"The vampires beheaded them."

Poros and Hestie turned to one another with looks of shock on their faces.

"Oh, my gods," Hestie murmured.

Poros fell to his bottom and raked a hand threw his hair. "Poor, Mina. I can't believe it.

Hestie sat on the floor beside him as tears flooded her eyes.

"Where were you?" Hermie asked them. "Why weren't you there?"

Before they could answer, someone entered the hull and raced toward them. It was the girl who'd beheaded Mina.

"That's Mina's killer," Hermie said angrily as the girl approached their cage.

"This is *your* fault!" the girl shouted, pointing a finger at Hermie.

"Now, wait a minute!" Hestie hollered.

"*My* fault? How in the hell is any of this *my* fault?" Hermie wanted to know.

"You saw us last night as you sailed past," she said. "And not two seconds later, Poseidon was on our trail. We nearly died trying to lose him."

"I thought vampires were immortal," Poros said dryly.

"Yes," the girl said. "But unlike you, we can be destroyed."

"I can't wait to find out how," Hermie said beneath his breath.

"Who are you?" Poros asked. "And why have you taken us?"

Hermie punched his fist against the cage. "What did you do with my bird, you thieving, murdering…"

"And our coins?" Hestie shouted.

"I'll ask the questions," the girl said. "You are gods, and yet I have never heard of you. Who are you, and why have you been spying on us?"

"Don't answer," Hestie said to Hermie and Poros. Then to the girl, she said, "If you want answers, set us free."

"We don't talk to thieving, murdering vampires!" Hermie added with tears of anger in his eyes.

The girl shrieked with frustration and flew from the hull.

"Where's Mina?" Jinsoo asked again.

Gertie turned to Morpheus, because she thought it should come from him.

"We buried her at sea," the winged god said.

Jinsoo jumped from his bed. "What? You can't do that! Poros is going to make us gods. Get her back!"

"Jinsoo, it's too late," Morpheus said.

Gertie wanted to disappear. She turned to Hector, whose face was white, as though he were thinking about the day that he had lost his mother.

"Hermie's dad can fix this!" the boy shouted. "Where Hermie? Where Captain?"

"Maybe we should wait above deck," Gertie said to Morpheus.

"Who are those people?" Jinsoo asked Morpheus. "And where are your cousins?"

"They're demigods," Morpheus said. "They have experience with vampires."

"Vampires?"

"Vampires took my cousins and Poros, and they killed your sister and Prometheus," Morpheus said.

"Captain can't be dead," the boy said, faltering.

"No," Morpheus said. "When his body has healed, it will call to his soul, which is waiting in Tartarus."

"Take me to Captain, Please!"

Morpheus shrugged and led the others from the room, down the narrow corridor, to a larger room in the bow, where Prometheus lay, white and stiff, with a red ring around his throat.

"Not here," Jinsoo said angrily. "Take me to Tartarus! I need to talk to Captain!"

"I can't do that," Morpheus said. "Look, I know you're hurting."

"My sister is going to be a god! We need her body!" the boy broke down in tears.

Morpheus shook his head. "I'm sorry. We can't bring her back. But we can find her killers. Will you help us?"

"Why didn't you keep her body?" Jinsoo asked. "Hermie's father could fix her."

Gertie flinched when another god appeared in the room from thin air. She recognized him as Thanatos, the god of death.

"Thanatos?" Hector whispered.

Gertie found it more and more difficult to breathe.

"Mina isn't coming back," the god of death said to Jinsoo. "The Fates wanted her. There's nothing I can do."

The death god vanished.

Jinsoo collapsed onto the floor and covered his face and wept. Gertie wished she knew what to say to comfort him.

"I need you to take over as captain," Morpheus said to the boy. "Just until Prometheus recovers."

The boy looked up at the winged god with narrowed eyes. "I can't be captain."

"Yes, you can," Morpheus said. "Gertie and Hector can help. They have powers."

"Powers?" the boy asked, wiping his eyes. "Then *they* can run the ship."

"We don't know how," Gertie said.

"Then what good are your powers?" Jinsoo asked. "Can you bring my sister back, like Hermie did?"

"I'm afraid not," Morpheus said. "No one can. You heard Thanatos."

Hector crossed his arms. "I have super speed and strength, and Gertie can see the future and shapeshift."

Gertie blushed. She rarely talked about her ability to shapeshift, since it had only happened once.

"Like a werewolf?" Jinsoo asked, as he leapt to his feet and backed into a corner. "Are you a werewolf?"

"No," Gertie said. "I'm a…well, I can turn into a bull."

"Oh," Jinsoo said. "Can I see?"

"Maybe some other time," Morpheus said. "Right now, I need you to captain this vessel, Jinsoo."

Jinsoo shook his head and clenched his fists as more tears fell down his cheeks. "I can't. I can't do anything."

Just then, Gertie heard a bird chirping. It sounded close, as though it were in the hull with them.

Jinsoo crossed the room and entered the corridor. "Chidori?"

A yellow canary landed on Jinsoo's shoulder.

"Chidori! You poor girl! You're back! You're back!"

CHAPTER SEVEN

A New Crew

Hestie would not allow her and Poros and Hermie to remain prisoners to some lowlife vampires. She was determined to find a way out. The adamantine cage made it impossible to god-travel or to break out, but there were other ways.

Not wanting to be overheard by vampires who may have supernatural hearing, she tried to communicate her plan telepathically, but neither Poros nor Hermie seemed to hear her.

"No one knows where we are," she whispered.

"You're not helping," her brother complained.

"But nothing stops Death," she added.

Her brother raised his brows. Poros furrowed his.

"I volunteer," she said, realizing they knew what she meant.

"No," Poros said. "If we do this—and I'm not saying we should—it should be *me*."

"It was *my* idea," Hestie said.

She didn't say what she was thinking: that Mina might be alive if Hestie hadn't convinced Poros to look for the *Tarantula*.

"How?" Hermie asked. "With what?"

They stopped talking when the ship began to spin and rock, throwing them against the bars of the cage.

"What's happening?" Hestie wondered aloud.

"We're lifting up into the sky," Poros said.

"It may be how they travel from one point to another," Hermie speculated, "to avoid being tracked on the water."

"I wonder where we're headed," Poros said.

"We need to think more about your plan," Hermie said. "We need to consider all the possible consequences."

"Why?" Hestie complained. "Why wait a moment longer?"

"What if Dad gets trapped here, too? No one will know where we are."

"When my body calls to my soul…"

"And if the vampires throw you overboard and feed you to the sharks?" Poros said. "I don't like this idea. Forget it. We need a new plan."

Hestie sighed. She hadn't thought of the possibility of the vampires feeding her to the sharks. With her body ripped to shreds, she'd have to live out the rest of eternity in Tartarus.

Maybe she deserved it.

"This spinning is making me sick," Hermie said, clutching his stomach.

"We're descending," Poros said.

The spinning slowed, and the vessel came to a halt.

"I wish I knew where the hell we are," Hestie said.

"And why we're here at all," Poros added.

Hestie took a deep breath, trying to control the chattering of her teeth. "Hermie, there's something I need to tell you."

Hermie looked across the cage at her from where he sat in one corner. "What?"

"It's my fault that Mina's dead." Hestie's entire body shuddered into one massive sob. "I wanted to look for the pirate ship. Poros wanted to stay, but I convinced him. If we'd been there…"

"Mina might be alive," Hermie finished.

The look of repugnance in her brother's eyes felt like a knife in her chest. What had she expected? Forgiveness? Well, she should have known better. Her brother hated her now, and she didn't blame him, because she hated herself. She dropped to the floor and allowed Poros to hold her as she allowed her guilt, sorrow, and grief to overwhelm her.

Gertie watched in awe as the yellow canary called Chidori chirped and flapped her wings, and the god of dreams listened.

"She's saying she was caged on the *Tarantula* in the captain's quarters," Morpheus said to Gertie, Hector, and Jinsoo where they stood together on the flybridge. "She barely escaped with her life."

"You're safe now," Jinsoo said as Chidori settled on his shoulder. "Are you hungry? Want some seeds? Hermie bought a swing for you!"

"She wants to know where the others are," Morpheus said.

Jinsoo bit back tears as Morpheus explained to the bird what had happened. Gertie's eyes welled, too. She couldn't imagine what the boy must be going through.

"This is Gertie and Hector," Morpheus said to the bird. "They're demigods with powers, and they're here to help us find Hermie, Hestie, and Poros."

The bird chirped and flapped her wings enthusiastically.

Morpheus's face transformed into an expression of excitement. "Chidori knows where they are! She can take us to the *Tarantula*!"

The teens got busy preparing the *Marcella II*. Hector had more experience than Gertie, so she followed his lead in hoisting the sails. They pulled up the anchor and buoy and unfastened and coiled the lines. A half hour passed before Jinsoo returned to the helm and shouted, "Away we go!"

Gertie was nervous as they sailed from the marina. The navigation lights on the masts and around the perimeter of the boat illuminated the darkness in all directions, allowing them to see about a hundred yards from any angle. She was surprised to see so many other boats coming and going at night. She only hoped Jinsoo knew what he was doing and didn't get them shipwrecked before they'd had a chance to find the vampires.

Once the *Marcella II* was free of the other crafts around the port and was sailing in the wide, open sea, Gertie felt less uneasy. The yellow canary gave Morpheus directions, and Jinsoo put them on a course to the pirate ship. Then Gertie and Hector joined Jinsoo, Morpheus, and the bird on the flybridge at the helm to discuss what to do next.

"Chidori says we're hours away," Morpheus said. "Gertie, you and Hector should get some sleep."

"I don't think I can," Gertie said.

"Me, either," Hector said.

"I can't believe vampires are real," Jinsoo said. "I feel like I'm in a nightmare. This can't be real."

"Most gods blame my father," Gertie said. "My father is Dionysus, god of wine. But I blame Zeus. If Zeus had never cheated on Hera, my father would never have been born."

"And neither would you," Hector pointed out.

"What did your father do?" Jinsoo asked. "How he make vampires? And why?"

"It was an accident," Hector said. "He didn't make them on purpose."

"He was lonely," Gertie explained. "Hera hated him and got him banished from Mount Olympus. He used his wine to create a troop of beautiful immortal women, his constant companions, known as the maenads."

"Maenads?" Jinsoo repeated. "What are maenads?"

"They are the oath enforcers," Hector replied. "The wine of Dionysus makes them immortal and strong but also wild and crazy."

"According to my research," Gertie began, "when a god breaks an oath on the river Styx, that god is given to the maenads as punishment, to be ripped into pieces."

Jeno had told her as much, but Gertie had looked it up, to make sure his information had been accurate.

"Let's just say it isn't pretty," Morpheus said.

Gertie shuddered. "My father didn't know what his wine would do to these women. He was reckless. That first night, the maenads went home and ripped their husbands and children from limb to limb."

"Oh, my gods," Jinsoo said.

"This happened in the ancient city of Athens," Hector added.

"Zeus and the other gods weren't happy about it," Gertie said. "My father tried to heal the families with his wine. After trying different things—none of which worked—he soon discovered that they could be saved with human blood."

"That's how the first vampires came into being," Hector said.

"How do you know this?" Jinsoo asked.

"My friend Jeno told me," Gertie said. "He was the first vampire I ever met."

Jinsoo took several steps back from Gertie. "Friend? The vampire was your *friend?*"

"You're not in danger," Morpheus said. "You have nothing to fear."

"She's a *friend* to vampires," Jinsoo said as tears filled his eyes. "Vampires are monsters. How could she be friends with one?"

"There are good vampires and bad vampires," Morpheus explained. "Just like people."

"And gods," Gertie added.

At that moment, a gray owl dropped from the sky, and, as it landed on the upper deck a few yards away from them, it morphed into the goddess Athena.

Gertie wondered if Athena would recognize her from the vampire war.

"Where is he?" Athena asked. "Where's Prometheus?"

"I'll show you, goddess," Jinsoo said.

"But who'll captain the ship?" Gertie objected.

"Don't worry," Hector said as Jinsoo led Athena below deck. "I know what to do."

Gertie wasn't reassured. She wished she had been smart enough not to tell Jinsoo about Jeno. Now, the boy didn't trust her. She was glad she hadn't mentioned that she had lived for a time as a vampire. He never would have spoken to her again.

"Listen," Morpheus said. "I didn't want to say this in front of Jinsoo, but you guys need to be prepared." He held out his palms, where two swords and scabbards appeared—one in each hand. "I've got daggers and shields for you, too." They appeared on the table beside them.

Hermie wanted to go home—not to the Underworld, and not even to the *Marcella II*. He wanted to go to his old house where he grew up in Colorado—a log cabin in the San Juan Mountains across from a beautiful reservoir. And, best of all, the house was down the road from his grandparents and cousin, whom he missed terribly. As he sat in the corner of the adamantine cage in the bowels of the *Tarantula*, he wanted his old room, his old bed, and his old life. He may have been excited six weeks ago about making the transition from demigod to god, but he would give up his immortality to be back home in Colorado living his old life.

Maybe Mina would still be alive.

He had been excited about helping Prometheus to deliver medicine and modern technologies to underdeveloped areas, but couldn't Hermie do that some other way? As the god of technology, he should be on a computer inventing new software, or in a lab developing new hardware, or at an agency leading a team of engineers.

He should be anyplace other than on a ship at sea.

Besides, he was terrified of the ocean. He was a land lover through and through. Dear gods, why had he joined the crew of the *Marcella II*?

Hermie knew the answer. He had joined the crew to be with Mina.

She hadn't wanted to train. Hermie had pushed her, wanting to prepare her to be a god. If he hadn't been training her, she wouldn't have picked up his sword and threatened the vampire.

Mina was dead because of him.

The vampires would pay for what they'd done. Hermie couldn't wait to find out how to destroy them. First, he needed to find a way out of this cage. He glanced at his sister and Poros, who were holding one another in the corner opposite him in what Hermie estimated to be a six-feet-wide, four-feet-long, and five-feet-high cage. Hestie was crying, and Poros was trying to console her.

Let her cry, after what she'd done. Morpheus had warned them that something could happen to Mina and Jonsoo, and Hestie had left, anyway. If she'd been there, maybe…

His thoughts were interrupted by the repeating image of the vampire's blade slicing across Mina's neck and the look of shock on Mina's sweet face as her head fell with a thud from her severed body.

It was quiet above deck and had been for hours. Without a portal, Hermie couldn't be sure if the ship was moving. It seemed to be sitting still. If the vampires were gone, now was the time to escape. He pushed against the bars of the cage, to see if it was tethered to anything. It was possible to fly with adamantine cuffs. Was it possible to lift their cage and fly away in it?

Gertie woke up just before dawn from where she had fallen asleep on the couch on the flybridge near the helm. Jinsoo and Hector sat quietly in the swivel seats near the control dashboard and steering wheel, each staring out to sea. Gertie glanced around for signs of Morpheus and Athena. The dream god was nowhere in sight, but Gertie recognized the graceful gray owl perched on the top of the center mast.

"Are we close?" she asked Hector, rubbing her stiff neck.

"According to Chidori, we should be there by now," Hector said. "Morpheus has gone ahead to look around."

"How are you doing, Jinsoo?" Gertie asked gently. "Do you need food or sleep or anything?"

"I'll sleep after we kill the vampires," he said.

Gertie blanched. "I don't think the plan is to kill them."

"It should be!" Jinsoo shouted with clenched fists. "The goddess agrees with me."

Gertie glanced back up at the owl.

"Athena refuses to leave until Prometheus has rejoined his body," Hector explained to Gertie. "But, yeah. Her plan is to kill and ask questions later."

"I thought our job was to recruit them for Hades," Gertie said.

Hector gave her a wry grin. "It is."

Jinsoo jumped from his seat and stared at his phone. "I just got a text from Hermie!"

Gertie and Hector leapt to their feet, too, just as Morpheus appeared from out of nowhere.

"What does it say?" Morpheus asked.

"It says, *Are you there?*" Jinsoo read.

"Ask him where he is!" Gertie said.

Jinsoo sent the text, and the three teens and the winged god eagerly awaited Hermie's reply.

"He doesn't know," Jinsoo said. "He says the ship moved by flying."

"A flying ship?" Hector arched a brow. "Are the vampires lifting the ship from one location to another? Can they do that?"

Gertie shrugged. "They have super-strength and the power to fly. I guess it's possible."

Athena descended from the mast. "That would explain Poseidon's inability to track the vessel's whereabouts."

Chidori tucked her beak into Jinsoo's hair and shrieked. Gertie didn't need the power of a god to know that the bird was upset.

"It's okay, Chidori," Morpheus said. "We'll find them."

"Wait," Gertie said, suddenly remembering something. "I saw Charybdis in my dream."

"What dream?" Jinsoo asked.

"She had a prophetic dream," Hector said. "That's why Morpheus came to her."

"Charybdis lives in the Strait of Messina," Athena said. "It's worth a look."

"Jinsoo, can you set us on a course for the Strait of Messina?" Morpheus asked.

"We have to turn around, into the wind," Jinsoo said. To Hector and Gertie, he asked, "Can you handle the tacking?"

"Just tell us what to do," Hector said.

Jinsoo took off for the main deck. "Follow me. It's best to show you."

At the hatch, Jinsoo took out his phone and tapped on it. "I'm telling Hermie not to worry, we're on our way."

Gertie glanced back at Morpheus and Athena. "Can we agree not to kill any vampires without first asking questions?"

"You might get me to agree to that," Athena said, "but I doubt Poseidon would comply, after all the trouble these pirates have caused."

As Gertie followed Jinsoo down the steps to the main deck, fingers of dread crept up her spine. With the gods at odds with what should be done about the vampires, this rescue mission seemed doomed from the start.

CHAPTER EIGHT

A Plan Is Born

Hestie opened her eyes and blinked. Hermie sat slumped in the opposite corner of the cage from her and Poros. She glanced around and listened. All was quiet. She wasn't sure how much time had passed since she had fallen asleep.

"Are they back yet?" she whispered.

Poros shook his head.

Then she heard the familiar beep of a text notification. It wasn't her phone. She'd left it on the *Marcella II*. And Poros didn't have a phone. She turned to Hermie.

"Is that your phone?" she asked Hermie. "Are you texting?"

"I know. It's crazy. I wish I would have thought of it sooner. Jinsoo said not to worry. They know where we are."

Poros and Hestie looked at one another with their mouths hanging open.

Poros chuckled. "The vampires warded the cage against prayer but, apparently, not a cell signal."

"This is amazing!" Hestie cried as, for the first time since they'd been captured, hope bloomed in her chest.

"But how can Jinsoo know where we are? And who's *we*? Is Athena helping him to sail the ship?" Hermie tapped on his phone—probably texting those very questions to Jinsoo.

"Maybe Hecate performed a location spell!" Hestie said.

"Or Apollo may have had a vision," Poros suggested.

Their speculations were cut short when the vampires burst into the hull in a giant swarm and landed on the wooden caskets, where a few of them wiped blood from their lips. It was obvious to Hestie that they had just returned from feeding. Had they been drinking human blood?

"Of course," the girl who had killed Mina said. "We cannot live without it." Then, she added, "Wait, is that a phone?"

She reached her thin hand through the bars of the cage and tried to grab the phone from Hermie, but he jumped to his feet and evaded her reach.

She drew her dagger and said, "Hand it over."

Another vampire—a teenage boy—flew over and stood beside the girl. Hestie was shocked by his beauty. Tall with sandy-colored hair, blue eyes, pouty lips, and flawless skin, he looked more like an angel than a demon.

The boy vampire grinned.

He had the power to read her mind. She'd have to be more careful.

"Yes and yes," the boy vampire said to her with a wink. Then to Hermie, he said, "Hand it over."

"Why don't you come in here and get it?" Hermie challenged.

"That is a tempting offer," the boy vampire said with a flirtatious grin.

A third vampire flew like a bullet from a casket, stuck his hands through the cage, and held Hermie by the throat. He had dark stringy hair that fell over his striking face and dark eyes. Like the others, he appeared to be in his teens. Not a single vampire among them appeared to be older than seventeen.

"Get off me!" Hermie struggled but couldn't get free.

"Is that necessary, Raimo?" the boy with the sandy hair and pouty lips asked.

The one named Raimo did not loosen his grip on Hermie's throat. "Shut up, Alastair. Your tongue is too loose."

Before Hestie and Poros could come to Hermie's rescue, two other vampires grabbed them from behind through the cage.

"Hello, darling," another girl vampire said as she pulled a fistful of Hestie's hair. She was round and busty, with big brown eyes and curly brown hair tied high on her head. "I am Penelope, but my friends call me Penny. Oh, but we are not exactly friends, are we? Though I must say, I am in love with your long red curls."

"Quit flirting," a third girl vampire, who held Poros's hair in both fists, muttered softly to Penelope.

"Do not be so sensitive, Sophia," Penelope said. "I am only teasing."

The first girl vampire, the one with the long dark curly hair and dark skin, said to Hermie, "Cooperate, or you will suffer the same fate as your friends."

"Technically, I *cannot* suffer the same fate as my friend, because she was *mortal*. Thanks to you, she's gone forever. I, on the other hand, can't be killed."

"There are worse things than death," Raimo said, tightening the grip on Hermie's throat.

"Hurt him and you'll be sorry," Poros warned as he wrenched himself away from the vampire's grip.

"Just give them the phone," Hestie said to Hermie.

Hermie handed the phone to Raimo, who then released him and gave the phone to the girl with the dark curly hair. The other vampires returned to their caskets, where they perched and stared.

"I would not have killed your friend if I had known she was not a god, like you and your captain," the first girl vampire said, turning the phone over in her hands.

Hermie gripped the bars of the cage and narrowed his eyes at her. "You really expect me to believe that?"

"I do not care what you believe," she said. "It is the truth. I am not a murderer."

"You're the *definition* of a murderer," Hermie insisted. "A murderer is someone who kills people. You kill people. Ergo, you're a murderer."

"Look, *you* threatened *us* by putting Poseidon on our trail," the girl said. "We had to find out why."

"Um, maybe because you're murdering, thieving pirates?" Hermie spat.

"Enough!" Raimo shouted as he returned to his wooden casket.

The girl glared at Hermie. "You do not know anything about us."

"I know enough," Hermie snapped.

"Ignore them," one of the other vampires called from across the hull. "Your efforts will get you nowhere."

Hestie noticed that the others had climbed into their caskets and had pulled their lids closed. Were they going to sleep?

"Some will sleep," Alastair, who had remained near the cage, said with his beautiful pouty lips. "Others will entertain themselves until dusk."

Hestie couldn't think of many ways one could find entertainment in a wooden box.

"Some of us read, one of us knits, some draw, some compose songs or poetry, and others listen in on what people are thinking," he said, still grinning.

"Because you can't tolerate the sun?" Poros asked.

Alastair frowned. "We were a choir in Athens a long, long time ago. We are a cultured people of many talents who find it easy to entertain ourselves."

"But you stay in the boxes because of the sun—isn't that right?" Poros asked.

"That is enough talking," the girl vampire said as she fiddled with Hermie's phone. "Tell me the password."

Hermie said nothing, but the girl said, "Thanks."

Hermie's mouth dropped open.

Then the girl vampire said, "Someone knows where we are."

The lids opened on their hinges before the other vampires sat up, wearing looks of concern.

"It is too late to move now," one of them said.

"Get ready to fight," Raimo said as he flew from his casket.

"Our lord said to lay low for a while," the girl vampire said. "So, that is what we will do."

"We have no choice but to defend ourselves," Penelope said.

"What do you want from us?" Poros shouted.

"Nothing," the first girl vampire said. "We want absolutely nothing from you."

"Then let us go!" Hestie insisted.

"Believe it or not," Alastair said—again with a flirtatious grin—"we do not have a death wish."

"We promise not to harm you," Poros said.

"Speak for yourself!" Hermie shouted.

"Hermie!" Hestie hissed.

"Enough!" the girl vampire said. "We await instructions from our lord."

"And who is your lord?" Poros asked.

"You would like to know, yes?" the girl said.

Hestie felt her cheeks grow hot. She'd never wanted to strangle someone as much as she wanted to strangle the vampire bitch smiling back at her.

Hermie was overwhelmed with disgust. What kind of person killed people and then claimed not to be a murderer? Was she using mind control on him? If vampires needed human blood to survive, that made them predators, and predators of humans were murderers, plain and simple.

"We do not kill our prey," the girl said from where she sat, waiting, on top of her casket. "And we prefer the word *crate* to *casket*. A crate is a safe place to rest. A *casket* is something to be buried in."

"Quit listening to my thoughts," Hermie said.

"It is hard not to. You are shouting them at me."

"Just ignore them, Del," one of the other vampires said to her.

So that was her name—Dell. Like the computer company?

"It is Del, with one L," she said. "Short for Delphine."

Hermie returned to his corner of the cage and sat down, trying to breathe, trying to calm down. He needed to clear his head.

But then Poros asked, "If you don't kill your prey, what do you do with them?"

"We drink one pint, and one pint only," Alastair said, from where he sat on the floor with his back against a casket. "That is the rule."

"Your lord's rule?" Poros asked.

"The gods of Olympus made the rules," Del said. "They created us, and they let us live, as long as we stick to the rules."

"Why would the gods create *vampires*?" Hestie asked with obvious disgust in her voice.

Del frowned. "It was an accident. You do not have to be rude."

"You killed our friend," Hestie said angrily. "You stole our coins— and probably our bird—and abducted us. So, yeah, I'm going to be rude."

"Try to stay calm," Poros muttered.

"Is our bird *here*?" Hermie asked through a tight throat. "I haven't heard her."

"She was," Del said. "She escaped."

Hermie sighed with relief. Poor Chidori. She must have been terrified. He hoped she had found her way back to the *Marcella II*. What if a sea creature leapt from the sea and snapped her out of the air? He wished he had his phone so he could ask Jinsoo if he'd seen her.

Del took his phone from her trouser pocket and wrote out a text.

"Chidori made it back safely," Del said after a beat. "And your friends are headed to the Messina Strait."

Hermie wondered if she were speaking the truth. He hoped so.

"Are we anywhere near that area?" Hestie asked.

"Maybe," Del said with a shrug. "Maybe not."

Alastair moved closer to the cage, so that he stood in front of Hermie. "Poseidon is the real enemy to the human race, Hermie. Not us."

Hermie shook his head and chuckled. "Bullshit."

"It is no use," someone called from across the room. "Ignore them and be prepared to fight."

As Gertie worked the tacking on the front mainsail, she glanced over her shoulder at Hector near the center mast and at Jinsoo on the upper deck near the back mast. They were using the rigs to zigzag their way toward the Strait of Messina, to avoid heading directly into the wind.

She found it more and more difficult to focus on the rigging, however, because the main deck had become crowded with arguing gods. She recognized most but not all. Among them was her father, Dionysus, who had not so much as acknowledged her presence.

"My children's safety is a priority," a red-haired goddess called Therese argued. "And why are mortals aboard? They're in danger!"

"They're demigods with powers," Hades explained. "And they've dealt with vampires before."

"We don't need to *deal* with the vampires," another god, with long sun-bleached hair and beard, bellowed. "We need to destroy them!"

"Hear, hear!" Athena cried.

"We agreed not to, Poseidon," Gertie's father argued. "Have you forgotten?"

So, the god with the sun-bleached hair and turquoise eyes was Poseidon, Gertie thought.

"That was before they attacked Prometheus, killed an innocent mortal, and captured three gods!" Athena argued.

"There may be a logical explanation for their behavior," Hades said. "They deserve a chance to explain themselves."

"Lord Hades is right," Hermes said. "We can't just wipe them out without giving them a chance to explain."

"The hell we can!" Poseidon bellowed.

"Even the most heinous criminals deserve a chance to be heard," Hades said. "You have my word that, if found guilty, the vampires will get their just desserts."

"Oh, they're guilty," Athena said. "We have a witness."

"He didn't actually see what happened," Morpheus said. "He was hiding in the pantry."

"I was referring to Prometheus," Athena snapped. "And don't forget that *I'm* your elected leader. That should mean something."

"*Hades* was elected first," Hermes argued. "You got your position when Hades abdicated his, to remain in the Underworld."

"Nevertheless," Athena said sternly, "I'm your leader."

Ares folded his arms at his chest. "If Zeus were here, he would…"

"But he isn't," Hades said.

Poseidon lifted his hands in the air. "Are we not a democratic council? Or will we revert to the old ways at the first sign of conflict?"

"You and I are aligned on this," Athena said to the god of the sea. "It doesn't happen often, but it has now. Why are you fighting me?"

Poseidon's answer, if was going to make one, was cut off by the appearance of three goddesses—two of which Gertie recognized: One was the Fury Alecto, mother to Lajos. The other was the Fury Megaera.

"The *Tarantula* is not in the Messina Strait," Megaera said. "My sisters and I searched every mile of it."

The gods turned to Morpheus.

"That's where we thought they'd be because of Gertie's dream," the winged god said. "It was prophetic, through the gates of horn. I saw it myself."

"Call us when you have their true location," Hades said before he put on his helm of invisibility and disappeared.

"Wait!" Gertie cried.

Hades reappeared, with his helm in his hand, and all gods turned to her. She felt small and stupid, but she had an idea.

"I've thought of a plan," she said, clasping her trembling hands behind her back.

Ares and Poseidon rolled their eyes, but the red-haired goddess called Therese said, "Let's hear it!"

Gertie wondered if she should have waited for the gods to leave. She could have presented her plan to Morpheus, who could have told her whether it was worth mentioning to the others. But now that everyone was staring at her, it was too late not to spit it out.

"Like Morpheus said, I had a dream from the gates of horn, and, in it, I saw Hermie, Hestie, and Poros in an adamantine cage in the bottom of the *Tarantula*."

"Did they seem harmed?" Therese asked.

"No," Gertie replied, realizing that Therese was Hestie and Hermie's mother. Hestie had the same vibrant red hair.

Therese leaned against the rails. "Oh, thank the gods."

Other gods also seemed relieved.

Gertie continued, "I also saw Charybdis return to her cave."

"So?" Athena wanted to know.

"The *Tarantula* may not be in the Strait of Messina at the moment, but it will be, eventually," Gertie said.

Poseidon thrust his fist into the air. "We'll ambush them!"

"Good plan!" Ares clapped his hands.

"It's a terrible idea," Hades argued as he paced in the center of their circle.

"Wait." Gertie shook her head and tried to regain the floor by waving her hands.

"Let the girl speak," Dionysus said.

As the crowd hushed, Gertie glanced with surprise at her father. His standing up for her might be a little thing, but it was something, and she was grateful. "You can't hide from vampires. They have x-ray vision and the ability to read thoughts. They'll sense you before you can ambush them."

"Not if we have the helm of invisibility," Athena pointed out.

"Let her finish," Hades said.

Gertie cleared her throat, her mouth suddenly dry. Again, she clasped her trembling hands behind her as she said, "Hector and I could take the dinghy to the Messina Strait."

"Alone?" Athena asked.

Gertie nodded.

"That sounds too dangerous," Therese said.

"And you have no idea when the pirates will move into the area," Megaera pointed out.

"You could be waiting for days, weeks," Alecto added.

"I don't think so," Gertie said. "Besides, we could always take the dinghy back to the *Marcella II*, if the vampires didn't show."

"I'm more worried about what happens if they *do* show," Hermes said. "What would you do?"

Gertie lifted a shaky finger into the air. "If they take us to their ship, we might be able to rescue the gods from the inside."

Alecto flew closer to Gertie. "What if they don't take you to the ship?".

"What if they feed on you and leave you there?" Megaera asked.

"We would pray to you," Hector said. "And alert you to their location."

Ares folded his big arms across his big chest. "Why not just go with plan B?"

"We'll just have more teens to rescue," Poseidon complained, lifting his arms, as if he were directing an airplane.

"First, we would attempt to befriend them and gain their trust," Gertie said.

"Like spies," Ares said, seeming to warm up to the idea.

"Exactly," Gertie said. "We'll look for a way to rescue the gods, and we'll also collect evidence that could be used to either defend or to incriminate the vampires."

"What if the vampires kill you?" Athena said. "What good are you to us then?"

"We'd be worth more to the vampires alive than dead," Hector said. "As a food supply."

"And yet they killed the mortal girl, Mina," Poseidon pointed out.

"Maybe one of you could watch over us, beneath the protection of the helm," Gertie added, "just in case."

"It should be me," Hermes said. "No god, and certainly no vampire, can outrun or outfly me."

"I like it," Hades said.

"Only because you'd love the opportunity to recruit the vampires to your band of reapers," Poseidon said angrily.

"That's true." Hades took up his pacing once again. "I don't deny it. The vampire reapers in my charge are faring well, are they not?"

"I never liked the arrangement," Athena said. "I worried about some of them going rogue and causing trouble, like these pirates."

"These pirates were never among my reapers, I assure you."

"It's a good plan," Hermes said. "Let's stop bickering and put it in motion."

Hades stomped his feet. "Agreed!"

"Hear, hear!" Dionysus said as he winked across the deck at Gertie.

"Fine!" Poseidon said curtly.

When the other gods agreed, Gertie returned her father's smile. She may not like him very much, but she wouldn't mind proving something to him. And maybe—just maybe—at the end of this, Poros would agree to turn her and Hector into gods, too.

CHAPTER NINE

A Plan Goes Awry

As the hours passed, the vampires grew less vigilant, and all but one of them—the one called Raimo—returned to their boxes and closed the lid.

Hestie lay curled against Poros in the corner of their adamantine cage and listened to the lapping of the water against the still ship. Her brother sat across from them with his eyes closed. She wondered if he'd ever forgive her for not being there. She wiped another tear from her cheek and took a deep breath before slowly exhaling. She focused on her breathing and on the lapping of the water. Just as she was about to doze, she thought she heard weeping coming from the wooden box belonging to Del.

What would a vampire pirate have to cry about? Maybe her lord had been hard on her. Maybe she was asleep and having a bad dream.

Hestie then noticed Raimo leave the hull. She strained to listen to what he might be doing above deck—had he gone to meet someone? She held her breath but heard nothing but the weeping vampire and the lapping waves.

Moments later, Raimo returned just as the lids of the caskets opened on their hinges and the other vampires climbed out. Hestie noticed that Del's beautiful lashes were wet with tears.

"I have orders from our lord," Raimo said to them.

If he conveyed those orders, he did so in silence, for Hestie heard nothing more, until one of them said, "This is asinine!"

"Watch your tongue, Mahdi!" Del snapped.

"But this is bullshit!" Mahdi, whose black curly hair and dark skin glistened with sweat, complained. "How does he expect us to complete our other more important mission if we have to make this extra journey?"

"Where are we going?" Poros asked.

Mahdi flew like a bullet to the cage and grabbed the adamantine bars. "Looks like we will be meeting your friends after all."

"What is that supposed to mean?" Hermie asked.

Mahdi ignored him and, after closing his casket, as the others had done, followed the herd from the hull.

Hestie listened for the vampires above deck. Once again, the ship spun and lifted into the air, and she and her brother and Poros fell against the bars of the cage until the ship stopped spinning.

When the *Tarantula* landed back on the water, Hermie fell against one side of the cage, causing the entire thing to move a foot from the wall, pulling the chain taut.

"That chain," Hestie said, noticing it for the first time. "That's not adamantine."

"No," Poros agreed.

"Which means we can break it." Hermie climbed to his feet and stood beside Hestie to get a closer look.

"Is this chain the only thing tethering the cage to the boat?" Hestie wondered out loud.

She stretched her hand through the bars and yanked the chain free of the stud it had been anchored to.

Poros shook his head. "Thank the gods you didn't put a hole in the ship."

"That didn't even occur to me," Hestie said. "That could have been bad."

Hermie moved to the front of the cage—the side facing the wooden crates. "Come on. Let's fly out of here."

The three of them lined up, and on Hermie's count, they applied pressure against the side of the cage. The cage turned like a hamster wheel until it hit against the front row of wooden crates and came to a stop. Hestie managed not to get thrown about too much. She couldn't say the same for the boys.

"You guys okay?" she asked as Hermie rubbed his head and Poros his thigh.

"Let's do it again," Hermie said.

"But push upward this time," Poros said. "Let's fly the cage to the hatch."

"It will never fit," Hestie pointed out. "Is the plan to bust through to the upper deck?"

"There's no other choice," her brother said. "Come on. Ready?"

Hestie and Poros nodded.

As they sat at dusk on the dinghy with their fishing rods in the rough waters of the Messina Strait, Gertie wondered why Hector was so quiet. Perhaps he wasn't comfortable talking with Hermes nearby, beneath the helm of invisibility—though, for all she knew, Hermes could have left her and Hector there to deal with the vampires alone.

Maybe Hector was focused on blocking his mind from the vampires. Gertie had been surprised by how easily the skill had returned to her after a year of not needing it. But maybe it wasn't so easy for Hector.

It was cold, and the white caps tossed the dinghy about. Although she was bleeding, Gertie wasn't too worried. It was a surface wound, and it was only a trickle of blood running down her arm, which was full of goosebumps from the chilly night. It was enough blood to catch the attention of a vampire. She knew from experience.

When Selene appeared in the night sky, Gertie felt comforted. Gertie had never met the moon goddess, but she'd often found herself praying to her. According to Gertie's research, Selene tended to remain neutral in the conflicts among gods and, like Prometheus, cared more for the human race than her own kind. Seeing the moon up in the sky overlooking the earth often reminded Gertie that she wasn't alone.

She felt a twitch on her line, so she reeled up, finding nothing but the rubbery lure on the end of it.

"I thought I had something," Gertie said before she cast the lure back into the water. "I guess I don't know what I'm doing. I've only been fishing one other time."

When Hector said nothing in reply, she asked, "Is there anything on your mind that you can talk about?"

"Were you happy to see your father?" he asked.

Gertie was taken aback. "I don't know. A little, I guess."

"I wonder why Hephaestus didn't come."

"I'm sure he must have been busy."

"*All* of them are busy."

Gertie wasn't sure what to say to that.

"Lajos sees his mother once a year—more than that, now that his father is gone."

"Hephaestus probably didn't know you'd be there," Gertie said.

Hector shrugged. He reeled up his line and cast it back out.

"Hey," she said, wanting to change the subject, "have you ever wished you could be a god?"

"No way."

Gertie frowned. "Really? Why not?"

"I would never want to put my kids through what my parents put me through. I want a normal life with a typical family—children, little league, regular jobs, regular bills, all of it—all the things I didn't get as a kid."

"My childhood sucked, too, you know."

"I know," he said. "We were both robbed by neglectful parents. I don't want to be that kind of parent."

"You won't be," Gertie said as she squeezed his hand. "No matter what you become."

"Why do you ask? Is that something *you* want?"

She shrugged, even though she knew her answer. She would do almost anything to become a god, now that she knew it was possible. "I want to be with you."

The adamantine cage hovered above the wooden crates below.

"This was a dumb idea," Hermie said. "I was so desperate that I didn't think it through."

"But we're almost there," his sister said. "We can bust through. I know we can."

"Don't you see?" Hermie said with a sigh. "Without the key, we'll be trapped in here, whether we're on this ship or someplace else."

"Maybe Hecate knows a spell," Poros offered.

"And what if she doesn't?" Hestie said. "Hermie's right. What if the vampires throw away the key when they come back and find us gone?"

"We have to find it before we leave," Hermie said. "Come on. Let's put the cage back exactly as it was."

The gods worked together to manipulate the cage through the air toward the stern, where they settled it on the floor in its original position. Then Hermie slumped back down in his corner.

"Did you see who locked us in?" he asked.

"I think it was Del," Poros said.

"We need to find a way to get her to let one of us out, so we can see where she keeps the key," Hermie said. "Maybe if Hestie says she needs to take a crap."

"They'd just tell her to use that bucket." Poros gestured toward the empty bucket at the back of the cage.

"Hestie could say she's too shy to crap in a room full of people."

"She could," Poros said. "But I doubt they'd care."

"Think," Hestie muttered to herself.

Poros rubbed her shoulders. "We'll think of something."

Gertie and Hector had reeled up their fishing lines and had lain the rods in the bottom of the dinghy and were now huddled together, shivering against the cold night as the waves lifted them up and down, lulling them to sleep.

"Should we turn back?" Hector asked.

"Just a few more minutes," she said.

The lights on the boat shone no more than thirty feet in each direction, and, past that ring of light, the world seemed to end. It was spooky, not knowing what lay beyond.

A movement in the water near them caught Gertie's eye. Could it be a vampire? A shark? Charybdis?

Two brown hands reached up from below the surface and grabbed the side of the boat, threatening to capsize them.

"What the hell?" Hector leaned in the opposite direction, using his body weight to offset the weight of the person clinging to their boat.

Then a face, wearing a mask and headlight, emerged.

"Jinsoo?" Gertie asked once he'd lowered the mask from his face. "What are you doing here?"

"I want to help," he said. "I want to avenge my sister's murder."

"That's not why we're here," Hector said as he and Gertie lifted the boy and his oxygen tank into the boat.

"I know," he said. "It's why *I'm* here. I snuck away after the others left."

"We need to take him back to the *Marcella II*," Gertie said to Hector. "He's going to ruin everything. They'll read his mind. He'll blow our cover."

Hector started up the motor. "Agreed."

"No!" Jinsoo said. He pulled off his mask and unstrapped the oxygen tank. "Do you know how long it took me to get here?"

"We have no choice," Gertie said. "It doesn't look like they're coming tonight, anyway. I'm cold and hungry and want to go to bed."

Suddenly they were surrounded by a swirling black cloud that seemed to drop from the sky, like a tornado. Gertie and the boys were lifted from the boat in the arms of strangers whose grins exposed fangs. The vampires had come, after all. Gertie immediately blocked her mind, knowing that it would do little good, because Jinsoo's was an open book. As the vampires carried them to their ship—which was twice as large as the *Marcella II*, Gertie prayed to Hermes to protect them from harm.

They were taken into what appeared, by the soft glow of Jinsoo's headlamp, to be a dining hall. Gertie imagined that it had once been quite elegant, but that day had long passed. The wooden tables and chairs were rotted and broken. The windows, painted over with black paint, were full of cobwebs. And the couches along the perimeter of the room were full of holes.

At the back of the room was a large wooden bookcase. The doors on the case had only a few glass panes still intact. The other panes were broken or missing. Gertie's eyes followed Jinsoo's light to the rows of old, dusty hardback books. She wondered what they contained and if they were of any value.

On the floor near the bookcase were three wooden chests. One of the lids was partially opened, revealing a bronze bust, a jeweled dagger, a silver ornamental box, and red velvet fabric frayed along the edges.

"Have a seat," one of the vampires said as he and his cronies forced Gertie, Hector, and Jinsoo into chairs around one of the tables in the center of the room.

The vampires used rope to tie Gertie's wrists together. The same was done to Hector and Jinsoo. Then all but two of them—a girl and a boy—returned to the deck outside.

The girl, who had dark curly hair and dark skin, used her index finger to scoop up the line of blood trickling down Gertie's arm. She put her finger into her mouth, sucked off the blood, and said, "Tasty."

"You killed my sister!" Jinsoo said through trembling lips.

The girl vampire stared into Jinsoo's eyes. "I need you to calm down. Take a deep breath and relax."

Jinsoo was mesmerized. He did exactly as the vampire commanded.

"I'm here to help you," Gertie said to the girl. "I lived for a time with vampires in caves beneath the acropolis in Athens. I have some insight into your point of view."

The girl glared at her. "You know nothing about me."

Gertie sucked in her lips as blood from embarrassment rushed to her cheeks.

"Listen Gertie," the boy vampire began. He had short blond hair, full lips, and gorgeous blue eyes.

"How do you know my name?" she asked. Then she glanced at Jinsoo.

"I know all of your names," the vampire said. "Gertie, Hector, and Jinsoo, yes?"

Jinsoo gave him a slow nod. Gertie could tell the boy was still under the spell of the first vampire.

"Maybe you will feel better if you know my name," the vampire said. "I am Alastair. And this is Del."

Del rolled her eyes. "We have an important mission to carry out and do not have time for this nonsense."

"What kind of mission?" Hector asked.

"Nothing for you to worry about," Alastair said. "Just stay put, and we will be back in a jiffy."

It took most of Gertie's strength to keep her mind blocked as the vampires left the room.

As soon as they were alone, Gertie turned to Hector. "We have to stay calm. Keep your block up."

He gave her a smile and showed her his hands, which he'd broken free from the rope. He quickly untied her and Jinsoo.

"They're below deck," Gertie said of the young gods who'd been taken prisoner. "Come on!"

Gertie led the way from the old dining room to the main deck, where Selene hovered in the night sky. Gertie found the hatch that led below, where it was dark and musty, just like in her dream, until Jinsoo entered from behind and illuminated the space. The wooden coffins were there in rows, and the other crates were stacked against the walls of the ship. And, like in her dream, there was a metal cage at the very back with three teenagers in it.

"Guys!" Jinsoo cried as he ran to his friends. "You okay?"

"Jinsoo?" the blond boy called Poros said. "How did you get here?"

"Where's Chidori?" Hermie asked.

"I left her with Captain," Jinsoo said. "He still not back in his body yet." Then he turned and pointed to Gertie and Hector. "These demi-gods came to help. Gertie and Hector, this is Hermie, Hestie, and Poros."

"Hello," Gertie said.

"Thank the gods!" Hestie said. "Hurry! Look for the key! It might be hidden in one of those caskets."

"I'm so relieved to see you, Jinsoo," Poros said. "I can't tell you how sorry I am about your sister."

"I can't think about that right now." Jinsoo lifted the lid of the coffin closest to the cage. Then he lifted another.

Gertie did the same, starting with the back row. Hector searched the middle row.

"It might not be here," Hermie said. "It might be with the vampires."

Gertie opened a crate stacked against the wall and found a painting inside. The face of a haggard woman wearing a kerchief and holding a baby looked up at Gertie from the portrait. Gertie returned the lid and searched several more and found a different painting in each. What were the pirates planning to do with them?

She prayed to Hermes, hoping he'd know what to do, but she got no reply. She was beginning to believe he wasn't there.

"If we don't find the key, don't worry," Gertie said. "I'll try to get the vampires to trust me, and, as soon as an opportunity presents itself, I'll…"

"But they know about you," Hermie said. "They know you and Hector are demigods."

Gertie's stomach tightened. "What?"

"How?" Jinsoo asked. "How can they know?"

"There must be a mole among the gods," Hector said.

"Then why would the vampires take our bait?" Gertie wondered. "If they knew we were demigods, why would they capture us in the first place?"

"It's a trap," Hector said.

Jinsco's face was pinched with pain and anger when he said, "Just one more reason to kill them."

"No." Gertie said. "We're here to investigate."

"That's ridiculous," Hestie cried.

"Investigate what?" Hermie said. "I saw one of them murder Mina in cold blood."

"The gods have a traitor among them," Hector said. "If we wipe out the vamps, that traitor will just recruit more."

"We need a name," Poros agreed.

"Maybe Hermes knows," Jinsoo said. "Hermes? You here?"

Gertie's stomach dropped. "You weren't supposed to tell anyone, Jinsoo. Now the vampires will know."

"They'll read Jinsoo's mind anyway," Hector said.

"Hermes is *here*?" Poros repeated.

"He's watching over us beneath the helm of invisibility," Gertie explained.

"He's here to help," Hector said.

Hestie clapped her hands. "Good news, for once!"

Gertie crossed her arms, feeling sick. Everything was going wrong. "Try not to think about it, so we don't give him away to the vamps."

"Someone's coming," Hestie said.

Gertie glanced across the room at Hector.

"Stay close," he said, moving toward Jinsoo. "I'll do my best to protect you."

Jinsoo nodded as Gertie joined them near the cage and waited for the vampires to return.

CHAPTER TEN

Unusual Cargo

Hermie's heart seemed to thud in his throat when he saw what the vampires carried into the hull. Surely Hermes would put a stop to this.

"Oh, my gods," Poros whispered.

Hestie covered her mouth and stared.

"What are you doing?" Hector demanded, but the vampires ignored him.

Hermie counted eight little boys. By his estimation, they were no more than six years of age. The vampires sucked blood from their necks or wrists and then laid them inside the wooden crates before closing the lids. Then they sat on top of the caskets, panting, as if they'd just finished running a race.

"That was close," Alastair said to Del, who nodded as she licked fresh blood from her lips.

The little boys pounded on the lids, crying and screaming to be released. Hermie recognized their language. It was Pashto.

"How can you live with yourselves?" Hermie said through gritted teeth.

"What can you possibly have to gain from this?" Hector asked. "Are they your new food source?"

"No," Dell said. "We have nothing to gain from this."

"Then why?" Hermie cried as he locked eyes with Del. She was supremely beautiful—a beautiful devil. "Why do this to innocent children?"

Del averted her eyes.

"We have just saved their lives," Alastair said.

Hermie shook his head and laughed.

"Ignore them," Raimo said. "They cannot understand."

"Try me," Gertie said to Raimo.

The trapped boys continued to pound on the lids, crying to their mothers and begging to be set free. The vampires stubbornly, morosely sat on the lids to prevent their escape.

"Get in the cage," Raimo said to Hector, Gertie, and Jinsoo.

Hermie saw an opportunity. Over half of the vampires were occupied with preventing the boys from leaving their crates. If there were ever a time to attempt to escape, this was it. He and his sister and Poros could charge the door to the cage as soon as it was opened.

"Wait," Del said to Raimo.

"Yeah, I got it," Raimo said. He turned to Gertie. "Get in the crate instead."

Hermie frowned. They'd heard his thoughts as soon as he'd thought them. How in the hell would they ever escape?

"Get in!" Raimo said again to Gertie.

"What? Why?" Gertie asked.

Raimo lifted the lid of an empty crate and pointed. Gertie climbed in. Two other vampires made Hector and Jinsoo climb inside two other empty crates.

"Hurry," Del said. "We need to move before daylight."

Hermie watched in disgust as the vampires quickly wrapped chains around the wooden crates containing the eight boys and the three mortals before flying above deck.

"This isn't ordinary chain," Hector said as he pounded against his lid.

"If your super strength can't break it," Gertie said, "then…"

"It must be adamantine," Hermie finished for her.

"How did the vampires get so much of it?" Poros said. "It's supposed to be rare, according to my sister."

"According to my research," Gertie said from inside the box, "adamantine was mined from meteorites that fell to the earth outside of Delphi in ancient times. Perhaps vampires found the source and forged their own chains and such."

"Let's hope not," Hestie said.

Hermie closed his eyes and cringed at the pitiful sounds of little boys begging to be freed.

In Pashto, Hestie said, "My friends and I will find a way to help you. We'll get you out of here—you'll see." Then she turned her worried face to Hermie. "What do we do? We have to do something to help them."

"Hermes?" Hermie asked. "Now would be a great time to reveal yourself."

He and his sister and Poros glanced around, but the messenger god did not appear.

"We'll think of something," Hermie said, though he wasn't so sure that they would.

Just then, the ship spun, and he and his sister and Poros were thrown against the sides of the cage again. Nausea swept over him.

"What's happening?" Jinsoo cried from his box.

"We're moving," Poros said.

"The vampires spin the ship and make it fly," Hestie explained.

In a few minutes, it was over, and the *Tarantula* was once again resting on the sea.

Hermie listened for the vampires. It wasn't long before Del, Alastair, Raimo, Penelope, and three others—a girl with big brown eyes whose name Hermie believed was Sophia and two boys—returned and sat on their wooden caskets. The two boys were opposites in every way. One was long and lanky with short curly red hair, and the other was short and thickly muscled with his black hair cut in a buzz.

The little prisoners were less vocal now—though Hermie could still hear some of them whimpering for their mothers.

"Where are we?' Hermie asked. "And where are the others?"

"Why should I answer your questions, when you refuse to answer mine?" Del said dryly.

Hermie bit his lip and sighed. "I'm sure you found your answers from me, anyway, by reading my mind."

"True," Alastair said.

"Will you please let us out of these crates?" Gertie asked. "It doesn't smell very nice in here."

Penelope laughed and turned to Raimo. "Poor girl. You put her in Kagan's crate."

The other vampires laughed, too.

"Kagan cannot help it," the girl with the big eyes said.

"Oh, Sophia." Penelope kissed her cheek. "My sweet softie."

"How can you be so cavalier while those little boys are crying beneath you?" Hestie asked.

"They cannot understand anything we say," Del said. "What do you expect us to do?"

"Gods can speak all languages," Hestie said. "Tell me what to say to them."

"Fine," Del said. "Tell them that we saved them from the slavers and will have them home with their families in Pakistan tomorrow night."

"What?" Hermie said with his mouth hanging open. "Are you really going to lie to them?"

"Just say it," Del said. "And let them know that the reason they feel strange is because the vampire virus is in their system, healing them from the damage caused by months of starvation."

Hermie glanced at Hestie, who asked Alastair, "Did you really save them from slavers?"

Alastair nodded. "They were being smuggled to a coastal town in Egypt to be sold in the black market as camel jockeys."

"Camel jockeys?" Poros repeated.

"Camel racing is big money," Penelope added. "And bad people will pay good money for tiny, malnourished boys who can be trained to ride."

"I've read about this!" Gertie cried from inside her box.

"Tell them," Del said to Hestie. "Let them know that the others have gone to get them food."

Hestie glanced at Poros and Hermie.

Hermie shrugged but Poros said, "Tell them. If it's not true, it may still give them hope."

Hestie spoke in Pashto to the boys. When they asked why they couldn't come out of their dark boxes, Hestie asked Alastair, "Why can't they come out of the crates and wait for the food out here with us?"

"The virus in their blood does not only heal them. It gives them the powers of a vampire—temporarily," Alastair explained. "It is dangerous for boys so young."

"They can easily kill themselves or one another," Del said. "Everyone is safer if they remain in these crates until the virus has passed from their systems."

"How long does that take?" Poros asked.

"Six hours," Gertie called from her crate.

"But there's no reason to keep me and my friends trapped in these caskets," Hector said.

"Please!" Jinsoo cried. "Let me out of here!"

Hestie translated Del's message to the boys, explaining why they had to wait. She recommended that they close their eyes and try to sleep. It would make the time go by faster.

"Did you save the lives of the boys so you could feed on them?" Hermie asked again.

Del shot Hermie a look of reproach. "I already answered that question."

Alastair raked his fingers through his sandy hair. "We did feed on them, but only long enough to heal them from the damage caused by months of starvation."

Alastair unwrapped the chain from Jinsoo's crate and lifted the lid. "You can come out, cutie pie—if you do not cause trouble."

Without a word, Jinsoo climbed out and scrambled toward the cage, to stand by his friends.

"What about the others?" Jinsoo asked.

"No one deserves to lie in Kagan's crate," Penelope said to Del. "Where is she going to go? She lacks the strength of the boy—Hector."

Del shrugged. "Whatever you think."

Penelope removed the chain and helped Gertie from the box.

"Thank you," Gertie said. "But won't you please let Hector out, too?"

"If he unblocks his mind," Raimo said. "It is hard to trust someone with super-strength when his mind is shielded from us."

"Fine," Hector said. "I'm an open book. Better?"

"There's a way to block your thoughts?" Hermie asked Gertie.

The demigod nodded.

Raimo freed Hector, who joined Gertie and Jinsoo on the floor by the cage.

"If you block your mind again," Raimo said to Hector, "you are going straight back into the box."

"Got it," Hector said. "I'm not so good at it, anyway."

Jinsoo wiped his eyes with trembling hands. Hermie could only imagine how terrified and angry and sad his friend was feeling.

"Don't worry, Jinsoo," Hermie whispered to his friend as he glared at Del. "You'll have your freedom and your revenge, if it's the last thing I do."

"We can hear you," Dell said as she rolled her eyes.

Gertie sat on the floor beside Hector, leaning her back against the cage. So much for her plan to infiltrate and to gain the trust of the vampires. She doubted the gods would consider making her one of them after this poor showing. Hopefully, they would consider her role in the vampire uprising when making their decision.

Gertie's thoughts were interrupted when Del said, "I know who you are. You two fought with Jeno against the vampires."

"Not against," Gertie started.

"You do not have to explain," Del said. "Hector's thoughts have shown me. You were in love with Jeno."

Gertie's face grew hot.

"You look delicious when you blush," Alastair said.

"You can drink from me, if you want," Gertie said. "I don't mind."

"No," Raimo said. "We do not know how powerful she is with the virus and her demigod powers combined."

Gertie shrugged. "Suit yourself."

"When will the others be back with the food?" Hector asked.

Del looked up—perhaps using her x-ray vision to see outside. "Soon. It is nearly dawn."

"Why do you have so many paintings?" Gertie asked. "What are they for?"

"They're pirates," Hermie said. "They steal things."

"That is true," Alastair said with a grin.

"But it's not the whole truth, is it?" Gertie asked. "There's more to the story."

"Do not say anything," Raimo said. "We cannot trust them."

"We already told them too much," Penelope agreed.

"Then there is no reason to hide anything," Del said.

"I think there is," Riamo said.

"I agree with Del," Alastair said. Then, turning toward the cage, he said, "You are familiar with the custom of the art and treasures of the conquered being taken by the conquerors?"

Gertie glanced at Hector, who was nodding.

"Like when the Nazis took everything from the Jews?" Hermie asked.

"That is one example," Del said.

"The same thing happened to slaves in America before the Civil War," Gertie said. "Black American writers and artists didn't own their work. Their owners did."

"There are many more examples," the lanky red-haired vampire said.

Penelope stood up and moved closer to Sophia. "It is terrible when oppressors profit from art created by others."

"It's even more terrible to kill innocent people!" Hermie said.

Del glared at him. "How many times must I say it was an accident? I thought she was a *god*, like you! I was defending myself!"

"Can we get back to the paintings?" Gertie said. "Shouting gets us nowhere."

Hermie folded his arms and fumed in silence.

"Please, continue," Hector said to the vampires.

"We have recovered art and treasures once belonging to Bosniaks and Albanians. It was taken by the Serbians," Alastair said.

"Are you referring to the Yugoslav Wars?" Gertie asked. "I remember reading about that."

"I do not think this is a good idea," Raimo said again.

"Is that what's in those crates?" Gertie asked. "Art from Bosniaks and Albanians?"

"And others," Del said.

"We take the art when it is being shipped by the oppressors," Alastair began, "and we return it to the oppressed—if not to the individual artists, then, at the least, to their local museums."

Hermie shook his head and muttered, "I find this hard to believe."

"How do you do it?" Hestie asked. "How do you know where to find the stolen art and where to return it?"

"Our lord helps us," Del said.

"Careful," Raimo warned.

"What did you mean yesterday when you said that Poseidon was an enemy to the human race?" Poros asked Alastair. "Is he somehow involved with the selling of stolen art?"

"I really do not think this is a good idea," Riamo said again.

At that moment, the other vampires—Mahdi and two others—returned with bags in their arms. They settled on top of the caskets and began showing off the food they'd brought: loaves of bread, a tub of peanut butter, a bag of apples and another of oranges, and lots of canned food. Gertie hadn't eaten for hours. Neither had Hector or Jinsoo. She felt guilty for coveting the food when it was meant for the little boys whimpering inside the caskets.

"The boys will not be able to eat for a few more hours," Alastair said to Gertie and her friends. "You should have some."

At first, Gertie scolded herself for lowering the block on her mind. Then she realized Alastair had read the thoughts of Hector and Jinsoo.

"There is plenty," Del said.

Del grabbed three apples and lobbed them across the room. Gertie and Hector caught them, but Jinsoo crossed his arms and let his apple fall on the floor.

"You should eat while you can," Gertie said to him.

"I'll vomit if I accept anything from my sister's murderers."

Knowing she couldn't force him, Gertie said nothing more. She bit into the sweet apple and finished it in no time. Penelope brought her and Hector bread and peanut butter. They gobbled it down. Jinsoo sat beside them with his arms crossed over his chest and his head down, refusing to look at anyone.

Gertie was surprised when Del flew from the hull to the upper deck. Wouldn't the sunlight burn her skin?

Sophia and Raimo followed. Gertie wished she could hear what they were thinking. A moment later, the three vampires returned. Del's dark eyes were full of tears.

"Has something happened?" Gertie asked her.

Del lay down on her back on top of her crate and crossed an arm over her face. "Mind your own business."

Something had *definitely* happened to upset the vampire. Had she been given orders by her lord that she didn't want to carry out? Did the orders involve Gertie and her friends?

In a few more hours, the vampires lifted the lids from the caskets and helped the boys to some of the food, including canned fruits, which the vampires opened with their sharp claws.

Hestie spoke to the boys in their native tongue, and that seemed to comfort them. After they finished eating, they fell asleep.

Gertie leaned against the cage beside Hector and allowed herself to close her eyes. She hadn't slept in ages, it seemed. She rested her head on Hector's shoulder and drifted off.

CHAPTER ELEVEN

Under Attack

With a gasp, Hermie awakened from a troubling dream. He'd been chasing Mina from the salon on the *Marcella II*, across the main deck, and down the hatch toward her cabin. Her flirtatious laughter had echoed throughout the narrow corridor as he'd caught up to her. He'd taken her into his arms, had carried her into her cabin, and had flung her down on her bed, where they'd kissed. But when he lifted his chin to look down at her beneath him on the bed, it had been Del who had smiled up at him.

"You okay?" Hestie asked from across the cage.

Hermie shrugged as he glanced at Del, who sat on the floor with her back against her crate. Her cheeks had turned pink, which he hadn't thought possible for a vampire. Had she seen his dream? Or, worse, had she caused it, with her vampire mind tricks? She looked down at the little boy she was cradling in her lap. The boy was sleeping. Had she been feeding on him? Hermie didn't see any signs of blood on her lips or on the boy.

Hermie caught Alastair staring at him with an arched brow. Alastair glanced from Hermie to Del with a slight grin. Hermie wished he could wipe that grin off the vampire's face with his fist.

Alastair cleared his throat and began to sing in Greek with a surprisingly beautiful bass voice that carried throughout the hull like the sad strumming of a cello. Hermie, who understood all languages, translated the words in his head:

I, too, wish to sing of heroic deeds
(about the Atreides and about Kadmus),
but my lyre's strings
can only make sounds of love.
Recently, I changed the strings,
and then the lyre itself,
and tried to sing of the feats of Hercules,
but still the lyre sang songs of love.
So, farewell, you heroes!
*My lyre sings only songs of love.**

Other vampires soon harmonized with Alastair's deep bass, including a surprising soprano from Del, producing a beautiful orchestra of voices, unlike anything Hermie had ever heard before:

My lyre sings only songs of love,
only songs of love it sings.
I changed the strings and the lyre itself
and tried to sing of heroic deeds,
of Achilles and Telemachus,
of Odysseus and Hector.
I tried to sing of Theseus and Perseus and Jason,
but still the lyre sang only of love,
only songs of love it sings.

Hermie had been so moved by the lovely voices that he nearly missed seeing the shiny metal key appear on the floor of his cage beside his knee. The only explanation he could think of was that it had been stolen and placed there by Hermes.

He hid it inside his trouser pocket, trying to block his thoughts. Since he didn't trust himself, he recited his multiplication tables, silently to himself, beginning with *one times one is one.*

"That was beautiful," Gertie said, when the song had ended.

"It was," Hector said. "I recognize it. I sang it with my mother when I was young."

"We were chosen among the orphans in Athens to tour with the priests," Alastair said. "They took us from village to village, from temple to temple, to sing at the religious rites."

"That was before we were turned," one of the others said. "Life was better then."

"How can you say that, Kagan?" Penelope asked. "We were orphans with nothing."

Kagan, whose long brown hair was tied at the nape of his neck, sighed. "I felt closer to the gods back then. Now, all but a few have abandoned us, even though we did nothing to deserve it."

Hermie frowned but continued with his multiplication tables: *two times five is ten…*

Kagan's speech reminded Gertie of Jeno. He'd been a melancholy soul who, in the end, had felt death was better than the life of a vampire.

"Do you no longer sing before an audience?" Gertie asked.

"Only for ourselves," Alastair said. "It is a comfort, you see?"

Gertie nodded. "It's a shame that such talent goes to waste. I tell Hector the very same thing. He has a voice, too."

"Is that so?" Alastair asked.

Hector shrugged. "I used to write my own songs and perform them for friends. I haven't done that in a long time."

"You must sing for *us,*" Alastair said.

Kagan straightened his back. "Please, do. We are bored to death."

"Why should he?" Raimo pointed out. "We hold him against his will."

"Please?" Gertie asked Hector.

"I'm not as good as they are," Hector said.

"*I* think you are," Gertie said.

It had been a long time since he'd sung, and Gertie missed seeing that part of him in action. Since she'd gone to the conservatoire and he the police academy, they'd both stopped doing things they loved. He'd stopped singing, and she rarely read for pleasure.

"You have a slight bias, Gertie," Hector said with a grin.

"Please?" Jinsoo, who sat on the opposite side of Hector from Gertie, asked.

"What should I sing?" Hector asked.

"My favorite," Gertie said. "Dreamer."

Hector nodded. To the others, he said, "I wrote this song a few years ago, before my mother died, before I had to grow up and face reality. It's not how I feel anymore, but it's how I felt at the time that I wrote it."

(To hear Hector's song, click here: https://soundcloud.com/travispohler_dreamer):

Before you close your eyes,

After you shut the door and you turn out the lights,

Remember all the days gone to waste.

Let 'em go, your shoulders know sleep's your only break.

And stay a dreamer, every day.

Dream every moment you're awake.

You may feel so far from space,

But someday the stars will remember your name.

Before you accept your fate,

After you got a job and your dreams are far too late,

Remember all the days gone to waste.

Don't hesitate, surely your job can wait, live for today.

And stay a dreamer, every day.

Dream every second you're awake.
Money will mean nothing in the grave.
You'll die no matter how much you're paid.

Dreamer,
The ground's so far beneath you.
Dreamer,
Someday they'll believe you.

As Hector sang, Gertie recalled the early days of their relationship, when they fell in love. Lately, they hadn't been as connected as they'd been in those first months. She'd felt them growing apart, focusing more on school and other responsibilities. They spent most evenings together at his house—it was true—but she'd been feeling as though something was missing. Hearing him sing as he had in the old days warmed her heart and made her long to feel closer to him again.

When Hector had finished his song, the vampires applauded.

Hector turned to Gertie and laughed.

"That was nice," Alastair said.

"Inspirational," Kagan added.

Penelope climbed to her feet from where she'd been sitting on her crate. "You are way too modest, Hector. You are as good as any of us."

At that moment, the ship began to groan, low and loud, like a frightened mother bear. Then the bow lifted dangerously high as a thunderous roar vibrated along the wooden planks. The crates and chests slid and tumbled toward the cage. The *Tarantula* turned nearly vertical in the air, bow over stern.

Grunts and screams filled the hull, along with the clatter and thud of moving crates.

Gertie feared the ship would capsize as it teetered and wobbled like a spinning top that was losing momentum.

Holding tightly to the bars of the cage, Gertie, Hector, and Jinsoo dodged the tumbling wooden crates. Two of the little boys were flung through the air. They would have been severely harmed had Penelope and Kagan not flown over and caught them.

"What the hell is happening?" Poros shouted from inside the cage.

The ship howled, like an enraged monster, and then cracked, like thunder, before the bow dropped, and the ship leveled, causing everything, including the adamantine cage, to fly toward the bow. Gertie's cheek was struck by something, nearly knocking her out. Hector saved Jinsoo and one of the little boys from being flung in the air. The vampires flew about the hull, trying to help the other little boys in the chaos. As she clutched her stinging cheek, Gertie prayed to Hermes, Hades, Poseidon, and Gaia for help.

Then the *Tarantula* screeched, like a train abruptly breaking on a steel track, as the deck overhead split open. The morning sunlight burst through a crack three feet wide and nearly the length of the craft. The vampires shrieked and cursed and flew to the corners, to avoid the sun.

Through the split in the vessel, Poseidon descended with his sword drawn, followed by Athena and Ares.

Before Gertie had fully taken in what was happening, Athena spun around with her blade and cut off Kagan's head. It fell with a thud at Gertie's feet. His eyes bulged up at her in shock. Gertie screamed.

"That was for Prometheus!" Athena growled.

Gertie blinked, trying to understand the scene before her. Gods and vampires darted through the air and leapt from one side to another. Their swords clashed. A vampire whose name Gertie didn't know was trapped in the sunlight in the center of the hull, where she screamed the most blood-curdling scream as the sunrays fried her. The girl's foot was caught on something. She struggled to free herself as she burned.

"Chloe!" Penelope scrambled from the opposite side of the ship toward her friend.

But Penelope was attacked by Ares and was forced to defend herself.

"Chloe, no!" Del cried as she defended herself from Athena.

Each vampire that tried to come to Chloe's rescue was deterred by a god. Gertie didn't know what to do.

Chloe caught fire and fell to the floor, until she was nothing but a heap of ash.

Hector tugged on Gertie's arm, snapping her out of her shock. He was guarding Jinsoo and Alastair in the dark recesses of the stern. Suddenly, Gertie had an idea.

"Bite me, Alastair," she whispered. "So, I can help you."

Alastair wasted no time sinking his fangs into her outheld wrist. It took only a moment for the temporary paralysis to be replaced by a powerful euphoria. Gertie could feel the strength surging through her muscles and bones. She could hear the thoughts of those whose minds weren't blocked—mainly the young gods. She could sense every movement, every smell, every sound with extreme clarity.

Ares charged. Gertie told Alastair to bite Hector next as she ran toward the god of war. She remembered what it was like the one time she'd transformed into a bull. She'd been running then, too. Now, she ignored her stinging flesh as she jumped over little boys and crates and fallen vampires toward Ares, who came at her from the bow with his sword drawn. When she was within ten feet of him, she leapt up with her arms out, and she felt the transformation take hold. The sun's rays no longer stung. With her great bull horns, she rammed Ares through the crack in the deck and out into the morning sky.

When the *Tarantula* had busted open above, and the sunlight had poured into the hull, Hestie had shouted at Del to set her and the other gods free. Del, who had flown into the darkness, reached in her pocket but came up empty. That's when Hestie noticed Hermie already had the key and was working it into the lock. Within seconds, she and her brother and Poros were free and in the midst of an all-out battle.

With her sword drawn, Del defended herself against the goddess Athena while shouting to Hestie, "Save the Pakistani boys! Take them to safety!"

Hestie was shocked that the three attacking gods seemed more intent on destroying the vampires than on saving the little boys.

She stopped in her tracks when one of the vampires got stuck in the sun. Should Hestie help her?

"This way!" Poros cried as he scooped up one of the boys and perched him onto his back.

Hestie and Hermie followed.

"Where's Jinsoo?" Hermie cried.

Hestie spotted him crouching in a corner behind Hector.

"I'll get him," she said, dodging Poseidon, who was chasing a vampire through the air.

"Take as much of the art as you can carry!" Del shouted from her sword fight with Athena. "The other things can survive the sea, but not the paintings!"

Before Hestie reached Jinsoo, Gertie darted through the air toward the bow and turned into a massive bull. Hestie was dumbfounded until Poros shouted, "Hurry, Hestie! We need to get these boys out of here!"

Hestie reached Jinsoo. "Climb onto my back. We're getting the hell out of here."

Hector's eyes were red. Blood dripped from his arm. It also dripped from Alastair's lips.

As much as she wanted to help Hector, her priority was Jinsoo. She helped him onto her back—piggy-back style—and held his legs, crossed in front of her, as she searched for the Pakistani boys.

"Over here!" Poros called.

Poros had three of the boys—one on his back and two on each hip. He pointed to another curled among the fallen crates. She pulled him onto her hip.

"Hold on to my neck," she said to the little boy as she dodged a flying vampire.

"There's another!" Poros said of a boy in the arms of one of the vampires, who was hiding behind a large chest.

The vampire, whose name Hestie thought was Sophia, handed the boy over to Hestie.

"Thank you," the vampire said. "Safe travels."

Hestie didn't know what to say.

"Grab those!" Poros said of the crates. "Hermie's ahead of us. Let's go!"

Hestie scooped up five crates containing paintings and followed Poros across the hull to the gap overhead, through which Hermie was already ascending with three boys and a stack of crates. As Hestie followed, she glanced down at the battle below. Water was pouring in from a crack in the bottom of the ship. She hoped Gertie and Hector would make it out alive.

CHAPTER TWELVE

Flight

After Gertie rammed Ares into the sky, she turned to see Athena clashing swords with Del and Alastair in knee-deep water while Poseidon fought Penelope, Raimo, Hector, and a vampire whose name Gertie didn't know. More water crept into the cracked hull. Some of the crates were floating. Then Athena knocked Del's blade into the water. Del stumbled back into the sunlight, screaming with pain, to avoid Athena's sword. Gertie spun and rammed against the back of Athena, shoving her into the adamantine cage. Gertie pulled the gate shut using the tip of her horn, and Athena was trapped inside. Del scurried to the shadows to recover from her burns.

No sooner had Gertie accomplished this than Ares pierced her flank with a dagger from behind, causing her to shift back into her human form and stumble to her knees, submerging underwater. She clambered into the shadows to avoid the stinging rays of the sun. Because the vampire virus still coursed through her system, her wound healed in no time. Yet, as she stumbled to her feet and tried to shift back into a bull, nothing happened. She wondered if she had to be running and stretching out her arms for the transformation to take place.

Before she could decide what to do, Ares raised his sword to finish her off, when suddenly she was swept out of harm's way by…Hermes? He wore the helm of invisibility.

Telepathically, he said to her, *We must save as many vampires as we can. I'll help you and Hector fight off Poseidon and Ares while the vampires take to the sea for their escape. Understand?*

Gertie nodded.

Take your bull form, Hermes said. Then he disappeared again beneath the helm.

Gertie used her vampire powers to relay Hermes's message to Hector as she took off running into the air, stretched out her arms, and transformed into her mighty bull form. She snarled at Ares whose brows shot up when he saw her charging him again. The remaining vampires dove through the crack in the bottom of the hull and scattered. As Gertie rammed against Ares for a second time, she prayed the vampires would make it to safety.

Hermie shouted in Pashto to the three screaming boys clinging to his neck as he flew through the bright sky over the tumultuous sea. "Just hold on! I'll get you home as soon as I can! It's going to be okay!"

He hadn't meant to shout, but he was scared that the boys were going to fall. Because his hands were full of wooden crates, he couldn't hold the boys. They needed to hold on tight, or they'd fall to their deaths.

And, as much as he hated to admit it, he was scared for Del. A part of him—a part he didn't understand—had wanted to protect her, had wanted to save her. He hated that part of himself. And he hated Del for making him feel it, because the only explanation for it was that she had used her vampire tricks on him.

"Hold on!" he shouted to the boys in Pashto again.

He searched below to get his bearings, wondering where in the hell they were. Then he recognized the port of Said, Egypt in the distance. It had only been three days—though it seemed a lifetime ago—since he was there with his crew enjoying juicy burgers at a restaurant at that very port. He'd cried tears of joy, because he hadn't eaten good food in weeks. And now, here he was, flying past it again, but this time with vomit in his throat and terror in his belly.

To Poros and Hermie, who were following close behind him and who were also carrying three kids each—not to mention the wooden crates of paintings in their arms—he shouted, "Head for Italy, this way. Search for the *Marcella II*!"

The boys were slipping. They were tired, and though the vampires had healed them, they were weak from months of starvation. Hermie prayed to every god he knew to help them.

"Don't let go!" he shouted to the boys in Pashto again, feeling helpless.

He was about to ditch the paintings so he could help the boys to hold on when suddenly, a few yards in the distance, a chariot appeared. Hermie recognized Swift and Sure—Hades's black stallions. Behind them, holding the reins was Hades. And riding along were Hip, Jen, and…Hermie's mother! When he met his mother's eyes, Hermie wept. He'd never been happier to see her.

Once all nine boys, including Jinsoo, were safely in the chariot with Hades, the other gods followed behind until the *Marcella II* appeared in the distance. Hermie smiled with relief at the sight.

Hades brought the chariot to a halt on the main deck and helped to carry the boys into the salon. Then he and Hip left for the *Tarantula*.

"Chidori!" Hermie cried when his yellow canary appeared.

She flapped her wings with excitement and chirped, "You're back! You're back!"

"Oh, Chidori!" Hestie clapped her hands. "What a relief!"

Hermie noticed Jinsoo break into tears. His entire frame shuddered with sobs.

"You okay?" Hermie asked him.

"That was scary."

Chidori landed on Jinsoo's shoulder and touched her beak to his ear.

"I love you, Chidori," Jinsoo said. "I'm so happy to see you."

While they were having their reunion with Chidori, the other gods stowed the crates of paintings on the table and arranged the boys—who had fallen asleep because of Hip and were just now waking up—on the couches in the salon.

Poros and Jen went to get blankets from below deck.

"What the heck, Mom?" Hestie finally asked. "What were Poseidon and them thinking? These boys could have been killed!"

Being back on the ship reminded Hermie that Mina was gone. He still couldn't believe it. Exhausted, he sat on the floor beside Jinsoo and put his face in his hands.

His mom knelt beside him and rubbed his back. "Hermie?"

Although her touch was comforting, Hermie shrugged and didn't look up.

"Mom, seriously, what happened?" Hestie asked again.

"Give us a minute," their Aunt Jen said to Hestie as she returned with the blankets. Jen snapped her fingers, and everyone's soaked clothes were dry and clean, including Hermie's. Then Jen spoke to the boys in Pashto, "We're taking you home soon. Try to rest," as she and Poros gave them the blankets.

"We don't have any answers," Hermie's mother said to his sister. "We had no knowledge of Poseidon's plans to attack the *Tarantula*."

"We didn't even know where it was," Jen said.

"We've been searching and searching," Hermie's mother added. "I can't believe Athena went behind our backs."

"It was a nightmare," Poros said. "I'm not sure if the two demigods made it out."

"Poseidon will protect them," Jen said.

"The demigods were defending the *vampires*," Hestie said. "Gertie transformed into a giant bull and attacked *Ares*."

"They were following Hades's orders," their mother said.

"What?" Hermie looked up from his hands. "Why would Hades want to protect the vampires? They killed Mina!"

"Take a deep breath, son," his mother said as she rubbed his back again. "You don't have the full picture."

Hermie shook his head and covered his face.

"Wasn't Hermes helping the demigods?" Jen asked.

"I think so," Poros said. "He was beneath the helm, so I'm not sure."

"I wonder why he didn't share your location with us," Jen said.

"I was just wondering the same thing," Hermie's mother said.

Hermie had wondered it, too. Why wouldn't Hermes have done everything in his power to protect them? Then his throat tightened, and he could barely breathe. Was Hermes the *mole*? Was *he* the god that was working with the vampire pirates?

"Maybe we should go, Therese," Jen said. "Hades and Hip may need our help."

"You're right," Hermie's mother said. "You kids rest. We'll come back as soon as we can."

Hermie didn't look up as his aunt and mother left. Frustrated, confused, exhausted, and angry, he ignored Poros and his sister's attempts to comfort him. Instead of acknowledging them, he sat on the floor beside Jinsoo and Chidori and prayed. He prayed to Hermes for understanding. He prayed to his father to let his friends live. He hated himself when he realized what he was praying for. The vampire must have done something to his mind, because Hermie found himself weeping in his hands, not for Mina, but for Del.

Still in her bull form, Gertie guarded the gap in the bottom of the hull, to prevent Ares and Poseidon from following the vampires—though not all had escaped. Penelope and a dark-haired boy, whose name Gertie didn't know, had been rammed with spears through their torsos and were pinned to the wall of the vessel. The hull was quickly filling with water and would soon be completely submerged.

Hermes and Hector were busy fighting off Poseidon and guarding the opening above, to prevent Poseidon and Ares from chasing the other vampires. Hector was limited, being sensitive to the sun. Sometime during the battle, the helm had fallen from Hermes's head, and now Poseidon disarmed him, grabbed him, and pinned his arms behind his back. Ares had been about to decapitate the messenger god when Hades stormed into the hull from above and shouted, "What do you think you're doing?"

Hypnos appeared and quickly disappeared with Hector. Gertie had been about to attempt to rescue Penelope and the dark-haired boy when Hermes told her telepathically to protect the other vampires. While Hades and the other gods bickered, Gertie transformed into her human form and swam through the gap in the bottom of the ship. With her improved vampire vision, she could see the others swimming below, so she followed them down into the depths of the ocean.

They were at least fifty yards ahead of her, but the combination of her demigod blood and the vampire virus coursing through her gave her a slight edge, and she was able to close the distance between them in no time. As she was about to ask them where they were headed, she noticed three sharks swimming at high speed directly toward them.

Sharks! she cried to them, telepathically. *Sharks at three o'clock!*

They'd been sent by Poseidon, no doubt. She prayed to her favorite gods, and to Clymene, Prometheus's mother, and to Morpheus and Hypnos and Therese. She also prayed to Gaia, who had helped her so many times before.

Please help us, she prayed.

The vampires shifted direction and were now swimming away from the sharks. Gertie followed, and was soon near the front of the group. Four figures came into view dead ahead. At first, Gertie thought they were allies, but as the goddesses neared, she could see by the look in their eyes that they were not. Their fish tails from the waist down indicated that they were merfolk. They were no doubt sent, like the sharks, by Poseidon.

Gertie halted, causing one of the vampires to bump into her from behind.

Danger ahead! she said to them telepathically. *This way!*

Gertie led them in the direction they'd been swimming before the sharks had appeared, but the merfolk were faster, and soon the vampires were under attack by both merfolk and sharks. Gertie turned around and used her vampire claws and fangs to defend herself and the others.

Gertie screamed when the lanky vampire with the curly red hair was snatched up at the torso by one of the sharks. Alastair and Raimo tried to help, but the shark's teeth had a firm grip on the lanky redhead. Like a dog playing tug-of-war, the shark thrashed and ripped the screeching vampire in half. His remains were left, uneaten, to float in the sea around them.

Gertie wanted to vomit, but there was no time. Two of the mermaids had a hold of one of the vampires—Gertie believed his name was Edric. One mermaid had a stranglehold on Edric's neck while the other gripped one of his ankles. Edric kicked with his free legs and thrashed his arms through the air. Gertie grabbed fistfuls of one of the mermaid's hair and tried to pull her off. Del sank her fangs in the neck of the other. But then a third mermaid gripped Gertie's hands and tried to pry her fingers free of the other mermaid's hair. When Gertie resisted, the mermaid bit her, sending a sharp stinging pain up Gertie's arm.

Before Gertie knew what had happened, Edric's head had been severed from his body, and the mermaid holding it shoved it at Gertie.

Gertie blanched and screamed until something nudged her from behind. Gertie turned to fight it off and was relieved to see Therese, the red-haired goddess and mother to Hermie and Hestie.

An army of gods, including Morpheus, Hypnos, and the Furies, had appeared to fend off the merfolk and sharks and to rescue Gertie and the vampires. Therese held Gertie's hand and god-traveled with her. The pressure of god-travel was familiar but disorienting, and Gertie stumbled to her knees when she landed in a space the size of a large kitchen in what appeared to be the hull of a ship, but more modern than that of the *Tarantula*. She saw a washer and dryer with overhead bins on one side and a sink with more storage bins all around it. There was also a portal to the sea on the exterior wall, through which Gertie saw a colorful school of fish swimming past, and there were new-looking floorboards leading to a clean corridor. One of the doors across the hall was open, and Gertie recognized the room. It belonged to Jinsoo, which meant she was on the *Marcella II*.

In the next instant, the other gods appeared with six of the vampires—Del, Alastair, Raimo, Sophia, Mahdi, and a boy whose thoughts revealed that he was named Taavi. Like her, they were soaking wet. Hypnos, the Furies, and one other god quickly left, leaving Morpheus and Therese behind.

"Be ready, in case they track our signatures," Therese said.

"Where are the others?" Gertie asked.

Morpheus sighed.

Therese shook her head. "I'm so sorry. We couldn't save everyone."

Sophia broke into tears. "Penny is gone?"

"I don't think she's dead," Gertie said. "She and a dark-haired boy were alive when I left."

"Bach." Del said. "Penny and Bach were speared by Ares but not killed."

"Then maybe they're still alive," Morpheus said.

"Hades will report back as soon as he can," Therese assured them.

"Gertie?"

Gertie turned to see Hector walking in from the corridor. He was clean and dry and smiling at her. She ran into his arms.

"Thank Gaia, you're okay!" she cried.

He pulled her close. She could read his thoughts, which were racing and complicated. There was something dark, there, too—a doubt. He was thinking he loved her, but…She couldn't pick up on the *but*, yet the fact that there *was* a but made her stomach hurt.

Hypnos and the Furies reappeared with six caskets, which they laid side-by-side on the floor, taking up most of the space in the room.

"Oh, thank you!" Alastair said to Hypnos as he helped the gods to arrange them on the floor.

The vampires claimed a casket by sitting on top of it.

"Any word?" Gertie asked the Furies and the god of sleep.

"Hermes and two vampires were taken to Mount Olympus," Hypnos said. "Athena, too. She's still trapped in an adamantine cage, until the key turns up."

The vampires turned to Del, who said, "I do not have it."

"I hope she rots in that cage after what she did to Kagan," Raimo said.

"Gods don't rot," Morpheus said.

"Figure of speech," Raimo muttered angrily.

"Thanks for helping us," Del said to the gods.

"And for getting our crates," Alastair added. "We cannot get good rest without them."

"You're welcome," Hypnos said before he vanished.

"He left so as not to put us to sleep," Gertie explained. "He's the god of sleep."

"We know who he is," Mahdi said.

"And sleep is what we need," Taavi said. "We need rest."

Hypnos reappeared. "First, you all need dry clothes."

The god snapped his fingers, and their wet and dripping clothes were instantly clean and dry—though their hair remained wet.

Therese found fresh blankets in cabinets above the dryer and gave them to each of the vampires. They wrapped themselves in the fresh blankets and thanked Therese.

"Climb into your caskets," Hypnos said, "and I'll help you fall into the deep boon of sleep."

Del opened the lid of one and climbed inside. "We prefer the word *crate* or *box* to *casket*."

Mahdi shook his head. "I will not sleep. One of us needs to be alert. We can trust no one, after all we have been through."

"Suit yourself," Taavi said with his charming smile. Then, as he lifted the lid of one of the crates, he turned to Morpheus. "I do not suppose you would give me a sweet, kick-ass dream? Maybe one involving a beautiful girl? I need a distraction from all this shit, you understand?"

"You got it, man," Morpheus said with a grin.

"Ah, hell," Mahdi said as he climbed inside his crate. "I want one, too."

"Your wish is my command," Morpheus said.

"You should get some rest, too, Gertie," Therese said. "Hector, why don't you take her to the guest room?"

Before Gertie turned to leave, she said, "It doesn't seem fair that we get a *room* and they have to sleep in wooden boxes."

Alastair sat up in his crate and smiled at Gertie. "We are more comfortable in our crates. I promise."

"They lock from the inside," Raimo added. "And the wood is thick and hard to penetrate."

"Go get some sleep, Gertie," Del said. "You deserve it after all you did to help us."

Gertie smiled and then followed Hector from the room to a cabin down the hall. She was relieved to be back on the *Marcella II*, safe with Hector, but she was sad for those who didn't make it and was anxious about what would happen next. To make matters worse, she couldn't stop wondering about Hector's doubt. He loved her, but *what*?

CHAPTER THIRTEEN

Aftermath

Hestie held the smallest of the Pakistani boys in her arms and softly sang to him in Pashto. She didn't have a voice as lovely as the vampires or as Hector, but, being a goddess, she could carry a nice enough tune. Her mom and Poros also comforted the boys, by either holding them or by stroking their hair.

Morpheus had only been gone for a few minutes, when he returned with Iris via her magnificent rainbow. The rainbow extended from the deck of *Marcella II* all the way to Karachi, a coastal city in Pakistan, where Jen believed the boys had been taken from. Jen was flying over Karachi now, listening to the prayers of families who were praying about their lost boys. They hoped that Jen would locate the boys' homes by the time they arrived.

Each time Hestie saw Iris, she was reminded of how beautiful she was. Not quite three feet tall, she was half the size of her husband, Morpheus. And while his wings were large and silver and his skin a dark bronze, her wings were small and gold and her skin fair. They made a beautiful couple. Not many other gods had wings—Selene and Nike came to mind, and the Furies sometimes transformed into winged creatures, but not very often—so it seemed right to Hestie that Morpheus and Iris had ended up together.

"Are we ready?" Iris asked.

"The sooner we get these boys home, the better," Hestie's mother said.

"Come along," Poros said in Pashto as he took two of them by the hands. "It's time to go home."

As she helped the boys toward the main deck, Hestie glanced back at her brother, who hadn't moved from where he sat beside Jinsoo and Chidori on the floor. Both boys were angry that some of the vampires had been saved.

"Come with me," Hestie said to the boys in Pashto.

Iris led the way to the rainbow arch. Inside, it was four feet wide and at least ten feet tall and had stair-steps that sparkled like diamonds.

"It's too far for the boys to walk," Iris said. "We'll have to carry them."

As if on cue, Hip appeared and multiplied himself into three, so each of them would only have to carry one boy. Only two gods had the power to multiply themselves—Hestie imagined her mother correcting her, as she'd done many times, by saying, "Not multiply, *disintegrate.*" Hestie recalled the first time her mother had described her father and her uncle's ability to *disintegrate*—or to be in many places at once. "Only Death and Sleep," her mother had said, "Thanatos and Hypnos." She'd explained that Morpheus had been gifted with the power of being in two places at once, but one of him must always be in the Dreamworld.

It wasn't long before the presence of Hestie's Uncle Hip put the boys to sleep and made carrying them across the vast distance easier.

Hestie was grateful for the rainbow, as a protection from Poseidon and his allies, who might want to capture and use the boys as leverage in exchange for the vampires. Her father and her Uncle Hip had disintegrated into an army and were guarding the entrance on the other side of the arch, as a precaution. But if any one of her father or uncle's forms were wounded or trapped, they would reintegrate, and the army would be lost.

Because her mother and the other gods believed it was more likely that Poseidon and Ares would attack the *Marcella II*, to kill the vampires, than the rainbow, the Furies and Hecate had been sent to guard the ship. Hermie was supposed to be helping, too, but Hestie wasn't so sure that he'd protect the vampires. She was worried about Hermie helping Poseidon, now that the little boys were out of harm's way.

It had shocked her, to see Poseidon so bent on destroying the vampires that he hadn't taken precautions to ensure the safety of the little boys. She'd been especially surprised that Athena had joined him. Ares hadn't been such a shocker. He was acting in his usual form. But Poseidon and Athena's behavior had troubled her.

Hestie's mother had told her that Hades had gone to make his case to the other gods on Mount Olympus, trying to recruit others to his side. Hestie wasn't exactly sure if her side and her grandfather's side were aligned, because he seemed to care more about the vampires and less about justice for Mina, which made absolutely no sense, whatsoever.

Poros, who was ahead of her, turned back to check on her. She gave him a smile and a wink. It felt good to be helping people again. Poros winked back and grinned. As much as she enjoyed helping humanity, she couldn't wait to be alone with him.

The trip across the rainbow took less than half an hour for the gods, but Hestie was exhausted by the time they came to the end of it. If it weren't dangerous to god-travel, she'd use it for the return trip instead of flight. But she'd been taught since she was a little girl that god-travel left a signature that could be tracked by enemies wanting to trap you. She'd been taught that flight was safer and that travel by chariot was safest of all.

After the boys had been handed over to Aunt Jen and to the disintegrated army of Uncle Hip, who would deliver the boys to their homes, Hestie hugged her father. He couldn't join her on the *Marcella II* without killing the demigods. He would be joining Hades on Mount Olympus to help organize a council meeting to negotiate the terms of release for Hermes and the two vampire prisoners, into the custody of Hades.

She was about to follow Poros back up into the rainbow when Ares and his twin sons—Phobos and Deimos—appeared with their swords drawn.

"Go!" her father shouted at her as he fought against their attackers.

"But—" She didn't want to abandon them.

"Go with Poros and Iris!" her mother, who was also fighting said.

Poros refused. He turned back toward the battle, conjured his sword, and attacked.

Once they were alone in the cabin aboard the *Marcella II*, Hector took Gertie into his arms and kissed her. She sighed, happy to be safe and alone with him, at last. She could feel the anxiety that had been causing her muscles to tense finally leave her body, until she felt like a wet noodle.

They grinned at one another and kissed again, making their way to the bed. He pulled off her shirt, so she pulled off his, and they fell on the mattress side by side and laughed.

He used his fingers to comb her hair away from her face. Then he propped himself on one elbow and leaned over her, touching his lips to her nose, then to each cheek, before landing smack on her lips.

"This feels nice," he said against her mouth.

"Mmm, hmm."

He fingered the strap on her bra. "Pretty."

"A girl should always be prepared," she said, "even when going into battle with gods and vampires."

"Is that something you read in a book?" he said with a grin.

"Probably."

They laughed again. It was something she heard once on *Hestie's Style*.

Then she said, "It was so great to hear you sing."

"It felt good. I hadn't realized how much I miss it."

She sat up. "Then you should do it more."

"Yeah, I know."

Although the vampire virus was beginning to wear off, she could still hear the doubt in the back of his mind.

"Hector?"

"Yeah?" He laid on his back, with his head on the pillow.

She could tell he was tired. She was, too. She decided this might not be the best time to ask him about his doubt.

She curled up against him and said, "I love you."

"I love you, too."

"Maybe we should get some sleep."

"Yeah. Good idea."

She closed her eyes and enjoyed the warm feel of his bare chest beside her. But it took a long time for her to fall asleep.

"You guys should get some rest," Hecate said in the salon of the *Marcella II*. "Hermie, help Jinsoo to his room."

Hermie climbed to his feet. He wanted to hug Hecate and to ask her how things had come to this. He wanted to know how Mina could be gone and how the vampires had not been brought to justice. He wanted to know why Hermes, one of his favorite gods and the one his parents had named him after, could possibly have been working with murdering, thieving vampires. But, instead, he held out a hand to Jinsoo and helped him to his feet. Chidori was perched on Jinsoo's finger.

"Let's get more seeds for her first," Jinsoo said as he headed for the kitchen.

After grabbing a handful of sunflower seeds, Jinsoo followed Hermie below deck.

Hermie stopped in the corridor below when he reached the laundry room. Six wooden caskets lay side-by-side on the floor, taking up most of the space.

Then he put a finger to his lips and led Jinsoo across the hall to Jinsoo's room.

Jinsoo sat on his bed. "I can't believe we're letting the murderer live."

"Me, too!" Chidori chirped. "Me, too!"

"I can't either," Hermie said, though there was still a part of him that wanted Del safe. He tried to ignore it, since he knew it wasn't a *real* feeling. "She did say it was self-defense. She thought Mina was a god."

"So? Intentions don't matter. Mina is still gone."

Hermie had an idea. "Maybe we can take matters into our own hands."

"What? How?"

"I heard Hip say that he put the vampires into the deep boon of sleep. Maybe we can open each casket, until we find Del, and then put a dagger through her heart."

"Will that kill her?" Jinsoo asked. "I thought you had to use a wooden stake."

"Oh, you could be right. I don't think we have a wooden stake lying around. Well, then I'll cut off her head. We know *that* works."

Jinsoo jumped to his feet and hugged Hermie as Chidori flittered excitedly overhead. "Thank you! Thank you so much!"

"You wait here with Chidori," Hermie said. "They can kill you but not me—at least, not forever."

"Okay, Hermie. I wait here. I *will* wait here."

Hermie patted him on the back. "Your English is improving."

"Yeah. Thanks."

Hermie conjured his sword. It had been in his room down the hall, and he could have flown down and took it from his closet, but why, when, as a god, all he had to do was call to it? The scabbard appeared around his waist. He unsheathed the blade to make sure it was sharp.

"Yes, this will do," he said as he touched his finger to one edge and accidentally drew blood.

He stuck his finger into his mouth.

"Be careful, Hermie," Jinsoo said. "I'll be waiting here."

"Be careful!" Chidori chirped.

"I will," he assured them.

Hermie flew from the room, so as not to make a sound, and entered the laundry room, wondering which box contained Del. Having no way of knowing, he decided to start on one end and work his way to the other, beginning on the end closest to the corridor. But when he tried to lift the lid, he found he couldn't. It was stuck, as if it had been locked on the inside.

Not ready to give up, he flew to the bin beside the laundry-room sink, where Prometheus kept his tools. He searched for a crowbar but, not finding one, settled on a flathead screwdriver.

When he turned around, he found Del hovering in the air not two feet away from him.

"What are you doing?" she asked.

He dropped the screwdriver and drew his weapon. "Getting justice for Mina."

He swung, but the vampire ducked, and he missed. He followed her into the corridor, which put him at a disadvantage, because the passage was too narrow for him to work his sword effectively.

"I told you, it was an accident," Del said.

"Quit using your vampire tricks to make me feel something for you," Hermie said as he swung again and missed.

"We can read your thoughts, but we cannot control them," she said as she dodged him again. "We cannot control the minds of gods—only mortals."

"I don't believe you."

She arched a brow. "Are you saying you have feelings for me?"

Enraged, he used both hands to take a swing at her but missed. Then he felt the sting of fangs penetrate his neck from behind.

"Huh?" He gasped, unable to move.

"Sophia, no! His blood is poison!" Del cried.

"I did not drink much," the vampire who'd attacked him from behind said just before she stumbled to the floor, and Hermie, who was limp, was caught by Del. "Only enough to paralyze him."

"Sophia?" another vampire—maybe Raimo—said.

The paralysis lasted for nearly a minute before a feeling of exhilaration coursed through Hermie. Was it Del who caused him to feel so good? Is that why she was smiling at him? He felt like he'd been drugged.

"It is the virus," Del said, still holding him in her arms. "It feels good, does it not?"

He didn't want to admit it, but, hell, yeah. It felt amazing.

Del laughed. "I was not sure it would work on a god."

"Oh, something's working, all right." He wondered if she could feel his boner. He was too lit to hide it.

Del laughed again. "Soon, you will have the powers of a vampire, I think. And, since you are a threat to me, I hope you will understand why we have to do this."

Before Hermie could ask Del what she meant, his arms were pinned behind him by Raimo, his sword was taken from him by Sophia, and he was shoved into one of the wooden caskets.

"Wait!" he cried. "Let me out of here!"

He pushed on the lid, but he could feel the three vampires pushing back.

"I will let you out on one condition," Del said.

Hermie stopped pounding. "Okay. What?"

"I am going to open my mind to you," she said. "And I want you to read it."

"Are you sure about this?" Raimo asked.

"It is the only way to make him understand," Del replied. Then, she said, "Hermie?"

Hermie closed his eyes and took a deep breath. He supposed reading her mind was better than another fight, especially since he was outnumbered, as he could hear the other vampires climbing from their caskets to see what was going on.

"We prefer the term *crate* or *box* to *casket*," Del said to him though the wooden lid.

There you go, reading my mind again, he said to her telepathically. *Now, shut up, and let me read yours.*

Fine, she said directly to his mind. *But just know, this is not easy for me. It is the most vulnerable thing one vampire can do for another. For this reason, it is rarely done. I am telling you this, because I want you to understand what a big deal this is.*

Can you be quiet now and let me in? I don't want to be stuck in here all day.

Fine.

He took another deep breath and reached out to her mind. It was a strange feeling. He felt as if he had to dig around to pick up on something. It was like trying to listen to a single person in a crowded room where multiple conversations were happening at the same time.

That is a good analogy, she said.

He groaned, wishing she'd stop communicating with him, so he could get on with it. Just when he was about to scold her out loud, he caught ahold of something.

It pained him to hear it. It was if he wasn't just *hearing* Del's thoughts, but he was *feeling* them, too. She was deeply upset over Mina's death and felt an overwhelming guilt for not testing the girl's mortality before striking. She'd assumed Mina, like Prometheus and Hermie, was immortal. She hated herself for it and wished with all her heart that she could fly back in time for a do-over. But such a thing was impossible.

She felt even worse for leaving a young boy without his beloved sister. And having to hear Hermie pine away for someone he loved had nearly destroyed her.

Her guilt, regret, and remorse, along with the grief she felt over losing her friends, overwhelmed Hermie. He felt like a panic attack was coming on. Even though he hadn't needed his inhaler since becoming a god, he couldn't breathe.

Then he caught another thread of a thought in Del's mind. It was a monologue she was having with herself: *Why does he affect me so profoundly? Am I confusing chemistry for guilt and remorse? When he looks at me, and I feel like he can see my very soul, and I* want *him to see it—is that guilt? If so, why do the others not affect me, too, especially Jinsoo? What is it about Hermie that makes me desperate for him to accept me, to like me, to…*

"That is enough!" Del said suddenly, as if she'd just realized what he'd been reading in her mind.

Hermie reached out to hear more, but it felt as if a concrete wall had been erected. No matter how much he reached out or pushed into her mind, he hit against a boundary that refused him entry.

"I said *enough*," Del said again.

Hermie lay there wondering what the hell? What the hell had he just experienced? And why was his heart beating so fast?

CHAPTER FOURTEEN

Difficult Feelings

Hestie was on a high—and not because she was flying through a rainbow. She was on a high because Ares and his sons had been forced to retreat. Although she and her allies had already successfully pushed Ares and his sons back, her father had delivered news from Mount Olympus of a truce.

It had been requested by Hades of Poseidon and had been approved by the council members, including Athena. Hermes and the two vampire prisoners would remain in the council's custody on Mount Olympus for forty-eight hours, until the council would reconvene to decide their fates. Meanwhile, the priority for the gods was to locate the key that would free their leader from the adamantine cage.

Hestie was proud of her performance against Ares, Phobos, and Deimos. She'd relished the chance to show her parents and Poros what she could do. Before they'd left for the Underworld, her parents had told her how proud they were of her—and of Poros, too.

She was glad they'd included him, because his parents weren't around to support him, and Prometheus, who'd been a surrogate father to Poros for so many years, was still in Tartarus, waiting for his body to heal.

So, reeling with the high of a victory, Hestie and Poros had decided to fly back rather than god-travel, so they could shout their hoorays with

Morpheus and Iris all the way back to the *Marcella II*, which was anchored in the Mediterranean Sea not far from Port Said, Egypt.

When they arrived, Morpheus and Iris said their goodbyes and then flew away, taking the rainbow with them. Hestie and Poros were surprised to find the decks and salon abandoned.

"Where is everyone?" she wondered aloud.

"Let's search below."

When they reached the corridor, they found Jinsoo standing in front of his cabin staring at the laundry room. Chidori was perched on his shoulder.

"Hey, Jinsoo! Hey, Chidori!" Poros said. "We're back."

Jinsoo didn't move. Chidori didn't make a peep.

"Um, are you okay?" Hestie asked as she got closer to them.

She turned to see what Jinsoo was staring at. All the vampires were hovering above their crates, in line with one another, like an army of soldiers, and among them was her brother. His eyes were red, and his mouth had…fangs?

Her jaw dropped open, and she jumped back. "Hermie? What's going on?"

"They turned him into a vampire!" Jinsoo said.

"I'm not a vampire," Hermie said. "I just have the virus in my blood. It will run its course, and I'll be back to normal in no time."

"Why were you bitten?" she asked. "Why are they lined up like an army about to strike?"

"He tried to kill me," Del said matter-of-factly. "It was only fair."

"Poor, Hermie!" Jinsoo said. "This is my fault!"

"I'll be fine." Hermie landed on his feet beside Jinsoo.

Chidori shrieked and flew into Jinsoo's cabin. Jinsoo followed and closed the door.

Hestie heard him press the lock.

"They're afraid of me," Hermie murmured.

"So am I," Poros said. "You look scary as hell."

Hermie turned to the vampires. "You can go back to sleep. I'll keep an eye on Jinsoo. You have nothing to fear."

Del put her hands on her hips. "And what about you? Do you still want to kill me?"

Hestie looked from Del to her brother, who said, "No. No, I don't."

Raimo nudged Del. "You were right. It worked."

"What worked?" Hestie asked.

"Nothing," Hermie insisted. "I'm going to bed."

"Wait," Poros said. "We have news from Mount Olympus."

"Is Penny alive?" Sophia asked.

"Yes," Poros said. "She and Bach, along with Hermes, are in the custody of the council."

"What about Farouk and Cade?" Del asked.

Poros shook his head. "I'm sorry. They didn't make it."

Hestie felt bad for the vampires as more tears welled in their eyes.

"If Bach and Penny are in custody," Alastair asked, "does that mean they are prisoners?"

"Only temporarily," Hestie said. "Hades was able to get a truce for forty-eight hours, so we don't have to worry about Poseidon attacking us again. Your friends on Mount Olympus are safe."

"Can we really believe that?" Mahdi said.

"And what happens in forty-eight hours?" Del asked.

"The council will decide what should happen to Hermes and your friends," Poros said. "I'm sure they'll come up with a fair verdict."

"Well, I am *not* sure," Mahdi said. "We need to get Penny and Bach out of there."

"We should wait to hear the verdict," Del said. "If it *is* fair, then great. If it is not, then we act."

"I agree," Alastair said.

"Okay," Mahdi said. "We wait. But let us hope the gods do not decide to execute them."

"They won't," Poros said. "Not with Hades and most of the Underworld on your side."

"Let us hope you are right," Raimo said.

"There's nothing more to do," Hermie said. "I'm going to sleep."

Hermie took off down the hallway to his room.

"We should all get some rest," Hestie said.

"Sweet dreams," Alastair said to no one in particular.

"Morpheus came through for me," Taavi said with a grin. "How about you, Mahdi?"

"Oh, yes. It was good. Maybe I can get back to it."

One by one, the vampires returned to their crates and pulled the lids closed.

Hestie turned to Poros. "That was weird."

"Yeah."

"You want to go rest with me in my room?"

"In a minute. I need to look in on Captain."

"Of course," she said. "See you later, then."

Hestie went to her room and changed into a long soft night shirt. Then she pulled back the covers and climbed into bed. She wasn't sleepy, but she was exhausted. She turned on the television bolted to her wall and clicked the remote to the fashion channel. She still hadn't processed everything that had happened—especially Mina's death. But she didn't want to think about anything right now.

"Did you hear that?" Gertie asked Hector.

Hector yawned, stretched, and blinked. He looked sexy as hell.

"No, I didn't," he said. "Hear what?"

"Poros had news from Mount Olympus. Hades got a truce for forty-eight hours. Then they're going to have a council meeting to decide what to do about Hermes and the vampire prisoners."

"Oh, good."

"You don't think the gods will vote to execute the vampires, do you?"

"No. No way. Worst case scenario, Del might be thrown into the Titan pit."

Gertie blanched. "You think they'd do that to her? Even though it was self-defense?"

"I don't think everyone will agree it was self-defense, Gertie. A vampire has no reason to behead a mortal."

"But Del didn't know Mina was a mortal."

"That's what she says, anyway."

"I believe her."

Gertie found her shirt lying on the floor and put it on, because she felt cold and vulnerable.

"You okay?" Hector asked.

She took a deep breath. "I don't know."

He sat up. "What's wrong?"

She searched for the right words. "Well, when I had the vampire virus in my system, I, well, I didn't mean to invade your privacy…"

"You read my mind?"

"Not intentionally."

"Bullshit, Gertie. It's impossible not to be intentional about it."

"Okay, you're right. I'm sorry."

Hector bit his lip. "Something I was thinking about bothered you, I guess."

"The virus was nearly out of my system. I couldn't get it all. Just this doubt—you love me *but*. It's the *but* that's bothering me."

"I see." He got up, found his shirt, and slipped it on. Then he found his shoes and put those on, too.

"Are you going somewhere?" Gertie asked.

"I need some air."

He walked from the room, closing the door behind him.

Hermie lay in his bed in his cabin aboard the *Marcella II* feeling more confused than he'd ever felt in his life. As tired as he felt, he saw no chance of sleep without an urgent prayer to his Uncle Hip. Hermie didn't pray to his uncle, however. He needed a minute to think about what the hell had just happened to him.

I am sorry. I am so, so sorry. Del's words entered his head. *I wish we had never met.*

You and me both, he thought.

That night I first saw you standing at the rail of this vessel staring back at me— you were a beautiful and perplexing sight, she said. *I was surprised that you could see me because I did not know you were a god.*

Hermie rolled over onto his side. A part of him wanted to figure out how to block her out; another part of him was desperate to hear what she had to say.

Should I continue? she asked.

I honestly don't know.

I was so surprised you could see me and the Tarantula, *because we vampires can make ourselves invisible to mortals. We can also work together—if there are enough of us—to make the ship invisible, too. You were a surprise, Hermie. I could not stop thinking of you.*

It had been the same for him. Since the moment he'd seen her, he hadn't been able to stop thinking of her.

After I killed your friend, I was tormented by guilt. Listening to your suffering overwhelmed me. I wished I could comfort you. But how could I when I was the cause of your pain? I considered destroying myself. I nearly did, but Raimo and Sophia talked me out of it. I had been about to expose myself to the sun.

Hermie gasped. *I didn't know.*

I did not want you to know. I cannot tell you how badly I wish I could go back in time.

Me, too. It was my fault that Mina went after you with a sword. I'd been training her. She was going to become a god.

She would have lived forever if it had not been for me.

My sister shouldn't have left. We might have had a chance if she and Poros had stayed.

It is no one's fault but mine, and I am so, so sorry. I do not expect your forgiveness. I know that is not possible. But maybe you can believe me when I say that I did not mean to take her life.

He believed her. He even felt sorry for her suffering. Mina was at peace in the Elysian Fields, but Del would be tortured by guilt for years to come.

Thank you for that, Hermie.

Are you being sarcastic?

No, I swear. Unlike mortals, whose guilt and regret are purged from them in Tartarus, we immortals carry all our guilt with us. Just imagine centuries and centuries of it.

Oh.

You are a new god. You do not understand yet.

I hope I never do. Hermie turned over in his bed, feeling restless.

This regret—what I did to Mina—is the worst of my lifetime, she said.

Have you never killed before?

I have killed, but always in self-defense.

Which is what you thought you were doing with Mina.

Yes.

He didn't know what to say.

It is a torment, as you have said, even worse than death.

He'd been inside her mind again, but the concrete wall was erected before he'd gotten very far. He wished he knew how to erect his own mind fortress.

I will teach you tonight, if you want, after the sun goes down, she said.

Thank you. That would be helpful.

I am glad to help.

I suppose I should try to sleep now.

Sleep well, Hermie.

You too, Del.

Hermie prayed to his Uncle Hip: *Please bring me sleep.*

As the drowsiness overcame him, Hermie knew his prayer had been answered.

CHAPTER FIFTEEN

In Memoriam

When a half hour had passed, and Poros hadn't come to her room, Hestie padded in her bare feet down the hall to check on him, passing the laundry room full of coffins on the way. She opened the door to the captain's quarters to find Poros pacing at the foot of Prometheus's bed.

Hestie hadn't seen Prometheus since the vampires had beheaded him. Seeing his lifeless body stretched out on the bed made her gasp. His skin was unnaturally pale, and his lips were blue. Although his eyes were closed, you could tell by his still chest that he wasn't sleeping.

"Oh, hey," Poros said.

"Hey," she said. "I was just checking on you."

"I don't know if he can hear me." Poros stopped pacing and stood at the foot of the bed, looking down at Captain. "Do you know? Can gods hear our prayers when their souls are in Tartarus?"

She shrugged. "I guess that's a question for my father."

"Well, I've been filling him in on all that's happened."

"Oh, okay. Do you need more time?"

"Maybe just another minute."

She rubbed her arm, suddenly feeling awkward. "Should I leave?"

"Um, no. No. That's okay." Poros went around to the side of the bed and knelt on the floor. "I just wanted to say…" he seemed to be fighting tears. "Captain, please come back. I miss your endless lectures and your extreme knowledge of trivia." Poros laughed and wiped his eyes. Then he took Prometheus's hand. "I want you to come home."

Hestie's eyes filled with tears. She hadn't realized how hard Prometheus's death—however temporary—had been on Poros. Now she worried that she'd been insensitive, that she should have been there for him. His real father, Zeus, had tried to kill him. And his mother, Metis, who'd lived for centuries inside the belly of Zeus, was out living her life, making up for lost time. Prometheus was the only person Poros had been able to rely on. Losing him must have been scary.

Hestie flinched when the fingers on Prometheus's other hand—the one Poros wasn't holding—twitched.

"Did you see that?" she whispered.

"Captain?" Poros asked, leaning close. "Can you hear me?"

Prometheus blinked. "That felt like an eternity."

"Captain! You're back! Welcome back from the dead!"

Prometheus smiled as he stretched his arms over his head. "Ugh. I can't remember the last time I died. I'd forgotten about the stiffness."

"You should probably drink some water."

Prometheus smacked his parched lips together. They were just returning to their natural color. "Yes."

Hestie took the cup on his nightstand and went to the bathroom sink, where she filled the cup with water before returning it to the captain.

He drank it down in seconds.

"More?" Hestie asked.

"Yes, please."

While she refilled the cup, she heard Prometheus say, "We should have a memorial service for those who were lost—for Mina and for the vampires."

"You heard me, then?" Poros asked.

"Yes, but I was also kept abreast of the situation by the Furies in Tartarus."

Hestie handed Prometheus the cup full of water. As he gulped it down, she said, "You aren't angry at the vampires for killing you? For killing Mina?"

"Not angry—sad. Mina was a good girl, a kind soul. Her death was a tragic accident. The vampires had good intentions."

Hestie lifted her brows. "And what were those?"

"To protect their mission—isn't that what you said, Poros?"

Hestie studied her boyfriend's face. "You've forgiven them?"

Poros shrugged. "It wasn't hard, after what they told us on the *Tarantula*."

"Jinsoo has a different opinion," Hestie said.

"How *is* Jinsoo?"

Hestie sucked in her lips.

"He's not taking it well," Poros said.

"Which is to be expected," the captain said. "What about Hermie?"

Hestie shook her head. "It hasn't been easy for him, either."

"A memorial won't take away their pain," Prometheus said, "but it will give them closure. They need that—you do, too. Even *I* need it."

"I'm surprised you can so easily feel sympathy for the vampires," Hestie said. "I thought you'd want vengeance, like Athena."

"Athena and I have never seen eye-to-eye on the value of vengeance," the captain said with a chuckle.

"So, when will we have this memorial, Captain?" Poros asked.

Prometheus returned the empty cup to his nightstand. "As soon as possible. Tonight, after the sun goes down, so we can have it above deck."

"That soon?" Hestie asked. "What should we do to prepare?"

"Let the others know. We can put out some food and wine for a small reception after we say a few words. I'll ask my mother to make some flower arrangements. I have candles here somewhere, too. Maybe we could sing a hymn."

"The vampires are a choir," Hestie said. "They sang for us on the *Tarantula*."

"It was incredible," Poros said.

"Yeah?" Captain raised his brows. "Then ask them to sing."

"Look at you," Poros said. "Back from the dead not five minutes and you're already running things."

Prometheus chuckled.

Hestie smiled. "It's good to have you back, Captain."

"It's good to be back."

Gertie had tried to watch the television mounted to the wall in the cabin, hoping to get her mind off the way Hector had left, but it hadn't worked. Now she turned off the TV, slipped on her shoes, and headed above deck to look for him.

She found him alone on the flybridge sitting in the captain's chair. He was staring out at the sparkling sea where the sun was about to set.

"Hi," she said.

"Oh, hi."

"Is it okay if I sit with you?"

He waved to the other swivel chair beside him. "Go ahead. We can watch the sunset together."

Relieved that he wanted her to stay, she relaxed a little as she took her seat. The evening breeze was cool, but not too cold. The air smelled like rain was on its way, though the clouds weren't dark. They were striped with the pinks, oranges, and purples of a setting sun.

The ocean waves were gentle, and, if they rocked the boat, it wasn't noticeable.

"I'm sorry about earlier," she said. "You were right to be angry with me."

"I'm not angry with you."

She met his smile. Then she leaned over and kissed him.

"Thanks," he said.

They were quiet for a moment as they watched the sky.

She wanted to ask him about the doubt, but she knew it would be a mistake to bring it up again.

She was surprised when he did. He said, "About earlier."

She held her breath and waited for him to say whatever it was he needed to say, guarding against the worse-case-scenario: He loved her, but *what*? Did he want to break up with her?

He scratched his chin as he kept his eyes on the horizon. He was probably enjoying the sunset, but she needed him to look at her.

"You were right about the doubt," he said. "I've been feeling like I'm, I don't know, failing you."

"You aren't failing me," she insisted.

"Just listen."

Her stomach bunched up into a tight knot. "Okay. I'm sorry."

"I'm failing you because I haven't been able to devote myself to you like I should, like I want to."

Wanting to contradict him again, she bit her lip instead.

"I feel like I'm kind of floundering right now and have been, trying to get my act together, to figure out what it is I want to do with my life. I thought it was the police academy. And maybe it is. But my heart hasn't been in it, even though my mind was made up about it."

"You'll figure it out," she said. "I feel the same way. We can figure it out together."

"That's just it. I don't think we can."

Her heart seemed to skip a beat, and her breath caught. Suddenly everything—the boat, the sea, the setting sun, and Hector sitting beside her—seemed unreal. She pinched herself, to make sure she wasn't having the worst nightmare of her life.

"I think this is something I need to do on my own," he said. "I can't be there for you and be there for me at the same time. Gods, I hope this is making sense."

"You don't need to be there for me. I can be there for *you*."

Tears had filled his eyes and had run down his cheeks. "I don't want you to."

She didn't know what to say to that. It was a total shock. He didn't want her to be there for him? She looked at the sinking sun unable to accept that this was happening. Unlike him, she had no tears. She felt numb.

"I love you, Gertie."

He finally looked at her, but she couldn't look at him.

"Please don't think I don't," he said. "I think I just need to be on my own for a while."

"For how long?" she asked.

"I don't know. I guess until I can figure out what I want to do with my life. Until I can get back on track."

"Can't I help you get back on track?" she asked, feeling feeble and needy. "We don't have to hang out as often. I could give you support when you need it, and…"

He shook his head. "That wouldn't be fair to you."

She wanted to say that breaking up wasn't fair. She wanted to say she'd do anything to keep him in her life.

"I just need some time alone."

"Like a week? A month?"

"Probably more. I don't know what the hell I'm doing. I can't worry about us and figure things out at the same time. I just can't. Please say you understand."

She didn't understand. "Of course. Take as much time as you need."

He leaned over and kissed her forehead. "I love you."

It felt like goodbye. She fought the tears stinging her eyes. She was angry. She hated him for what he was doing to her. "I love you, too."

"Hey, you two! Did someone put you in charge of my ship?"

Gertie jumped to her feet. "Prometheus?"

"In the flesh," he said with a laugh. "And it's about time. It's no fun to be separated from your body."

"We wouldn't know," Hector said, as he quickly wiped his eyes. "Welcome back. It's nice to meet you."

Hector stood and offered the captain his hand.

Prometheus shook it. "The pleasure's mine. Hector and Gertrude— am I right?"

"Gertie," Gertie said as she shook the Titan's hand.

"Thank you for your part with the vampires. I believe you've done all you can do, so, when you're ready, I'll have Morpheus take you home."

"Oh, okay," Hector said.

"We're having a memorial tonight for the people we lost. You're welcome to stay, or you can go now, if you're ready."

"I'm ready to go," Hector said.

Gertie frowned. "I'd like to stay."

"That's not a problem," Prometheus said. "Morpheus can take Hector home now and come back for you later."

Gertie looked from Hector to the Titan. "I'd like to stay until after the council meeting, if that's okay. I want to be here, to support the vampires."

Prometheus's brows lifted to his hairline. "That would be great of you. They could use a friend."

"Are you sure about this?" Hector asked her.

Gertie nodded. She'd already abandoned the conservatoire. She needed something to keep her busy, to fill the void from his absence in her life.

Morpheus appeared in the dying light. His luminous bronze skin was brighter than the sun, and his silver wings sparkled like his silver-rimmed eyes.

"Hey, dude," Morpheus said. "Ready to split?"

Hector turned to Gertie and gave her an awkward hug. "Call me when you get back."

"Okay," she said.

The reality of what was happening had begun to sink in as tears pricked her eyes. Her body trembled as she watched Morpheus spread his magnificent wings and carry Hector away.

"Are you okay?" Prometheus asked her.

She batted the tears from her eyes. "Yes. I'm fine."

Hermie stood between his sister and Jinsoo on the main deck beneath the starry night, where the gods, mortals, and vampires had gathered for the captain's tribute to the fallen. The deck had been decorated with flowers and candles. The cool, gentle breeze made the tiny flames dance, and it even extinguished a few, but there were enough that remained lit to evoke the cathedral-like ambience of a funeral.

They stood in an informal circle between the front and center masts. Everyone wore somber looks on their faces. Hermie was surprised to see a few of the vampires weeping, including Del, who, as always, looked supremely beautiful, especially when her dark eyes sparkled with the light of the moon. The vampire virus hadn't completely left his system, so he reached out to her mind, wondering what she was thinking.

It is considered rude and an invasion of privacy, Del said directly into his mind.

Talk about the pot calling the kettle black, he replied.

You were my enemy then.

I'm not your enemy now? he asked.

She glanced at him from where she stood between Sophia and Alastair on the opposite side of the circle from him. *I do not know what you are to me.*

Hermie chewed on the inside of his bottom lip. *We have chemistry, like an animal magnetism—that's all it is. It's science. It doesn't have to mean anything, or to make us anything to each other. We just have to ignore it.*

He waited for her reply, but she said nothing more.

"We come together tonight to remember our friends," Prometheus said, from where he stood in the middle of their circle. "Their names will now be said by those who loved them."

He gave Jinsoo a nod.

"Mina Huang," Jinsoo said.

Prometheus nodded at Alastair.

Alastair cleared his throat. "Kagan Kalogeropoulos."

Then Del said, "Edric Iraklidis."

Mahdi said, "Farouk Eliades."

Taavi said, "Cade Rokos."

And, lastly, Raimo said, "Chloe Persopoulos."

"We pray that the souls of our beloved find their way to the peaceful Fields of Elysium, where they will be happy and joyful for all of eternity," Prometheus said. "We also pray that our memories of them will be happy ones and that soon our grief will be replaced by peace."

Hermie wiped his nose and fought tears.

"And now, let us have a song to commemorate the occasion," Prometheus said.

Alastair began in his rich bass voice:

While you live, shine.

Have no grief at all.

Life exists only for a short while,

*And Time demands his due.***

Then the others joined in, with a lovely harmony:

The rain descends, and from high heaven

A storm is driven:

And on the running water-brooks the cold

Lays icy hold:

Then up! beat down the winter; make the fire

Blaze high and higher;

Mix wine as sweet as honey of the bee

Abundantly;
Then drink with comfortable wool around
Your temples bound.
We must not yield our hearts to woe, or wear
With wasting care;
For grief will profit us no whit, my friend,
Nor nothing mend;
Think not on what we have lost,
But rejoice that we once had.
For grief will profit us no whit,
*Nor nothing mend.****

Hermie still couldn't get over how beautiful the voices of the vampires were, and the sadness in their voices made it impossible to fight the tears that had been welling in his eyes. As Hermie glanced around, he didn't see a dry eye among them.

"That was beautiful," Prometheus said. "Let us now say a few words in memory of our loved ones. Who would like to go first?"

Raimo lifted his hand.

"Please, Raimo," Prometheus said. "Speak."

"Chloe always put herself last," Raimo said. "She was one of those people who saw to the needs of others before seeing to her own. She helped me more times than I can count. After singing, her next favorite thing was knitting. We all have sweaters and scarves that we will remember her by. We love you, Chloe."

Del looked up at Prometheus, who nodded.

"Edric was a comedian with a gentle spirit," she said. "In his heart, he was not a warrior, but he fought for justice. In his mind, he was not brave, but he did brave things. He was best at making the rest of us laugh. We will miss your joyful spirit, Edric. Goodbye, my friend."

Del glanced across the circle at Hermie. He averted his eyes. Her words had moved him, had made him feel the pain of her loss. But if he were to get past the natural attraction between them, he needed distance, not feelings of compassion.

"Farouck wasn't one to show emotion or to express feelings," Sophia said. "But he had a huge heart."

"Cade, too," Taavi said. "He was the kind of person who would do anything for anyone."

Alastair cleared his throat again. "Kagan was a philosopher who always made me think. He loved to analyze people and situations. He showed me new ways of seeing things. He cared about humanity but resented the gods because he felt abandoned by them. I hope and pray that Kagan will find peace in the Underworld, that he will be judged by his good deeds and not by his resentful heart."

Prometheus turned to Jinsoo. "Wouldn't you like to say something about your sister?"

Jinsoo nodded. "She was the brave one. I did not want to come on the ship with Captain. She talk me into it. I was afraid to scuba dive. She talk me into it. Everything in my life I did because she push me. I don't know how it will be without her. I miss her. Why did she have to die? I still don't understand. I don't understand why her murderer is not being punished."

Jinsoo didn't look up at Del—or any of the vampires. He clenched his fists and allowed his tears to flow freely.

Del broke from the group and headed to the hatch, but Sophia caught up to her and convinced her to stay.

Prometheus took one of the candles and, cupping the flame to protect it from the breeze, he said, "Follow me to the lower deck."

They crossed through the kitchen and salon, where they took three steps to the lower deck at the stern of the ship, which was at sea level and had a ladder in back, for when the crew wanted to go diving. Prometheus had six blocks of wood already waiting and soaking in lighter fluid.

He picked up one, held the flame to it until it caught fire, and said, "Chloe Persopoulos, may the perpetual light of the Underworld shine upon you and bring you peace."

Then Prometheus carefully set the burning wood onto the calm sea, where it floated into the distance.

Prometheus took up a second block, held the flame to it until it caught fire, and said, "Edric Iraklidis, may the perpetual light of the Underworld shine upon you and bring you peace."

He set the burning wood into the water. It followed the first, drifting like a tiny funeral pyre.

Prometheus took up the third, held it to the flame, set the burning wood into the sea, and said, "Kagan Kalogeropoulos, may the perpetual light of the Underworld shine upon you and bring you peace."

"Farouck Eliades, may the perpetual light of the Underworld shine upon you and bring you peace." The fourth block was set on fire and put on the water.

"Cade Rokos, may the perpetual light of the Underworld shine upon you and bring you peace." The fifth block was set on fire and placed onto the sea.

The captain took up the final block, set it on fire, and, as he placed it into the sea, he said, "Mina Huang, may the perpetual light of the Underworld shine upon you and bring you peace."

Hermie wiped his eyes as he watched the six burning blocks drift from the boat and out into the dark sea as the light from their flames lifted into the starry night, all the way up to the moon goddess, Selene.

CHAPTER SIXTEEN

Treasure Hunt

Hestie used the sleeve of her shirt to dry her eyes as she and the others left the lower deck for the salon, where she had helped Prometheus and Poros to set out food and drinks earlier. Although the vampires weren't interested in the food, they each had a cup of wine. The captain even allowed Hestie and the rest of his young crew to partake—though Jinsoo still refused to eat or drink.

Hestie and Poros stood together in one corner of the room, snacking on cheese and sipping their wine, when two of the vampires approached.

"Look at all the art you saved," Alastair said to them as he studied the stack of crates along the back of the room. "There must be at least twenty canvases here."

"We never properly thanked you," Del added. "It means a lot to us."

"We're glad we could help," Poros said.

"I wonder what happened to the other treasures, like my coins," Hestie said before taking a sip of her wine. Then she asked, "Why did you take, them, anyway? I hadn't stolen them from anyone."

"Those coins were ancient Persian darics," Raimo said from across the room. "They belong with the Persian people, in their museums in Iran, and not with some wealthy collector who has no ties to old Persia."

"Who died and made you the morality police?" Hermie challenged from where he sat at the booth with Jinsoo and Chidori.

Another vampire—Mahdi—joined the conversation. "We should search the *Tarantula* before the council meeting on Mount Olympus."

"That's a great idea!" Gertie said before popping a cube of cheese into her mouth.

"I am sure Poseidon and his minions have already cleaned out the wreckage," Del said. "I doubt there is anything left."

"It would not hurt to look," Taavi said.

"I agree!" Gertie said. "I'm happy to help."

Poros cocked his head to the side. "I'm still curious, Alastair. What exactly did you mean when you said that Poseidon is the real enemy to the human race?"

"He misspoke," Del said. "Poseidon is not an enemy to all humans—just to the disenfranchised."

Prometheus turned from where he was pouring more wine in the galley. "Be careful of making false allegations against gods."

"She speaks the truth," Raimo insisted. "Poseidon enables victors to take from the vanquished."

Prometheus scratched his chin. "Hermie was right to call this an issue of morality. It breaks no laws."

"What about the Pakistani boys?" Poros asked.

"Is there any proof that Poseidon had anything to do with that?" Prometheus asked.

Del put a hand on her hip. "He supports Sailfish Trading and Shipping, which controls almost everything imported and exported on the Mediterranean, including black market goods."

"And people," Raimo said.

"I'd be careful about accusing a god," Prometheus said again.

Alastair drank down the last of his wine before saying, "Even if Poseidon is unaware of the smuggling that goes on by STS, which I doubt, and even if there is nothing illegal about selling art made by and taken from the disenfranchised, anti-trust laws exist in most countries. Like Del said, Poseidon has made STS a monopoly in this area."

"And where there is a monopoly, there is corruption," Mahdi added.

"Regardless of Poseidon's guilt or innocence," Poros said, "it wouldn't hurt to search the wreckage, would it Captain?"

"I suppose not," he said. "But it's a long journey, and we don't have much time before the council meeting."

"What if we could shorten the length of the trip considerably?" Alastair asked with a gleam in his eyes.

"Do you mean by flying the ship, like you did with the *Tarantula*?" Hestie asked.

"Exactly."

Everyone turned to Prometheus, waiting for his reply. The Titan scratched his curly head. Then he scratched his curly beard. Finally, he said, "Okay. I'm curious to see how this works."

Hermie remained behind in the salon with Gertie, Jinsoo, and Chidori while Hestie and Poros followed the captain and the vampires out onto the main deck beneath the starry sky.

"We call the top," Taavi said, as he flew to the top of the center mast.

He was followed by Mahdi and Riamo.

"We call the center," Del said to the others.

Alastair and Sophia followed Del halfway up the center mast and grabbed ahold of it with their legs dangling just above Hestie, Poros, and Captain.

"Hold on with both hands," Del told them. "On my count, lift the ship into the air and then turn her in the same direction as the hand of a clock. Got it?"

Hestie and Poros nodded.

"How high are we taking her?" Prometheus asked.

"About one hundred feet," Alastair said. "Which is usually just enough to escape Poseidon's notice."

"What's the point of spinning?" Hestie asked.

"If we were to fly up *without* spinning, the ship would break apart," Del said from above. "The rotational force holds everything together."

"How interesting," Prometheus said.

"On my count," Del said. "Lift on three. Ready? One, two, three."

Hestie pressed up against the mast, along with the others. She laughed with excitement when the ship lifted from the sea. It moaned like a lost ghost and crackled like fireworks.

"We did it!" she cried to Poros.

"Turn!" Del shouted.

Everyone turned their bodies to their left and flew in a clockwise direction. Slowly at first, the ship made a revolution, and then, as the immortals picked up in speed, the ship began spinning like a top.

"Now press southeast!" Del shouted.

Hestie barely heard Del's voice over the howling air whipping past as she and the others flew in circles. It was exhilarating, like a carnival ride, and she was dizzy—so dizzy that she started laughing. Since she could no longer tell what was east or west, she let the others take the lead, and she followed.

After ten or fifteen minutes, Del cried, "This is it. Slow down and lower her down!"

Everyone turned to their right and pushed in the opposite direction, to slow the ship's momentum. This made Hestie's brain feel like it was spinning inside of her head. She couldn't tell what was up or down as nausea swept over her.

Once they had stopped and the *Marcella II* was safely floating on the sea, Hestie stumbled to the rails and was sick over the side.

Poros flew beside her. "You okay?"

"Yeah. My head just hurts now."

"Maybe you shouldn't go on the dive."

"Oh, I'm going on the dive, Poros. You can't get rid of me that easily."

"That was something, huh?"

"It was incredible," she said. "If it weren't for the part where I got sick, I'd want to do it again."

He put his arm around her and leaned in for a kiss.

She covered her mouth to stop him.

"I was just sick, Poros. At least let me rinse my mouth first."

He kissed the back of her hand. "I don't care about that."

"Well, I do. Gross."

He threw his head back and laughed. "I love you so much, Hestie."

Her eyes widened and her mouth dropped open. It was the first time he had said those words to her.

"Gods, Hestie. Say something. Am I way off here?"

She shook her head. "You're not way off. Oh, Poros, I love you, too. But your timing couldn't be worse!"

They both threw their heads back and laughed as they followed the others back to the salon.

As the vampires were deciding who should stay behind to guard the *Marcella II* and their crates, Gertie approached Alastair in the galley and tapped him on the shoulder.

"Yes?" he asked, as he poured a little more wine into his cup.

She grinned. "Can't you read my mind?"

"I do not want to be rude, now that we are friends."

Jinsoo, who had overheard from where he sat at the booth across from Hermie on the far-end of the room, glared at them.

"Well, I want you to bite me, so I can go on the dive."

"As lovely as you taste, I do not think that is wise."

"Why not? You saw how fast I was."

"It is nothing against you, my dear. I do not want to get addicted to you, or you to me."

"Just once more?"

"I will do it," Taavi said. "I am unbelievably thirsty and could use a pick-me-up."

Alastair stepped out of the way to join the group of vampires in the center of the salon.

"Thanks." Gertie held out her wrist to Taavi.

He was tall and wiry with dark wavy hair and golden-brown eyes and a few freckles on each side of a thin nose. His lips were also thin, and his brows were thick and dark. When he smiled, a dimple appeared in his left cheek.

He pressed his fangs into her wrist. Her momentary paralysis was quickly replaced by the all-too-familiar euphoria. She sighed with pleasure as the feeling overtook her. Next came the sharpening of her senses and her ability to read thoughts—though nearly everyone in the room had a block up.

"Thank you so very much!" she said to Taavi.

He laughed as he licked her blood from his lips. "My pleasure."

A few minutes later, they gathered on the lower deck, where Prometheus handed out four cross-body bags made of netting.

Gertie didn't get one.

"I'm sorry I don't have more," he said. "But if everyone stays with a partner, which I highly recommend, you can share."

Gertie glanced around as people partnered up: Raimo and Mahdi, Sophia and Alastair, Poros and Hestie. She was relieved when Taavi waved his index finger back and forth between them. She nodded gratefully and moved closer to him.

"Now, listen up," Prometheus said. "At the first sign of trouble, head back. The Olympians have called a truce, but that won't stop others from doing the same thing we're doing. Expect the worst-case scenario—not the best—and, that way, you'll always be prepared."

One by one, the vampires dove into the dark sea.

"Keep me abreast of what's happening," Prometheus said to Poros just before the young god pushed off.

It was Taavi's turn to dive. Gertie's heart raced as she watched his lean form gracefully fly from the platform into darkness. Then, she took a deep breath and dove.

Grateful for her vampire vision, Gertie followed the others into the dark depths of the ocean. Poros and Hestie quickly moved to the lead of the group. Gertie believed she could catch up to them but didn't want to abandon her partner, who appeared to be swimming at his top speed already.

Gertie shivered as they approached a massive whale hovering listlessly in the water. It appeared to be sleeping. As she wondered why the group hadn't put more distance between themselves and the whale, the creature opened its eyes and looked at her. She screamed and swam in the opposite direction as fast as she could go, leaving everyone else in her wake.

Gertie? Taavi called to her telepathically. *Where did you go?*

She stopped and glanced around, no longer able to see the rest of the group. *Didn't you see that whale?*

Whales do not wish to eat us. You have nothing to fear.

I know that. I've read quite a good deal about whales. I wasn't thinking.

I understand. You reacted instinctively.

Where are you? I can't see you anymore.

I am coming to you.

Taavi soon appeared in her line of vision with a smile on his face. He took her hand and led her back to the others.

When the wreckage of the *Tarantula* appeared in the distance below, Gertie slowed down to take it all in. She'd never seen anything like it before. The enormous ship sat on the bottom of the ocean floor nearly intact. She'd expected to find it in pieces.

"Oh, Gaia," she muttered. "What a sight."

"Sad, is it not?" Taavi said beside her. "That was our home for many years."

"I'm sorry," Gertie said. "Do you think it can be salvaged and repaired?"

"No way."

They followed the group until they were directly above the ship, where the huge crack down the center was now visible.

I sense others already inside the hull, Poros said telepathically.

Gertie imagined he said it to everyone in the group.

Let me go first, he said.

Not without me, Hestie insisted.

Gertie and Taavi hovered above the *Tarantula* watching with anticipation as the two young gods entered the hull through the gap. The minute that passed seemed long before Hestie and Poros emerged.

Furies and merfolk are searching for the key to free Athena, Poros said. *Most of the treasure was already taken to Poseidon, but we're welcome to what's left.*

Could this be a trap? Mahdi suggested.

Maybe we should turn back, Raimo said.

You go back, Hestie said. *Poros and I will continue the search.*

Some of us should stay here and keep watch while others of us help with the search, Alastair said. *Any volunteers?*

I want to search! Gertie said.

Taavi nodded his agreement.

Mahdi, Sophia, and I will stay here, Raimo said.

Alastair nodded and beckoned to Taavi and Gertie to follow him and the young gods. Gertie was filled with excitement as she swam toward the gap in the hull.

Hermie sat in the booth across from Jinsoo and Chidori, waiting for the divers to return. Del entered the salon and sat on one of the couches, where she tried to use the remote to turn on the television, with no luck.

"What is with this thing?" she murmured.

"Let her suffer," Jinsoo said to Hermie.

"Then we all suffer," Hermie said as he scooted from the booth to help her.

Once he reached her, he held out his hand for the remote. Without hiding her frustration, she handed it over.

"What do you want to watch?" he asked, as he clicked on the power.

"The news? Or a channel about nature or animals or outer space?"

"Seriously?" Those weren't the answers he would have guessed.

"I never get to watch, and I love to learn new things."

He put it on the space channel. Then he sat on the opposite end of the couch to watch, too. The vampire virus had left his body, so there was no fear of accidentally trying to read her mind.

"I expected you to go with the others," he said.

"I hate diving."

"Seriously? You're a *pirate.*"

"I do not like the way the saltwater makes my hair smell."

Hermie laughed. "You don't strike me as the kind of person to care about such things."

"You do not know me."

"True."

"What about you?" she asked. "Why did you not go?"

"Someone needed to stay with Jinsoo."

"Ah."

After a beat he added. "The truth is, I don't like swimming where there are creepy, crawling things."

Del shuddered. "I know what you mean. I hate it, too."

"Seriously?"

"Why do you keep saying that word *seriously*? I am almost nothing but serious."

"I get that."

After a few moments of listening to a description of the rings on Saturn, she said, "I never set out to become a pirate. It just happened."

"How does something like that just happen?"

"You already know that my friends and I were orphans, yes?"

Hermie nodded.

"A plague hit our village when I was twelve years old. My parents and two brothers died. I had no one else. It was the same for my friends. We were taken in by a temple devoted to Athena in what is now called Athens."

"How long ago was this?"

"A very long time ago," she said with a laugh. "Anyway, the children with the best voices were formed into a traveling choir. We did this for many years. Since I could hit high C and Alastair could hit low C, we were considered the leaders of the group."

"That's an interesting way to choose leaders."

"We were a *choir*."

"I get it. I was only kidding."

"One night, when I was seventeen years old, we came home to our orphanage, which was near the modern-day acropolis, and something was not right. We could hear screams throughout the village. Our priests told us to go to our beds, but none of us could sleep. We were terrified."

"Was it a war? Was Athens under attack?"

"Athens was under attack, but it was not a war, exactly. The first vampires had just come into being, and no one yet knew what this meant for humanity. The gods did not even know."

"So, Athens was being attacked by vampires," Hermie said.

Del nodded. "It was terrifying. It was even more terrifying *after* we were attacked. We found ourselves blood thirsty and possessing strange new powers that we did not know how to use. The only thing that helped me through that period in my life was the decision made by our choir to stick together. After five years of sleeping, eating, and singing together, we had become a family."

Hermie sighed as he realized how hard it must have been for them to lose Edric, Chloe, and Kagan.

"It was *very* hard," she said. "Especially when Athena destroyed Kagan. He had loved and worshipped her for so long."

"Did you just read my thoughts? I thought you said that was rude?"

"I did not pry. You threw the thought at me. There is a difference."

Hermie made a mental note that he needed to be more careful with how he handled his thoughts.

"Oh, listen," Del said, pointing at the television. "That is what the rings of Saturn sound like? How interesting."

Hermie glanced across the room at Jinsoo, who was feeding sunflower seeds to Chidori. Hermie supposed Jinsoo was listening to Del's story, too.

When the segment on the sounds of the rings of Saturn came to an end, Hermie asked, "So, how did you and your friends become pirates?"

Del laughed. "I have a way of drawing out a story, do I not?"

Hermie laughed, too. "It's okay. It's been interesting."

"Well, the priests who had taken us in had become vampires, too, and they were killed by villagers. The villagers were going to kill us, too, but could not bring themselves to do it, so we went into hiding. We went through a tough period when the gods were figuring out what to do with us. They finally settled on a set of rules for us to live by, enforced by demigods, whom they trained to destroy any rule-breakers."

"What kind of rules?"

"We can only drink from a willing mortal. We can only drink up to one pint from a single mortal. We cannot drink from the same mortal more than once per week. We cannot enter a mortal's home without an invitation. We cannot make any more vampires."

"How do you make a vampire?"

"The mortal must be drained of all blood," she said. "Then, if that mortal feeds on human blood, the transition is complete. Otherwise, the mortal dies."

"Have you ever made one?"

"Many, before the rules."

"And after?"

"A few who wanted it."

"Is it usually difficult to find a willing mortal?"

"Not as difficult as you think. You have seen Gertie, yes?"

Hermie chuckled. "She's pretty into it."

"People become addicted to the euphoria and to the temporary powers," she said. "Some mortals beg to be fed on more than once per week. It can be hard to follow the rules when both the vampire and the mortal wish to break them."

After experiencing it himself, Hermie understood why people became addicted. Even now, he wished for the feeling again.

"Food was scarce in Athens," Del said. "Alastair suggested that we go to Piraeus, a port in Greece where new people arrived almost daily. This was a good idea. After years of living there, we became well-known by the sailors who lusted for the effects of our bite more than those of their rum."

"What did the locals think of you?"

"Their feelings about us were mixed. Some thought we were good for the economy, because the sailors always wanted to stay in port for a while. Others felt we were making their home dirty and immoral and were possibly deterring tourists from visiting."

"I see."

"As the years went by, this second group of locals became larger and wanted to drive us away. We were invited by a large crew to join them on their vessel. Alastair was dying to go. So were Raimo and Mahdi and Penny, who craved adventure and became easily bored."

"And you?"

"I did not wish to go. But, after discussing it among ourselves, we decided it was for the best, so we went."

"Let me guess. The crew who took you in, they were pirates?"

"No. They worked for a respectable merchant. We were happy with them for over a decade. Then we were taken over by pirates who had lost their vessel in a storm. Our mortal friends were killed. So were a few pirates. But, needing a food source in the open sea, we let most of them live."

"Is that when you became pirates, too?"

"Not at first. When the mortals ran out of food and we were still days away from land, a smaller ship happened by, and the pirates killed the entire crew and took their supplies. We were told to drain the bodies of blood and dump them into the sea. Since they were already dead, we did what we were told. It was the first time in ages that we fed until we were full. Imagine how it would feel to be prevented from ever finishing your meal. After a few bites, you must push your plate away. That is the life of a vampire. But these pirates offered us a more fulfilling way of life."

Hermie shuddered.

"It was a low period in my life. We told ourselves that we were not responsible for the deaths of countless men and women. Sometimes there were children. But we knew better. By living in partnership with the pirates, we were culpable."

"How long did you remain with them?"

"For too long. We grew to despise ourselves and each other. It was an awful time. Our little family nearly broke up over it."

"What happened? What kept you from breaking up?"

"Hermes came along."

Hermie lifted his brows. "How long ago?"

Del shrugged. "When you have lived as long as I have, time becomes meaningless."

"Was it ten years ago? A hundred?"

"More than that."

"So, then what happened?" he asked.

Del jumped to her feet. "The divers have returned. Let us go and see what they found."

Hermie followed her from the salon down the steps to the lower deck, where the divers emerged from the sea.

"Hermie!" Hestie cried. "I found my little chest of coins! Poseidon's merfolk had already cleaned out the wreckage, but they didn't find my coins!"

"That's awesome!" Hermie said.

Prometheus, who was on the flybridge, cried out, "Excellent news! What else did you find?"

"Not much," Alastair said. "A few pieces of Albanian jewelry."

"The Furies were there," Poros said. "They and three mermaids were in a race to find the key to my sister's cage."

"Why were they racing?" Hermie asked.

"Because if the Furies find it, they'll give the key to Hades, who will then bargain on behalf of Hermes and the two vampires," Hestie explained.

"But if the mermaids find it," Poros began.

"They'll give it to Poseidon," Prometheus finished.

"You can guess who we are rooting for," Raimo said.

Hermie thrust his hands in his pockets and felt something in his right pocket, something he'd forgotten was there. Without pulling it out, he turned it over in his hand. It was the key to the adamantine cage.

So, you do have it after all, Del said into his mind.

Why are you in my head?

You speak to me without realizing it.

Hermie felt his face get hot with embarrassment. What else had he said to her without meaning to?

What will you do with the key? she asked.

I don't know.

CHAPTER SEVENTEEN

Confidants

After the excitement of the dive had dwindled, the ship had been prepared to set sail—this time, the old-fashioned way—and all but Prometheus and Hermie, who sat at the helm, had retired to their cabin or crate.

Gertie showered and changed into dry clothes and tried to sleep. But, as she lay in bed, she thought about Hector. She resented him for needing to figure things out on his own. They had done everything together for over a year. They had fought gods and vampires and even teachers who were unfair. They had been to dances and to festivals and to rock concerts. They had told each other everything about their difficult childhoods—the parental neglect and abandonment—and their need to prove themselves to the gods and to the world.

They had shared and had been through so much together. Certainly, they could figure things out together, too, couldn't they? She wanted to be there for him. And she wanted him to be there for her. She couldn't understand why, for the first time since they'd met, he didn't want the same thing as she.

Unable to sleep, and with the vampire virus still pumping in her veins, she reached out to Taavi:

Want to go flying for a little while?

I suppose you do not get to fly very often.

No. Are you up for it?

Within seconds, there was a knock at her door.

Taavi?

Are you coming? he asked.

Without changing from the nightgown that she had borrowed from Hestie, Gertie opened her door.

"Let's go," she said.

She led them above deck to the bow, from which she could see the distant island of Crete. Gertie recalled the nights of flying with Jeno over Greece.

"Ready?" she asked Taavi.

He leapt into the air, and she followed.

From the flybridge, Prometheus cried, "Where are you going?"

"I want to fly," Gertie said. "We'll be right back. I promise!"

When Prometheus didn't object, she followed Taavi across the sea toward Crete.

"Have you ever met Asterion and Ariadne?" Gertie asked Taavi, once they were flying side by side.

"Who?"

"The Minotaur and his sister."

"No. Have you?"

She laughed. "Yes, but that was an exceptional time in my life."

"And this is not?"

At that moment, Gertie realized that she had been dwelling on the past instead of living in the moment. Even her invitation to Taavi to go flying had been an effort to distract her from memories with Hector. What she needed to do, she now realized, was to live in the moment and to make new, exceptional memories.

"It is!" she finally said. "Come on!"

She led him to the snowy peak of Mount Ida, where she gathered up snow and formed it into a ball before throwing it at Taavi. He'd been standing there with an arched brow, wondering what she was doing, but, once it became clear to him, he wasted no time in forming his own snowballs. They chased each other all over the mountaintop—both on the ground and in the sky. They laughed so hard that they caused an avalanche. Fortunately, it was harmless.

They were having so much fun that they almost didn't notice the arrival of dawn. Once they did, they laughed and shrieked as they flew like bullets back to the hull of the ship. Not wanting to wake the others with their laughter over a close call, she invited Taavi to her room, where they lay on her bed, side by side, and watched episodes of *Avatar: The Last Airbender.*

Hestie crept down the hall in her night shirt and bare feet and stood outside of Poros's cabin.

Telepathically, she asked, *Poros? Can I come in?*

When she received no reply, she said again, *Poros? Can I come in?*

Please do.

Grinning, she opened the door.

He looked sexy as hell lying, shirtless, in bed in his striped boxers. His blond hair was smushed to one side, and his gray, sleepy eyes were hooded.

"I was going to invite you," he said, "but I worried that you might need your rest."

As she neared the bed, she asked, "Does that mean I won't get much rest if I join you?"

He threw his head back and laughed. "I don't know. I doubt it."

She sat on the edge of his bed and gazed down at him. "It looks like I woke you."

"I don't mind." He reached up and pushed her hair behind her ear. "Come here."

She curled beside him on the bed. He cupped his hand around her bottom and pulled her closer.

"I hope it's okay to kiss you now," he teased.

"My teeth have been properly brushed and rinsed."

"Well, thank the gods for that."

He pressed his lips to hers. She moaned against him as she kissed him back. He pulled her on top of him. She ran her fingers though his bedhead-hair and took his tongue into her mouth. His hands explored her body, touching her in places he hadn't before. Were they about to have sex for the very first time?

Though her actions said differently, Hestie teetered with indecision. When he rolled her onto her back and lay on top of her, kissing her neck and coming dangerously close to the top of her breasts, Hestie thought that maybe, yes, maybe, yes, this was it.

Then they heard giggling down the hall and the sound of a cabin door open and shut.

"Who was that?" she whispered.

Poros rolled onto his side and propped his head on an elbow. "I believe it was Gertie and Taavi. I heard them say they were going flying together."

"Hector hasn't been gone but a day," Hestie said.

"Maybe she and Taavi are only friends."

"Maybe."

"I guess it's none of our business," Poros said before he kissed her again.

Hestie had been glad for the interruption because it gave her the time she needed to think.

"Just so you know, Poros…I'm not ready for sex."

"Good," he said. "Neither am I."

She laughed hysterically as he tickled her and nibbled at her ear before pulling her on top of him again.

"No sex," he said with a grin. "But let's get back to where we were before we were so rudely interrupted."

Hestie laughed again with a heart full of joy as she pressed her lips to his.

"You should get some rest," Captain said to Hermie. "Dawn is coming, and we'll be leaving for the council meeting in a few hours."

"I guess you're right."

Hermie headed below deck. He was nearly knocked over by Gertie and Taavi as they flew past him. Hermie went to his room, changed into a t-shirt and fresh boxers, and climbed into bed.

He wished he could have heard the rest of Del's story. It had been interesting to learn about her past. He was dying to know how she and her family of vampires became associated with Hermes.

When sleep failed to come, instead of praying to his Uncle Hip, Hermie reached out to Del.

Are you awake? he asked her.

Yes, but you should not be.

Gods don't need as much rest as vampires.

I beg to differ.

Are we really going to argue over who needs less sleep? he asked.

No.

Will you tell me the rest of your story?

Okay. What do you want to know?

What happened when Hermes came into your life?

He taught us how to be pirates.

What? Hermie rolled onto his side and turned on the lamp on his nightstand, to make sure he was awake.

He called us his V-Team. Our mission was to reclaim stolen goods from pirates and return them to their rightful owners.

Oh. Like you're doing now.

Exactly. Our very first ship was the Water Beatle.

Cool name.

Next, it was the Mayfly. *Then the* Dragonfly. *Then, let me think, was it the* Water Strider? *I cannot recall them all. It brought Hermes pleasure to have a new ship built just so he could name it.*

I wonder why he named them after insects. Most people name their ships after women. Did he name the Tarantula?

Yes. He named our vessels after insects and spiders because Hecate believed a vessel named for a woman objectified all women. She even discouraged us from referring to a ship as a she.

That's interesting, I never thought about that before. So, do you mean to say that Hecate knew about you and what you were doing?

Yes. Her magic helped us to hide our existence from the other gods.

Oh, wow.

Without her, we might not have been successful.

How did it feel to give back the stolen goods?

Not always good. At first, we returned all stolen goods, even when the people who were robbed had more than they could possibly need. But, over time, Hermes began to make moral judgments about which pirates we should attack and which we should leave alone.

What do you mean?

When pirates who had nothing stole from the wealthy for their survival, Hermes allowed it. He had his V-Team focus on selfish, greedy pirates who stole for material gain.

I see.

We also stopped slavers, when we could, and some drug traffickers and other smugglers—again, Hermes made moral judgments about them, too. We followed his orders, and he kept us safe—he and Hecate both. In recent decades, we have focused our efforts on the enormous fleet belonging to STS—Sailfish Trading and Shipping. They have become so corrupt as to keep us busy all year long.

And you say Poseidon supports STS?

Absolutely. The company could not have taken over the Mediterranean without Poseidon's help. Hermes told us that Poseidon believes STS keeps the seas safer, because no other pirates can compete. If a buyer wants something from the black market, the buyer knows how to contact STS. Anything that can be smuggled—goods and people—are delivered by STS. Poseidon believes that it is impossible to prevent human corruption, but it can be controlled, and the way to control it is through STS.

Are you saying that Poseidon is aware of the smuggling that takes place on the STS ships?

Hermes says so, and I believe him.

To Hermie, it sounded as if *both* gods had crossed legal and ethical lines. Both gods wanted to help humanity but had different beliefs on how it should be done. Poseidon was more utilitarian in his support of what he believed would bring happiness to the most people, whereas Hermes was more liberal in his sympathy for individuals and disenfranchised groups.

Perhaps, Del said. *However, I would amend your conclusion with this: Poseidon cares less about bringing happiness to the most people than he does about aligning with and controlling the rich and powerful.*

You've given me a great deal to think about, Del. Thank you.

It has been my pleasure, Hermie.

Hermie didn't add that hearing her story had made him even more curious about her, but he supposed she knew it already.

As he closed his eyes, he prayed to Hades that Mina was at peace in the Elysian Fields. And he allowed himself to cry for Mina, even as he thought about Del.

<u>CHAPTER EIGHTEEN</u>

Mount Olympus

To protect the vampires from the sunlight, the captain met with his crew and passengers below deck. Everyone but the vampires had showered and changed into fresh clothes. Even Prometheus looked fancier than usual in a navy coat with brass buttons, with his hair and beard trimmed.

Gertie, who had fallen asleep beside Taavi, had awakened an hour ago to find him still lying beside her. He had hung out in her room to watch television while she had showered and changed, and now she felt awkward standing beside him. Although she'd enjoyed his company, she worried that she had given him the wrong idea. Her heart belonged to Hector.

Prometheus stood near her and Taavi across from the laundry room. The other vampires either sat on their crates or hovered in the air above them. Hestie and Poros stood at one end of the corridor, and Jinsoo hung back with Chidori on his shoulder behind Hermie at the other end.

"Most of the gods have a bias against vampires," the captain said. "To remedy this, I was hoping you could offer them a song."

"It would be our pleasure," Del said.

Alastair lifted his palms. "An honor."

The other vampires nodded their agreement.

"Have any of you ever visited Mount Olympus before?" the captain asked.

Gertie raised her hand and lowered it.

"They say the sun always shines there," Prometheus continued, "but have no fear. The light does not come from the sun god, Helios. It is a magical light that will cause you no harm."

"That's true," Gertie said as she lifted her chin. "I went there with Jeno, and he was fine."

"Getting there is another story," the captain said. "We will need to god-travel rather than fly, for obvious reasons. As I have no chariot, god-travel is our only option. Poros, Hermie, and Hestie can help me to get you there. However, we cannot travel directly inside the gates. And though the mountaintop sits high up in the clouds, the rays of Helios may reach us."

"Our clothing will protect us for short periods," Raimo said.

"I have umbrellas and hats and two raincoats," Prometheus said. "You're welcome to use them."

The umbrellas, hats, and raincoats appeared on the washer and dryer beside the vampires. The coats were too small to fit anyone but Sophia. Raimo and Mahdi each took a hat, and the rest took umbrellas.

"It goes without saying that, for the safety of all, we should be respectful to every god, even those who may treat us poorly," Prometheus warned. "Understood?"

Everyone, even the young gods, nodded.

"I hadn't planned on accompanying you," Prometheus continued, "but Hypnos has agreed to stay with Jinsoo. It is important that Athena hear from me."

"Captain! I want to go to Mount Olympus, too. Please?"

"It's not safe for mortals," Hermie said.

"*Gertie* is mortal," Jinsoo complained.

Gertie's breath caught. Would she be made to stay behind, too?

"Jinsoo should be allowed to speak at Mount Olympus on behalf of his sister," Del said.

"Del, why would you suggest such a thing?" Alastair asked with a voice full of concern.

"Del, please," Sophia murmured.

"It is right and fair," Del said.

Prometheus sighed. "She makes a good point. I suppose you can go with us, Jinsoo."

"And Chidori, too?" the boy asked.

Prometheus chuckled. "And Chidori, too."

"When are we leaving?" Hestie asked.

"There's no reason to delay," the captain replied. "If everyone is ready, we'll go now."

Gertie glanced around the room. Everyone seemed willing and eager to go.

They gathered in a circle to hold hands.

"Here we go," the captain said.

The familiar feeling of god-travel pressed against Gertie from all sides, and, in the next instant, she was standing with the others on a snow-covered mountaintop beside a large wall of clouds, which she recognized as the gates of Mount Olympus.

The vampires opened their umbrellas.

"Are you okay?" Gertie asked Taavi beneath his umbrella.

"Yes. Only nervous."

"Spring, Summer, Winter, and Fall," Prometheus shouted. "Please open the gates of Mount Olympus so that I, Prometheus, and my guests may enter."

A loud roar carried through the air, and a tunnel of cold wind lifted in front of them. At its center was a single rain cloud. As the wind settled and the rain cloud emptied its contents and then dissipated, the giant wall of clouds opened.

"This way," the captain said.

Taavi continued to hold onto Gertie's hand as they followed Prometheus inside.

The wall of clouds closed behind them, and, in front of them, at the center of a golden-paved plaza, was a round fountain. In the center of the fountain was the statue of a golden whale with water spraying from its spout. At the top of this fountain, where the water arched and fell into a pool bordered with golden bricks, was another rainbow. Gertie found it all quite breathtaking.

A giant palace of white stone and ornate columns stood tall and majestic. To the right and left of the palace were separate buildings, as tall, but not as wide or deep. The main palace of white stone was gilded and surrounded by a halo of gold. Rainbow steps led up to it.

"In here," the captain said as he climbed the rainbow steps.

Gertie and the others followed. The vampires closed their umbrellas before following Prometheus inside.

Inside the great hall, the blue sky—or *a* blue sky—hovered over them, and rays of magical sunlight shined down onto the marble floor.

"It feels amazing to stand in daylight without fear of being harmed," Taavi said beside her with tears streaming down his cheeks.

Gertie noticed the other vampires were weeping, too.

The massive hall held a circle of thrones along its perimeter, some of which were occupied by shining deities. They talked among one another. As Prometheus led Gertie and the others into the middle of them, the other gods grew silent.

Gertie, whose hands trembled with both fear and excitement, wanted to go down on her knees, but, instead, she bowed at the gods as she passed them. She recognized Aphrodite, the goddess of love, and Artemis, the goddess of the hunt. She recognized Hector's father, Hephaestus, the god of the forge, and Apollo, the god of music, healing, and prophecy. Beside Apollo, wearing adamantine cuffs, sat Hermes, chained to his throne. And beside him, in the adamantine cage from the *Tarantula*, sat Athena.

From one of the rooms leading from the great hall, more goddesses appeared. Gertie recognized Persephone, Demeter, and Hecate. From a door opposite them, Poseidon emerged. He took a seat on a throne next to Apollo.

Then Hades entered from behind Gertie and the vampires.

From her cage, Athena said, "Are we all here?"

One more goddess flew from the front of the hall to the back and took a seat on a throne near Athena's cage.

"We are now," the goddess said.

"Thank you, Hestia," Athena said.

Prometheus approached the cage. "It pains me to see you like this, Athena. The vampires have a gift for you and the other gods, before we begin, if you will allow it."

Athena narrowed her beautiful gray eyes as she studied the group of vampires. "Please tell me their gift is the key to my prison."

"I'm afraid it is not."

"How disappointing. Fine. I'll allow it."

Taavi dropped Gertie's hand and left her side to join the vampires in two rows of three.

At that moment, Ares entered with Penelope and Bach. They wore no chains or cuffs, and their wounds from the battle on the *Tarantula* had healed.

Gertie watched the glances exchanged between the vampires beside her and the two on the other side of the room. She suspected they were speaking to one another telepathically.

"May they be allowed to join our choir?" Del asked Prometheus.

Prometheus turned to Athena, who nodded.

Penelope and Bach joined the ranks of the others. Sophia was sobbing so much and so hard that Gertie wasn't sure how she would manage to sing.

Alastair took a deep breath and sang:

Listen, you who live in the deep-forested Mount Helikon,

The other voices joined on the second line:

Loud-thundering Zeus's fair daughters, come with songs

To celebrate Apollo of the golden-brown hair,

Who over the twin peaks of Mount Parnassus,

Accompanied by Delphic maidens,
Comes to the flowing Castalian spring
As he visits his mountain oracle.

Behold, Greece with its great city of Athens at prayer,
And dwellers on the unconquered land of the armed goddess Athena;
Where on the holy altars Hephaestus forges his blades;
And together with the smoke, Arabian incense rises to the heavens.
And the shrill, howling Aeolus weaves a melody with fluttering notes,
And the sweet-voiced Muses blend with the song of praise
At the delicate feet of Aphrodite.

Come to this twin-peaked slope of Parnassus,
Dancers are welcome to dance,
And singers are invited to sing.
Pierian Goddesses who dwell on the snow-swept crags of Mount Helikon,
Sing in honor of Pythian Apollo,
The master archer and musician,
Whom Leto bore, after his beloved sister, Artemis,
Beloved for both her beauty and her mastery,
Equal to his on the bow.

Come to us, Apollo of Delphi, and make our song ever sweeter,
Let us behold your golden-brown curls and silver arrows
And hear the true tenor of your masterful voice.
Lay your healing hands over us,
The hands that once slain the mighty Python
And defeated an army of marauding Gauls.
Oh, beautiful mistress of the Cretan bow,
We beseech you and your beloved brother,
Together with gray-eyed and glorious Athena,
*To protect Athens and Delphi as you have for so long.*****

Gertie watched Taavi with deep admiration as he sang his lovely baritone voice in harmony with the others. She glanced around the room at the gods on their thrones and at those gods standing beside her, finding their expressions mirrored her own. Even Jinsoo seemed moved by the vampires' voices. By the time the song was over, Athena's face had softened. Only Poseidon had continued to frown.

She wished the song had praised Poseidon. Maybe he'd be smiling now, too.

Apollo stood from his throne. "That was beautiful."

"A wonderful tribute to my brother," Artemis added.

"Your song is greatly appreciated by this court," Athena said as Apollo took his seat, "and properly sets the tone of our assembly, the purpose of which is to determine the innocence or guilt of you and your leader, Hermes, who stand accused of murder and piracy," Athena said. "Hermes? Do you have anything to say on your behalf and on behalf of these vampires?"

Hermes stood from his throne, pulling his chains taut. "Indeed, I do."

Hestie held tightly to Poros's hand as Hermes addressed the council on Mount Olympus. Wishing her parents were there, she sighed and said a prayer to them for comfort. They weren't on the council, so they were probably busy picking up the slack left behind by the gods who *were* present.

As she prayed to her parents, Hestie was distracted by Hecate, whose eyes were tightly shut and whose palms were facing up.

Look at Hecate, Poros. Hestie said telepathically. *Is she performing a spell? What is she doing?*

I don't know. How curious.

"As you know, I am the god of thievery *and* trade," Hermes said. "As such, I keep tabs on every kind of transaction you can imagine, all over the world. Some of these transactions are mutually beneficial, and some are not. Some of these transactions are fair and just, and others are not. In my judgment of them, I abide by no manmade law, but only this: does the transaction uplift or degrade humanity?"

"That seems rather subjective, if you ask me," Poseidon said.

"No one asked you," Hades said.

"Allow Hermes to continue with no more interruptions," Athena said.

"Thank you, Athena," Hermes said. Then, shooting a look of irritation at Poseidon, he said, "As I was saying, long ago, I recruited these vampires, and others whom we've lost along the way, to aid me in my governance over human thievery and trade. As I don't have the gift of disintegration, and therefore can only be in one place at any given time, I trained my lieutenants to carry out my orders on the seven seas. I have other helpers managing the railroads, while I attend to the air."

Fascinating, Hestie said telepathically to Poros.

I wonder if his other helpers are also vampires, Poros said.

Let's not forget to ask him.

"This isn't the first time Poseidon and I have bumped heads over actions being taken on the seas," Hermes said. "I try to be respectful of his position, but my efforts are, unfortunately, not reciprocated."

"I object," Poseidon said.

"You'll have your turn to speak," Athena said to Poseidon. To Hermes, she said, "Can you get to the main point?"

Ouch. Two points for Athena, Poros said.

Your sister holds nothing back.

Hermes blushed and cleared his throat. "Poseidon is interfering with my duty as god of commerce. His values and goals are different from mine, which puts us at odds with one another. The only way I've managed to have any control is to undermine him."

"So, you admit it!" Poseidon bellowed.

"Please!" Athena shouted at Poseidon. To Hermes, she asked, "Anything more?"

"Two more things: Poseidon is behind a powerful and corrupt shipping company known as Sailfish Trading and Shipping, which has become a monopoly and is responsible for human trafficking as well as smuggling stolen goods."

The other gods in the hall gasped.

Poseidon leapt to his feet. "How dare you!"

Ignoring Poseidon, Athena asked, "And your second point?"

Poseidon grumbled to himself as he took his seat.

"The mortal Mina Huang's death was an unfortunate accident," Hermes said. "My lieutenant believed she was acting in self-defense against a powerful god. I beg the court to find her innocent of murder. Please consider what she and the other vampires did to save the Pakistani boys. Please also consider their own loss—five friends who were like family to them."

Hermes sat down.

"Thank you, Hermes," Athena said. "Now, let's hear from Poseidon."

"It's about time," Poseidon grumbled.

Hestie glanced at Poros. *Here we go.*

No kidding.

Poseidon stood. "Hermes's main complaint against my shipping company is the redistribution of art and cultural artifacts of peoples who have been colonized, occupied, or otherwise oppressed."

"Along with human trafficking and downright smuggling," Hermes said.

"You had your turn," Athena said to Hermes. "You'll have another opportunity for a rebuttal." To Poseidon, she said, "Please continue."

"To the victors go the spoils," Poseidon said. "That's how it's always been. Even Achilles, beloved hero of our people, understood this when he made his case to Agamemnon to have Briseis, his war prize and concubine, returned to him. No one would begrudge that right to Achilles, would they?"

"Perhaps the Trojans would have," Hermes muttered.

"Nonsense!" Poseidon bellowed. "It's the way of the world!"

"Slavery was once the way of the world," Hades said, "but very few modern civilizations support it."

"You can't compare commerce to slavery," Poseidon argued.

"You're the one that used Briseis as an example of a war prize," Hermes said.

"And it was a ship from your fleet that was smuggling the Pakistani boys," Hades added.

"Silence!" Athena shouted. "Poseidon has the floor. The rest of you must keep your thoughts to yourselves until it is your turn to speak."

Poseidon took a deep breath and clenched his fists at his sides. "Do some of the people working for STS bend to corruption? Yes. Could I do more to prevent it? Yes, I admit that. But I do not condone illegal behavior. I merely wish to see order on the seven seas, which I accomplish by controlling the major shipping fleets. Hermes's tactics, by his own admission, undermine my efforts and create disorder and even *fear* on my seas. For this reason, he and his vampires should be punished. Hermes should be stripped of his powers for six months, and the vampires should be destroyed."

Hestie gasped. The faces of the vampires looked even paler than before.

The council wouldn't agree to destroy them, would they? Hestie asked Poros.

Let's hope not.

Poseidon returned to his seat.

"Who else wishes to speak on this matter?" Athena asked.

Jinsoo raised a shaky hand.

"You there," Athena said. "What is it you wish to say?"

Jinsoo pointed his shaking finger at Del. "She murdered my sister. Poros was going to make us gods. That vampire should be killed for what she did."

Hestie shot a worried look at Hermie, who returned her gaze with his mouth hanging open.

"Do you have anything else to add?" Athena asked.

"I-I have to go to the bathroom," Jinsoo said.

Hestie turned to him and whispered, "Why didn't you go before we left?"

"I was afraid you would leave me behind."

Hecate crossed the room and took Jinsoo by the hand. "This way."

Once Hecate and Jinsoo—along with Chidori—were behind closed doors, Athena asked, "Are there others who wish to speak?"

"I have something to say," Prometheus said.

"Then please do," Athena said with a nod.

"Although it's true that a vampire killed Mina Huang, who was beloved to me and my crew, I have come to agree with Hermes in seeing her death as an accidental tragedy. Her brother, Jinsoo, is not wrong to want justice, but I'm afraid it is vengeance he seeks. As you know, I cannot abide vengeance. That should be reserved for the Furies in Tartarus."

Athena's cheeks grew red.

Ouch. That's one for Captain, Poros said.

Hestie raised her brows. *That one should be worth two points.*

"The vampires have suffered enough by the loss of their friends. As Hermes said, Kagan, Chloe, Farouck, Cade, and Edric were more like family than friends to this group, having been together since ancient times in a choir formed as orphans. I should add that their songs were in praise of the Olympians. Furthermore, their current actions have been performed in service to Hermes. If these actions are to be judged by this council as wrongful, it is Hermes, and not his servants, who should pay the price."

"And do you find the actions of Hermes and his lieutenants to be wrongful?" Athena asked.

"I do not," Prometheus said.

Another score for Captain, Poros said.

I wonder if your sister will still want to be with him after this.

Even if she does, I doubt Captain will want to be with her, Poros said.

"Is there no one who'll speak on the side of reason?" Poseidon, red-faced, asked the council.

"I have something to say," Hades said.

Poseidon groaned.

Hermie thrust his hand in his trouser pocket and fingered the key to Athena's cage. Worried that Athena would be angry to discover how long he'd had it in his possession without telling anyone, he said a quick prayer to Hades:

Please don't tell, but I have the key to Athena's cage. I'll give it to you if you help Hermes and the vampires.

Jinsoo returned with Chidori to stand beside Hermie.

"Are you okay?" Hermie whispered to Jinsoo.

"I heard what Captain said. He betrayed me and Mina."

Prometheus gave Jinsoo a solemn glance before putting a finger to his own lips to indicate silence.

Hades walked to the center of the room, where he stood between Prometheus's group and Athena's cage. "I want to remind the council that our elected leader made a unilateral decision to attack the *Tarantula*, ignoring our newly instated democratic process. Our leader also executed a vampire without due process and was the cause of the deaths of two others."

Athena's face paled.

Hermie glanced at Del. *Hades knows how to shake things up.*

I cannot disagree, Del said. *Let us hope he proves to be an ally.*

Hades picked at his beard and paced between the cage and Prometheus. "I was originally going to recommend that we strip Athena of her office and of her powers for at least six months, but then the leadership position would revert to me, and I don't want it."

"So, what do you propose?" Athena asked gruffly.

"This court should find that Hermes was acting as the god of thievery and commerce and should be found not guilty of any wrongdoing, even though his position puts him at odds with another deity."

Thank you, Hades, Hermie said.

"Hear, hear!" Artemis shouted.

Poseidon narrowed his turquoise eyes at the goddess of the hunt. "This is an outrage!"

"Are you finished, Hades?" Athena asked.

"Not quite. As to our leader, I recommend that this court grant clemency for her crimes in light of the suffering she has already endured as a prisoner in this adamantine cage."

"Hear, hear!" Hephaestus cried.

"Anything else?" Athena asked in a less gruff and more contrite tone.

"I have one last recommendation. Although the general piracy performed by these vampires falls on the shoulders of Hermes, I cannot believe that he ordered the attack on the *Marcella II.*"

Hades? What are you doing? Hermie, overcome with a bad feeling, asked.

"If Hermes did order the attack, then he should be stripped of his powers for six months and made to work on a pig farm," Hades said. "If Hermes did not order the attack, then the vampires should be taken into custody and given the choice to serve as my reapers or face execution because, accident or not, they are responsible for the death of an innocent child."

Gertie covered her mouth.

The vampires glanced nervously at one another.

"Yes!" Jinsoo cried.

When Hermie gave his friend a look of admonishment, Jinsoo moved away, to stand beside Hestie.

We have our answer, Del said to Hermie. *Hades is no ally. He only wishes to use us.*

I told him about the key! Hermie said. *I need to get out of here before he and the other gods force me to give it up. It's my only leverage to help you.*

Why do you wish to help me? she asked.

It made him angry that he wanted to help her. It made him angry that he cared. *I don't know.*

"Hermes?" Athena asked. "Did you give the order?"

With sadness on his face, the god of thievery and commerce replied, "I did not, but they were trying to protect their mission."

"Would anyone else care to speak?" Athena asked.

Gertie raised her hand. "These vampires are good people trying to make a difference in the world. Their freedom shouldn't be stripped away because of one bad decision."

"What about Mina's freedom?" Jinsoo cried.

"Silence!" Athena shouted. "Is the council ready to reach a decision?"

"Let's get this over with," Poseidon said. "It's gone on long enough."

Del stepped forward. "I, alone, killed Mina Huang. Release the others and punish me."

Everyone in the great hall turned their eyes on Del. Hermie felt the urge to protect her, but he resisted taking any action as the faces around him gaped with a mixture of shock and admiration for this one vampire.

"Would that satisfy you, Hades?"

The god of the Underworld nodded.

"Poseidon?" Athena asked.

The god of the sea shrugged.

Athena straightened her back. "All council members in favor of re-solving this matter by placing the vampire responsible for Mina's death into the custody of Hades, to serve or to be executed, please say 'aye.'"

The hall resounded with aye.

"All council members opposed?" Athena asked.

Only Apollo and Artemis objected.

"So be it," Athena said.

No longer able to resist the urge to protect her, Hermie reached over and grabbed Del's arm before he god-traveled them out of Mount Olympus to the cave of the moon goddess, Selene. Then, to avoid being traced, he took her to the depths of the sea beneath the *Marcella II* be-fore ending their journey in the Minotaur's labyrinth on the island of Crete.

Once Del found her footing, she turned to Hermie. "Ugh. Sea water in the hair?"

"Are you really complaining about *how* I saved you?"

"A little."

"We can't afford for them to track us."

She wrung out her hair. "What now?"

"I don't know. Let me think."

CHAPTER NINETEEN

Fugitives

Hestie blinked. Had her brother really disappeared with Del?

I don't know how to feel, she said to Poros.

This is not good, he said. *Look at my sister's face.*

"Track them!" Athena shouted at no one in particular. "And get me out of this stupid cage!"

Hades did nothing.

Ares flew from his throne. "I'll get Phobos and Deimos to hunt them down."

"The Furies and Hypnos can help," Hades offered.

Ares disappeared.

Hermie? Hestie prayed to her brother. *Be careful. They're coming for you.*

"Hermie isn't answering me," Poros whispered.

"Me either."

She turned to Hades. "How could you do this?"

He frowned before turning his back on her. *Trust me. I know what I'm doing.*

Jinsoo, whose eyes were filled with angry tears, asked Hestie, "Why would Hermie do this? I thought he loved my sister. I guess I was wrong."

"He did love Mina," Hestie said.

"He's standing up for what he believes in," Poros said. "What I believe in, too."

"How can you say that, Poros? I thought we were friends."

"We *are* friends. But punishing Del for something she never meant to do won't bring Mina back."

"No," Jinsoo said. "But it will make me feel better."

"No, it won't," Hestie said. "You think it will, but it won't."

"How do you know?"

"I just do."

"Station guards at the gates, in case Hermie tries to return," Poseidon said to Athena.

"Nike and Nemesis!" Athena cried. "Join the seasons at the gates!"

"Where do you think they went?" Gertie whispered to Hestie and Poros.

"I wish I knew," Hestie said.

"Hold the others hostage until we get our prisoner back!" Poseidon demanded.

Artemis and Apollo flew across the hall to stand near Hestie and the others.

"Can someone get me out of these cuffs?" Hermes shouted.

"Athena, is this really necessary?" Prometheus said angrily.

This shocked Hestie, who had never seen Prometheus raise his voice before.

"The boy is guilty of treason," Athena growled. "Find him and the vampire and bring them here!"

"You know as well as I that Hermie has good intentions," Prometheus said.

"I'm tired of hearing about intentions," Athena said through gritted teeth. "People must be held accountable for the consequences of their actions, no matter their intentions."

My sister is a hypocrite, Poros said to Hestie. *What about the consequences of her actions? She's the reason Kagan, Chloe, and Edric are dead.*

Hestie squeezed Poros's hand and prayed to her parents, to Hades, and to Prometheus to please help Hermie. He hadn't meant to commit treason. He'd been trying to do what he thought was right, and she was proud of him.

Hermie heard his sister's prayers, but, before he could reply, a thundering roar came from the darkness around the corner, and the entire cave shook.

"What the hell?" Del flew off in the opposite direction.

Hermie raced after her. "Wait! Del! Hold up!"

Del whipped around a curve and came upon a fork. He followed her down the path to the right. "Stop, Del. Wait up! You'll get lost in here!" And then, as he continued to chase her, and as the Minotaur continued to chase *him*, he shouted, "Asterion, please! It's me! Hermie!"

The rumbling stopped.

Hermie caught up to Del and grabbed her ankle. "Wait! You're not in danger."

She glanced back at him. "Fine. Let go of my leg."

He released her ankle. "Asterion, I mean the Minotaur, is a friend of mine. You're safe."

The Minotaur caught up to them. He didn't look happy. Del crouched behind Hermie, ready to run.

"Why did you bring a vampire into my labyrinth?" Asterion asked in his deep, raspy voice.

"I need your help."

Hermie heard a fervent prayer from his mother, followed by another from his father.

Return to Mount Olympus, his mother said. *You're being accused of treason. Maybe if you go back with the vampire, they'll forgive you, or at least, show you leniency.*

The longer you stay away, the harder it will be for us to help you, his father said.

"What do you need?' Asterion asked.

"This is Del," Hermie said. "She's my…friend. The Olympian council wants to punish her for something she did in self-defense. Can you hide her here for me? I need to get back."

"What?" Del said with her mouth hanging open and her eyes wide with fear. "Hermie, please do not leave me here with this monster."

"I could say the same of you," Asterion said.

Hermie rubbed his eyes, feeling exhausted. He hadn't had good sleep in a long time. "Come on, Del. You should know better than to make snap judgments about people because of their appearance. Asterion is a friend, not a monster."

"Why should I help an ungrateful vampire?" Asterion asked.

"Do it for me. Please?"

"Why are you leaving?" Del asked. "What is the plan?"

Hermie pulled the key to Athena's cage from his trouser pocket and handed it to Del. "Keep this with you. I'm going to Mount Olympus to bargain for your freedom."

Hermie didn't wait for a reply. He god-traveled from the labyrinth back to the gates of Mount Olympus. When he arrived, Nike and Nemesis were waiting. He didn't fight them when they took him into their custody. He flew with them to the great hall, where the council was waiting.

I'm so glad you came back, Hestie said to him.

"Where's the vampire?" Athena demanded.

"I'll only tell you under certain conditions," Hermie managed to say calmly.

"How dare you try to bargain with the council!" Poseidon bellowed.

"What makes you think we would act according to your conditions?" Athena asked.

"Let the boy speak!" Hades shouted.

"I have the key to that cage," Hermie said.

What? Hestie prayed. *Did you find it? Or have you had it all along?*

Athena stood up and grabbed the adamantine bars. "Artemis, take the key from him and open this door."

"I don't have it on me," Hermie said before Artemis could react. "I have it hidden someplace safe."

Athena let go of the bars and took a step back. "Fine. Let us hear your conditions."

"In exchange for your freedom," Hermie said, "I want clemency for the vampires and me."

Thank you, Hermie, Alastair prayed.

Hermie received similar messages telepathically from the other vampires.

His sister said, *You rock. I didn't see this coming.*

"This is an outrage!" Poseidon shouted. "Will the crimes that took place on the *Marcella II* go unpunished?"

"Hermie, don't do this," Jinsoo said feebly.

"Perhaps Hecate could perform a location spell for both the key and the vampire," Hestia suggested.

Everyone turned to Hecate.

"I would need something that once belonged to Del," Hecate said. "Without it, my spell won't work."

Hermes stood up. "Accept his terms, Athena. The vampires may not have been acting under my direct orders when they attacked Prometheus's ship, but they were attempting to protect their overall mission. Poseidon has been trying to shut us down for months—decades, really. They felt threatened."

"Do not negotiate with a young god guilty of treason!" Poseidon said.

Athena glowered at the god of the sea. "Easy words to say when you're not the one in the cage."

Hermie raised his hand. "I didn't mean to commit treason, Athena. My act of civil disobedience was on the side of justice. I have witnessed you and other gods do the same. Please swear on the River Styx that this council will grant me and the vampires clemency, and I'll return with the key to your freedom."

Well played, Hades said directly into Hermie's mind.

Gertie clapped her hands when Athena and the council agreed to Hermie's terms. Athena and Poseidon glared at her.

Taavi took her into his arms and whispered, "What a relief."

Sophia embraced Penelope. Nearly every vampire there was in tears. Gertie was, too.

Hermie and Del returned with the key. The vampires huddled around Del in one big group hug. Gertie's heart was full of joy.

Once Athena was released from her cage, she sat on the double throne at the back of the hall, in the chair where Zeus once sat.

Gertie was surprised when Jinsoo stepped forward and said, "What about *my* justice? You said my sister's murderer would die."

"Jinsoo, please," Hermie said, catching up to him. "Don't ruin it."

"The boy is right to feel jilted," Athena said. "I have an idea."

Gertie squeezed Taavi's hand. The goddess wouldn't break her oath on the River Styx, but was there a loophole that none of them were aware of?

"My brother expressed his wishes to make you a god," Athena said to Jinsoo. "I know this won't bring back your sister or make up for her loss, but, as a god, you would have the ability to visit her in the Underworld as often as you wished."

Gertie noticed that Athena seemed much kinder now that she was out of her cage.

Jinsoo's brows disappeared beneath his black bangs. "Are you serious, goddess? I can become a god?"

"If the majority of the council will agree," Athena said, looking around.

Gertie noticed all but Poseidon nodding their assent.

To Athena, Gertie prayed, *What about me, goddess? Can I be made immortal, too?*

The goddess did not reply.

"Are you sure this is what you want?" Hestie asked Jinsoo.

The boy nodded enthusiastically. Chidori, perched on his shoulder, tweeted cheerfully.

Poros stepped forward while Athena gave Jinsoo a golden goblet.

"Take a drink of ambrosia," Athena said. "It will aid the process of apotheosis."

"Are you sure?" Hermie asked his friend.

With trembling hands, Jinsoo took the goblet from Athena and put it to his lips. He drank the ambrosia. Gertie watched on with envy as Poros then lifted his arms and turned into a ball of light.

Gertie closed her eyes but could still see Poros emblazoned on her lids. She heard Chidori chirp excitedly as the brilliance from Poros was mirrored by Jinsoo. Squinting against the light, Gertie was amazed by Jinsoo's transformation. He became larger, thicker, brighter, and more beautiful.

Poros dimmed himself and told Jinsoo to do the same. Finally, Gertie was able to open her eyes completely.

"You will need to discover your purpose," Athena said. "You have three months. If you do not declare what you intend to be the god of, your mortality will return."

Jinsoo bowed to Athena. "Thank you, goddess."

Then Jinsoo turned to face the vampires. Gertie did not like the look on Jinsoo's face. As he pointed a finger at Del, Gertie instinctively put herself between them. Something hit her hard in the chest. She fell to the marble floor, unable to breathe.

"Apollo!" Prometheus cried. "Help her!"

"Oh no!" Jinsoo cried. He bent over Gertie, where she lay on the marble floor. "I'm sorry! Please don't die!"

Gertie couldn't speak. She tried and tried to suck in air, but none came.

"Her lungs are damaged in too many places," Apollo said. "I don't know if I can heal her in time."

"Out of the way!" Taavi cried.

Jinsoo backed away as Taavi leaned over her and pierced her neck with his fangs. She felt the temporary paralysis overtake her body, but that was soon replaced by the most euphoric feeling in the world. Yet, she still could not breathe.

She closed her eyes, unsure if the virus had entered her system in time to save her. She prayed to the gods to help her, but, in the end, when the air finally came into her lungs, it was a vampire who had saved her.

CHAPTER TWENTY

The Underworld

As Hestie followed her father and Jinsoo onto Charon's skiff, Poros asked Hestie, "Did you ever ask Hecate what she was doing during the council meeting? Was she performing a spell?"

Charon lifted his white bushy brows but said nothing. Bald with frail, wrinkled skin, he stood thin and hunched, looking more like an elderly man than a god.

Hermie boarded the boat. "What are you talking about, Poros?"

Hestie turned to her brother. "When Hermes was making his speech to the council, Hecate had her eyes closed and her palms lifted."

Charon dragged his long, slender pole through the Acheron River.

"Whoa!" Jinsoo cried, pointing at the three-headed dog that guarded the gates of the Underworld. "Is that Cerberus?"

"Haven't you seen him before?" Hestie's father, Thanatos, asked.

"No, dude. Can I pet him?"

Chidori squawked.

"He wouldn't eat you, girl." Jinsoo turned to Hestie's dad. "Would he?"

Hestie, Poros, and Hermie laughed.

"He might," her father said.

"Achi-wawa, never mind!" Jinsoo stroked Chidori's feathers.

The giant black iron gates groaned as they opened. Cerberus looked down at them with his three tongues hanging out.

"He seems to be happy to see us," Thanatos said.

"Hi, boy!" Hermie cried.

"I wish we would have thought to bring him cakes," Hestie muttered.

Poros handed her a cupcake. "As a matter of fact."

"Smart thinking!" Hestie said as she took the cake.

It almost looked too pretty to eat with its swirling white frosting and pink sprinkles atop an extra-large yellow cake.

"Jinsoo should have the honors." Hermie said.

"Hermie's right." She handed the cake over.

"Thanks!" Jinsoo said with a smile that cracked his face in half.

The gates had already closed behind them when Jinsoo lobbed the cupcake through the air. It was instantly snatched and swallowed by Cerberus, who wagged his tail with glee.

The teens and Thanatos laughed. Even the corners of Charon's mouth twitched into the slightest of grins.

Hestie waved to the three judges who hovered above the river of fire in the House of Judgment, where the souls were told if they were destined to go to Tartarus, Erebus, or the Elysian Fields. The judges did not wave back.

Charon turned the skiff from the Acheron down the Lethe River—the river of forgetfulness—past Erebus, to the Fields of Elysium. Hestie could see the souls frolicking in the flowers in the distance. Some flew kites, others tossed a ball, and still others danced, or read books, or sang songs. Her parents had explained that the souls experienced a shared illusion. The Lethe River had wiped them clean of memories, and they spent eternity in delusional bliss.

"We'll get off here," her father said to Charon.

Charon brought the boat to a stop on the bank of the fields.

As Hestie and the others climbed out, Charon said in a low, gravelly voice, "Don't make a fuss over what you saw Hecate doing at the council meeting. She adores Hermes and was giving him the full support of her magic as he spoke."

Hestie glanced at her father, who seemed just as shocked as she—shocked to hear that Charon could, in fact, speak, and shocked that he cared enough about Hecate to speak on her behalf.

"Thank you, Charon," Hestie's father said. "I'm sure the children will do as you ask."

Hestie didn't like being called a child, but she nodded obediently, as did the others.

When all had climbed ashore, Charon pushed off with his long slender pole and continued down the Lethe River.

"This way," Hestie's father said.

Because Jinsoo was a natural at flying and had mastered it on his first day of lessons, they flew rather than walked across the fields. There were billions of souls, and the fields seemed to stretch on forever. How would they possibly find Mina?

As if he had read her mind, her father said, "Allow your soul to reach out to the soul of your loved one. Souls who are connected in life find their way to one another here, even if they have no memory of one another."

"Mina won't remember me at all?" Jinsoo asked.

"We talked about this, Jinsoo," Hermie said.

"Not even a little?" Jinsoo asked.

"I'm afraid not," Hestie's father said. "But your soul will guide you to her, as hers will to you."

"Look!" Hestie recognized her grandparents—her mother's mother and father. "It's Grandma Lynn and Grandpa Ger!"

Hermie followed her as she raced through the fields toward them and into their arms. Although they did not know who she was, they seemed to recognize that she was important to them—Hermie, too.

Then Jinsoo cried, "My mother and father! They're with Mina over there!"

Jinsoo flew over the fields to reunite with his family.

Hestie turned to see Poros looking forlorn beside her father. His bright gray eyes were hooded, and his mouth formed a straight line. Did he miss his parents?

I'm okay, he said to her telepathically. *But thanks for worrying about me.*

I will always worry about you, she said.

He smiled. *I know.*

Although Hermie would have liked to spend more time with Mina and his grandparents in the Elysian Fields, he was happy to see his mother and his childhood pets in the rooms they shared with his father. He and Hestie had rooms of their own down the hall, so if they ever wished to leave Prometheus's ship, they always had a home here.

Hermie had planned to come home for good. He was tired of the sea. But then he met Del. The attraction he felt for her still made him angry. He hated his inability to control his emotions. Hestie had always been the emotional one in the family. Now it was Hermie who felt completely at the mercy of feelings he wished he did not feel.

The idea of never seeing Del again was almost too much to bear.

They sat in couches around a hearth, where the fire from the Phlegethon River gathered into a pool of flames.

"It's good of Prometheus to allow the vampires to stay until Hermes can have another ship built," Hermie's father said.

"They were super happy about that," Hestie said. "They showered with real soap and shampoo for the first time in ages."

"And washed their clothes," Hermie added.

"Captain said we'll take them shopping in a few days when we go back to Malta, to sell Hestie's coins," Poros pointed out.

"We're taking the vampires shopping?" Jinsoo complained.

"Don't start," Hermie said to his friend.

"Can I get you anything to drink?" his mother offered.

"Do you have some of that ambrosia?" Jinsoo asked.

"I do. Would you like some?"

"Do fish swim?" Jinsoo said with a grin.

"Actually," Hermie began. "Not all fish swim."

"Don't start," Jinsoo teased.

Hermie wasn't amused when everyone laughed.

"Did you notice that Gertie was even worse than you, Hermie?" Hestie said with a laugh.

"What do you mean?" he asked as his mother handed them goblets filled with the drink of the gods.

Poros laughed and shook his head.

"Tell me," Hermie insisted.

"Dude," Jinsoo began. "She is a bigger know-it-all than you."

Everyone but Hermie laughed. He drank his ambrosia without comment.

"But she was more annoying," Hestie said—as a concession, he supposed, though he still wasn't amused.

Hermie lifted his finger. "I wasn't going to tell you this, but I heard her tell Hector that she thinks you're shallow and materialistic."

Boom, he said telepathically to Jinsoo, who hid his grin with his hand.

"What?" Hestie jumped to her feet.

"Sit down, Hestie," her mother said. "It's only one person's opinion, and she doesn't even know you."

"Your mom's right," Poros said, as he took Hestie's hand and pulled her back down onto the couch beside him.

"Did you see the three-hundred-dollar sneakers she wore?" Jinsoo said before he took a drink from his goblet. "Mmm. This so good."

"Better than kimchi?" Hermie asked with a laugh.

"Just a little," Jinsoo teased.

"Morpheus said Gertie drives a Porsche," Hestie said. "He saw it when he took her home last week."

"Sounds like *she's* the materialistic one," Poros said.

Hestie shrugged. "It doesn't matter."

Hermie could tell that his sister was bothered by what Gertie had said, and now he regretted telling her. "She doesn't know you. You're the least shallow and materialistic person I know."

"Hear, hear," his father said.

Hestie's face brightened. Hermie rarely paid her a compliment. He supposed he should do it more often—as long as it didn't go to her head.

Then Hermie said, "Mom and Dad, why do you think Grandpa—Hades, I mean—threw the vampires under the bus at the council meeting?"

"You heard about that, right?" Hestie asked them.

"I was wondering the same thing," Poros said.

"You need to learn to trust my father more," Thanatos said. "His plan was to get the vampires into his custody only to set them free."

Hermie's jaw dropped open. "Seriously? So, I basically ruined his plan."

"You didn't ruin anything," his mother said.

His father added, "Hades was proud of you for standing up for justice."

"It all worked out in the end." His mother reached over and patted him on the head.

"Jinsoo?" Hermie asked. "Are you okay with how things turned out?"

"I'll get used to it," he said. "And I already know what my purpose is."

"Really?" Hestie straightened her back.

Hermie moved to the end of his seat. "What is it?"

"Well, Poseidon takes care of the sea and everything in it, right?"

They all nodded.

"And Hermes uses the vampires to help landlubbers get their art and stuff back, right?"

"So?" Poros asked.

"Who looks out for the sailors?" Jinsoo said. "Poseidon should, but he doesn't—not really. I want to make sure the vampires and other pirates like them don't mistreat sailors. I don't want what happened to my sister to happen to anybody else."

"Jinsoo, congratulations, buddy," Thanatos said. "That sounds like an excellent idea."

"Captain will be so proud," Poros said.

"You'll need to return to Mount Olympus to declare yourself," Therese said. "I'm sure Poseidon will have a few things to say."

Hermie clapped his friend on the back. "I'm happy for you, man."

Jinso grinned. "You mean *god*, not *man*."

Everyone laughed.

"You still won't beat me at *Urban Fighter*," Hermie teased.

"We will see about that," Jinsoo said.

Gertie lay in her bed in her parents' mansion in Athens, curled beneath her covers with her ereader. She was trying to finish *Interview with a Vampire*, even though she had read it before. However, she found herself unable to focus. Checking the time on her phone, she decided it wasn't too late to call Nikita.

"Hey!" Nikita said when she answered her phone. "I miss you, girlfriend! You promised we'd have lunch this week!"

"I know," Gertie said. "We will. I promise."

"How about tomorrow, after my theater class?" Nikita asked.

"Okay. Our usual place?"

"You don't have to come to campus. We can meet someplace else."

"That's okay. I want to."

"Then it's a date. Can we talk *then*? We're in the middle of a show."

Gertie's stomach tightened as tears pricked her eyes. "You and Lajos?"

"Yeah."

"And Hector?"

"Yeah. I'm sorry."

"It's okay. I'm the one who asked. I'll see you tomorrow. Tell the guys I said hello."

"Will do."

Gertie hung up and rolled onto her back. Why did life have to suck so often?

She reached over for the bottle of melatonin on her nightstand and, after swallowing some down, prayed to Hypnos to bring her sleep. She turned off her lamp and her ereader and used deep-breathing exercises to empty her mind of thoughts about Hector.

When Gertie next opened her eyes, she found herself lying on the deck of a massive ship. It was freezing, and she couldn't stop shivering. She climbed to her feet and glanced around, recognizing the type of vessel it was from her research. It was a bulk carrier, designed for transporting grain, and it was moving fast across the sea. What was she doing here?

The deck, which took up most of what must have been a three-hundred-yard-long carrier, consisted of five giant bins that were each about a hundred feet wide and a hundred feet long. In between each of these enormous bins stood what appeared to be cranes dusted with snow. There were four of them towering as high as a mast but without sails. The arms of the cranes were roped together, so as not to move during transport, she supposed. A flybridge appeared at the back of the ship over a two-story enclosed salon and probably cabins. Was that where the crew members were?

She decided to head in that direction, to find out if someone could tell her what was going on. As she neared the flybridge, the writing on the flag waving from a mast at the stern became visible: Sailfish Trading and Shipping.

Why did that sound familiar?

Before she reached the entrance to the salon, two men wearing gloves and thick coats emerged and brushed past her.

"Excuse me?" she called.

They stopped and turned in her direction but seemed unable to see her.

"Did you hear that?" one sailor said to the other. "It sounded like a woman's voice."

The other one laughed and shook his head. "You've been away from land too long, bro'. That was just the wind."

Gertie realized she was dreaming. Armed with this new understanding, she followed the men.

"Do we really need to check every hold?" the one who thought he'd heard Gertie speak asked the other.

"You can bet the captain is watching, bro'."

"So, that's a yes."

"You're damn right it's a yes."

Gertie followed them to the bow of the carrier, where the two men opened the hatch to reveal a bin full of maze. But as one of the men used a gloved hand to move some of the grain around, a nuclear warhead appeared.

"Looks like she's still intact," the sailor said. "Can you believe this shit? A ballistic missile straight from Russia."

"And where are we taking it?"

"*It?* Bro', there's one in each hold. All five are going to some private buyer in Syria."

"You're shitting me."

"I shit you not. Come on."

The sailor closed the hatch and led them to the next, where a second missile was buried in the grain.

"They aren't paying us enough for this shit," the first guy said.

"Bro', we're lucky they're paying us at all, with what we know." Then he laughed. "A lot of good money will do us when these suckers blow."

Gertie hoped this wasn't a prophetic dream. She closed her eyes and prayed to Morpheus to tell her that the vision was coming through the gates of ivory.

When she opened her eyes, Gertie was back in her own bed in her own room in Athens, and the god of dreams was gazing down at her.

"We've got a problem," he said.

CHAPTER TWENTY-ONE

Malta

As much as Hestie enjoyed her visit with her family in the Underworld, she was glad to be back on the *Marcella II* and headed for the island of Malta.

By the time they reached the port, dusk had fallen, which was good, because the vampires were bored and ready to shop.

But, first things first: Hermie wanted to eat a delicious dinner. So, they went to a restaurant not far from the docks, where a waiter and waitress pulled a few tables together, and they sat down and opened menus.

"We have not been to a restaurant in years," Taavi said.

"I wouldn't think so, since you don't like food," Hermie said.

"But we love wine," Del pointed out.

"Then let's order some," the captain said as he flagged down a waitress.

After the waitress left with their drink order, Raimo asked the captain, "Are you set on selling those ancient Persian darics to that collector you know?"

Prometheus cocked his head to the side. He seemed to be reading his menu when he said, "Would it help you to know that my collector friend is Persian?"

"It would, if it is true," Raimo said.

"Is it?" Alastair asked.

"Professor Jamshid Gharib is as Persian as they come," the captain said. "He lives on crunchy rice with lima beans and loves to laugh."

"Crunchy rice sounds delicious," Hestie said. "I may have to order that for dinner."

"No nachos?" Poros asked with an arched brow.

"Not this time," Hestie said. "I hope you don't mind."

"I suppose we're strong enough to withstand the loss of what was once the cornerstone of our relationship," he teased.

Hestie threw her head back and laughed. "You're hilarious, Poros."

The waitress returned with a bottle of wine and thirteen glasses.

"I get to drink, too, Captain?" Jinsoo asked when he was handed a glass.

"Of course," the captain said. Then he whispered, "Now that you're a god."

Jinsoo smiled gaily as he put the glass to his lips. The face of disgust he made after tasting it had Hestie in stitches.

"I don't think wine is for me," Jinsoo said.

After they gave the waitress their order, the Captain said, "I think it's important that we make a distinction between cultural artifacts that are confiscated by an oppressive regime and those that are found at the bottom of the sea."

Raimo lifted his brows. "But the reason they're at the bottom of the sea is because the owner was fleeing from an oppressive regime."

Prometheus scratched his beard. "Let me think about that. You see, I need a way to produce an income for the medical supplies and technology we provide to the villages in the Sudan, Ethiopia, and other areas of Africa. We also deliver to a few places in India, Vietnam, and Korea."

"It's important work," Poros said.

"I'm sure it is," Alastair said before taking a sip of his wine.

"How long before the vampires leave our ship, Captain?" Jinsoo asked.

"Jinsoo, don't be rude," Hestie said.

She noticed Hermie glance across the table at Del for the hundredth time and wondered what was up with that. Was he developing a thing for her?

"We're waiting on Hermes to find another ship for us," Alastair explained.

Jinsoo screwed up his face. "Why can't Hermes make a ship by snapping fingers?"

"He can," Prometheus said, "but he won't. The gods avoid taking shortcuts because it's better for the human race if we purchase goods and services provided by people—that's why we're shopping for clothes and supplies rather than magically producing them."

Jinsoo nodded. "Oh, I see."

"Speaking of shopping," Hestie said, "I can't wait for you to see the fab styles they have at the supermarket here—of all places!"

Saying the words made Hestie think of Mina. She pulled out her phone and watched her most recent episode of *Hestie's Style,* so she could see her friend's sweet face again.

Jinsoo, who sat beside her, leaned close to watch it, too.

"We should make another video," Jinsoo said. "You could dedicate it to Mina."

Hestie wiped her eyes. "I love that idea."

Hermie enjoyed watching Del and her friends comb the racks for clothes in the supermarket. Hestie seemed even more excited than they because they cared about her opinion.

Del was always beautiful, but now that her long hair smelled clean, like shampoo, and her clothes were fresh, she was even more beautiful to him. He found himself staring at her way too often, especially when she came out of the dressing room in a short dress with thin straps.

"Wow," he said, gaping.

Del blushed.

Note to self, Hermie said. *Vampires can blush. And it's supremely beautiful when it happens.*

Del gave him a sideways glance. Had she heard his thoughts?

It was a little embarrassing, when Hestie took Del before a mirror, and only Hestie's reflection stared back at them.

Hermie felt a new peace wash over him when Jinsoo said to Del, "That dress looks sweet on you."

Del glanced across the racks at Hermie with a look of pleasant surprise on her face.

What would he do once she and her friends left the *Marcella II*? Would he ever see her again?

That depends on you, she said.

This gave Hermie an idea. He left the clothing racks to search for Prometheus and Poros in the grocery aisles.

"Captain," Hermie said when he caught up to them. "How would you feel about helping the vampires with their mission? Maybe they could help us with ours?"

Prometheus grinned. "I had a feeling someone would make this request of me."

"Does that mean you've considered it?" Poros asked.

"I thought about offering to help out, until they have another ship," Prometheus asked. "Is this something the vampires want?"

Hermie shrugged. "I could ask them."

"Let me give it some more thought. Don't say anything to them yet."

As Hermie returned to the clothing racks to watch Del and the others shop, a feeling of joy bloomed in his chest.

Gertie rushed around her room, packing. She was both excited and scared to be returning to the *Marcella II* with Morpheus, who sat on the edge of her bed picking his fingernails.

"That's almost everything," she said, as she shoved a few more shirts into her suitcase.

Her phone rang. She was about to dismiss the call when she saw it was from Hector.

"I have to take this," she said to Morpheus. "He hasn't called me in days."

He gave her a nod and went back to picking his nails.

"Hector?"

"Hey, Gertie. Do you have a minute?"

She really didn't. Morpheus was anxious to go, and she still hadn't found her other pair of sneakers. "Yeah. What's up?"

"I'm miserable. I miss you so much. I think I made a terrible mistake."

Gertie's jaw nearly hit the floor, but his timing couldn't be worse. "Oh, Hector. I'm so happy to hear that, but…"

"But what?"

Gertie took a deep breath. "Morpheus is here. He's about to take me back to the ship."

"Really? Why?"

"I had another dream."

"I wish I could come with you," Hector said.

"But I thought you needed time to figure things out," Gertie said as she searched for that second pair of sneakers.

"That's the thing," he said. "I think I have."

"Really?" she asked. "Tell me."

"I want to write music," he said. "You were right. It's what I was meant to do. In the two weeks since I've been back, I've written four songs—lyrics and musical composition. I'm back in the groove, and it feels good. It feels right."

"I'm so happy for you, Hector! That's so awesome. But why would you want to come with me on the ship? How would that be good for your music?"

"I miss you," he said.

Gertie closed her eyes and took a deep breath. "I think you need to stay, Hector. You need to keep working on your music. I'll be back as soon as I can."

Morpheus stood up. "We need to go, Gertie."

"I need to go, Hector. I'm so sorry."

"I love you, Gertie."

"I love you, too."

When they returned to the docks in Malta, Hermie was surprised to find his cousin Morpheus waiting for them in the salon with Gertie.

"What's going on?" Prometheus asked.

"Nice digs," Morpheus said to the vampires.

"What's up, Morpheus?" Hermie asked.

"Gertie had another dream from the gates of horn," Morpheus said. "You're all going to want to hear this."

"You should probably sit down," Gertie said.

Everyone but the captain took a seat on the couches while Gertie relayed her dream.

"Ballistic missiles?" Hermie repeated after Gertie had finished.

"With nuclear warheads," Gertie said.

"We need to inform Lord Hermes," Alastair said.

"Do you have any idea when this shipment is supposed to be made?" Del asked.

"There was snow on the carrier," Gertie said. "It can't have been anytime soon, right?"

"Could be as early as mid-October," Prometheus said.

"We need to prepare," Del said.

"We need Lord Hermes," Mahdi said.

The unexpected appearance of Hermes caused everyone in the room to flinch.

"Did someone call?" he asked.

Gertie relayed her dream to him.

"When will our boat be ready?" Raimo asked.

Hermes scratched his beard. "About that…I've run into a few difficulties."

"You're welcome to stay aboard as long as you need," Prometheus said. "My crew and I are prepared to help you in your missions, if you're willing to help us in ours."

"First things first," Hermes said. "Your crew needs to train."

"You'll find them to be excellent sailors," the captain said.

"Not as sailors," Hermes said. "They need to be trained as pirates."

THE END

Thank you for reading my story. If you enjoyed it, please consider leaving a review. Reviews help other readers to find my books, which helps me.

Please visit my website at www.evapohler.com to get the next book, *Pirate Academy*. The first chapter appears below.

The Code

As much as Hestie wanted to help save the world, she'd been hoping for a longer reprieve.

She sat beside Poros in the salon of the *Marcella II* marveling over how good everyone looked. They'd just finished shopping in Malta, and all of them—even the vampires—were sporting new digs. The stores had carried the newest back-to-school styles. Hestie had found a gray romper and wore it with a matching wide-brimmed hat. Beside her, Poros looked sharp in a white t-shirt with an unbuttoned blue plaid shirt and jeans, which brought out the gray in his remarkable eyes.

She wasn't sure she trusted Gertrude Morgan. To Hestie, the girl was an attention whore, who, for all Hestie knew, may have invented the prophetic dream just so she could return to the center of drama.

Alastair lifted his brows at her. *Morpheus confirmed her vision.*

Stay out of my head, she said to him telepathically.

You are broadcasting your thoughts to every vampire here.

Hestie glanced at the other vampires. Their eyes avoided hers. She nervously twirled a strand of her long, red hair with a finger and wished she knew how to keep her thoughts to herself.

We do, too, Raimo said without speaking.

Morpheus stretched his silver wings. "I'm headed to Mount Olympus now to inform the others."

"Thank you, Morpheus," Hermes said before the winged god of dreams disappeared.

Prometheus, their captain, turned to Hermes. "When do you want to begin?"

"Immediately," Hermes said.

"No offense, Uncle Hermes," Hestie said. "But my brother and I have been training since we were kids, and so has Poros. Maybe you should focus on the *mortal.*"

Alastair shot her another look, and Taavi, who'd become extra friendly with Gertie, frowned.

Hestie hadn't meant to sound snobby, especially since Jinsoo, the newest god in the pantheon, was also inexperienced. Yet, it wouldn't hurt Gertie to be taken down a notch. Hestie hadn't imagined there could be a bigger and more annoying know-it-all than her brother, but she'd been wrong.

You are angry at her for saying that you are shallow and materialistic, Taavi said to Hestie telepathically. *But she did not know you then.*

She doesn't know me now, Hestie shot back.

Gertie's face had reddened. "I fought in the vampire wars. I may not be as skilled as you, but I'm no rookie."

Prometheus patted Gertie's shoulder. "I don't think Hestie meant to imply otherwise."

Hestie had been about to insist that she *had* meant to imply otherwise when Poros squeezed her hand and said to her telepathically, *Is something bothering you?*

Before she could answer, Hermes moved to the center of the salon and, pacing, said, "I think you misunderstood me, Hestie. When I said you need to train, I wasn't talking about sailing, and I wasn't talking about fighting. In fact, my V-Team avoids fighting as much as possible."

Hestie's brother put his finger in the air, as if to speak, but before he could, Gertie said, "Thievery is the art of invisibility."

"Which *you* don't have," Hestie muttered.

Gertie scoffed. "I didn't mean *literal* invisibility."

"Can you two let our lord do the talking?" Del suggested, as she combed her long black hair from her beautiful bronze face.

"Thank you, Del," Hermes said. "That's a great idea! Why didn't I think of it?" Then, sarcasm rant over, he added, "First things first. You need to learn the code."

"I'm relieved to hear you have one," Prometheus said. "Because there are some things I won't abide on my ship."

Hermes scratched his dark curly beard. It looked almost identical to Prometheus's.

"Why don't you hear us out, Captain?" Hermes suggested. "Then, if you want to add anything, we'll hear *you* out."

Prometheus nodded.

"So that you don't have to listen to the drone of my voice," Hermes said, "I'd like each of my pirates to call out one of the rules in our code, one at a time. Who's first?"

The others turned to Del and Alastair since they were their leaders—after Hermes.

Del, who looked extra-stylish in her short dress with thin straps, spoke first: "Rule One: Only steal from greedy thieves."

"That's right," Hermes said. "Those who steal to survive are off limits."

Hestie bit her lip. The pirates' definition of "thieves" was a little vague. The vampire pirates took her ancient Persian coins, coins that *she found* at the bottom of the sea, because they believed the coins weren't rightfully hers—that they belonged to Persians. But *she* found them. What about finders, keepers?

Then Alastair, looking spiffy in his Marvel t-shirt and light gray vest with skinny black jeans, licked his pouty lips and said, "Rule Two: Land first, sea last."

"Exactly," Hermes said with a nod. "Transactions at sea are much more dangerous than those at port. Whenever possible, we follow the greedy thieves to land and, after they've left ship, we take the stolen goods."

"Hey," Jinsoo said. "That's what you did to us, when you took Chidori and the coins."

Chidori, perched on Jinsoo's shoulder, hid her beak in his hair.

The vampires turned a shade paler.

Even Mahdi, whose skin was as dark as the night sky, seemed to pale with mortification at the mention of the pirates' attack on the *Marcella II*. He cleared his throat and said, "Rule Three: Avoid confrontations."

Hermes nodded again. "Better to slink and hide than to fight."

Hermie cocked his head to the side. "A rule often broken?"

"Only when threatened," Del said coldly.

Hestie glanced at her brother. The sting of Mina's death had hurt him most, after Jinsoo. She wondered if he'd ever be able to forgive Del, even though everyone there but Jinsoo understood why she had done it.

Raimo's voice brought her from her reverie. "Rule Four: Scout and plan."

"Absolutely," Hermes said. "Avoid spontaneity and rash behavior. Always be smart and a step ahead of your victims."

Hestie blanched at the word *victims*. She hated the idea of becoming a *victimizer*. Not for the first time, she wondered if joining the pirates was the right move, even if they avoided people whom they considered innocents. Didn't stealing from thieves put you on their level? As much as she wanted to stop Sailfish Trading and Shipping from delivering the warheads to their buyer in Syria, the rest of it still seemed fishy.

Pun intended? Alastair asked telepathically.

What pun?

Sailfish, fishy?

Hestie grinned. Leave it to Alastair to lighten the mood.

You are welcome, he said. *And I will grant that* target *is a better word than* victim.

"Rule Five: No modern weapons," Bach said. "Only blades."

Poros turned to Prometheus. "That's a relief."

"Keep in mind that our targets usually have them," Raimo pointed out.

"Then why do you have this rule?" Gertie asked.

"As a precaution," Del explained.

"That's exactly right," Hermes said. "My vampire pirates are gifted, as are you and Prometheus's crew of young gods. But our targets are generally mortal, and it wouldn't be prudent to carry such weapons around those so vulnerable."

"*Generally* mortal? Hermie asked.

"Occasionally the gods get involved," Penny said. "You saw how it was when the *Tarantula* was destroyed."

"And Penny and I were taken prisoner," Bach added.

Penny and Bach exchanged glances in a way that made Hestie wonder if something had happened while they'd been detained on Mount Olympus. Was there more to their story?

As if in response to her thoughts, the faces of both vampires turned a light shade of pink—a vampire's blush, Hestie supposed.

"Sometimes you gods forget that we lost people, too," Penny said.

Hestie thought about Kagan, Farouch, Chloe, Edric, and Cade. The vampires had known one another—had been a family—for centuries. She could only imagine how hard it had been to lose almost half of their family members in one day.

Alastair glanced at her with moist eyes.

"The loss of loved ones should be all the more reason for working together," Prometheus said. "Right now, we need to focus on finding those warheads, before they end up in the wrong hands."

"If they're being sold to a buyer in Syria," Hermes said, "I would guess my brother Ares knows about it."

"He may even be the one orchestrating the sale," Prometheus pointed out.

"So, as always, we proceed with caution," Del said.

Despite her reservations, Hestie was glad she was there to help fight against corruption. When she'd first been transformed from a demigod to a god, she'd been shocked to learn that not all the Olympians were fair and just. It had been heartbreaking to watch the entire pantheon at odds with one another. She had been equally dismayed at the Olympians' destruction of the *Tarantula*. Even Athena, whom Hestie had admired most, had been a disappointment. Hestie wanted nothing more than to liberate people around the world, to fight against oppression. Bringing medicine and technology to those in need had been one step. Finding the warheads would be another.

"Rule Six: If forced to fight, fight to wound, not to kill," Penny said. "And before you mention our attack on this vessel *again*, we didn't kill Prometheus until we realized he was a god and would come back. We thought the same was true of Mina."

"Right," Hermes said. "We are *not* in the business of killing."

Hestie glanced at Jinsoo, who frowned.

"Rule Seven: Avoid taking prisoners," Sophia said. "Unless they are gods trying to kill you."

"We weren't trying to *kill* you," Poros said.

"Well, *I* was," Hermie said sheepishly.

"But that was *after* they took me and Poros," Hestie said.

Penny climbed to her feet. "Dude, you were trespassing on our ship."

"After you stole Chidori!" Jinsoo cried.

Hermes lifted his arms. "Enough. You all need to get over the past and focus on the present. There's a lot at stake."

"Sorry, Hermes," Poros said. "We're ready to listen."

Gertie stood up. "Rule One: Only steal from greedy thieves. Rule Two: Land first, sea last. Rule Three: Avoid confrontations. Rule Four: Scout and plan. Rule Five: No modern weapons—only blades. Rule Six: If forced to fight, fight to wound, not to kill. Rule Seven: Avoid taking prisoners. Is that everything?"

"Show off," Hestie murmured.

Gertie's face reddened as she sat back down.

"No," Taavi said with a grin, apparently impressed with his new girl-friend. "There's one more: Rule Eight: Be an expert at basic trickery."

"And that's where we'll begin," Hermes said. "I suggest you go to port and allow my team to demonstrate some basic schemes. Then try your hand at a few. Don't return to the ship until each one of you has stolen something without being detected. But do give whatever is taken back to its rightful owner. Tonight is for practice and nothing else."

"Aren't you joining us?" Hermie asked.

"I've got things to do and places to go," the god of thievery replied. "But call if you need me."

Hermes vanished.

"Is this really necessary?" Hermie asked Del as he followed her and the others from the salon. "I don't see how lessons in trickery will help us to steal the warheads."

"You might be surprised," Alastair said as he walked past.

Hermie flew in front of Del, forcing her to stop and to face him. When her dark eyes finally met his, he felt unnerved.

Before she could break away, he said, "I'm sorry I asked if the rule to avoid confrontations was often broken. It was insensitive of me."

Del shrugged and moved past him. "No worries."

Although she sounded sincere, there was something about her demeanor that made him feel as though she were angry with him. Why was she acting so coldly toward him? And why did it pain him so deeply?

Let it go, she said in his mind.

He followed her from the ship to the dock. *Let what go?*

She didn't answer. Instead, she picked up speed, making her way to the front of the group, where Prometheus, Poros, and Hestie were leading the way.

Hermie quickened his pace, nearly knocking Taavi into the sea.

"Sorry, man," Hermie said to the vampire.

Taavi shrugged. "It is nothing."

Hermie had never felt this way about anyone before, and he needed to pursue it, to find out where it would lead.

As Hermie was about to catch up to Del, Alastair grabbed him by the arm. "Leave it for now, my friend."

Hermie studied the vampire. "Do you know what's eating her?"

"We all do," Alastair said. "And she will tell you, when she is ready."

Hermie followed the others from the docks, nearly suffocated by his misery.

Jinsoo walked beside him with Chidori perched on a finger. "Where are we going, Captain?"

"There's a café I know a few blocks ahead," Prometheus called from the front of their group. "It's a popular area, especially at night."

Instead of heading inland, they walked along the marina toward the island point, where there was a plaza with a fountain surrounded by bars and cafés. When they reached The Black Pearl, they sat at round metal tables on the patio, splitting into three groups, but close enough to one another that even the mortal would hear what any one of them might say. Hermie and Jinsoo sat with Penny and Sophia. Hermie had tried to sit with Del, but the chairs around her table had been filled before he had reached them.

"I have questions," Hermie said.

Penny, who was round and busty with her curly brown hair tied high on her head, leaned forward, exposing her cleavage. "Shoot."

They were interrupted by a waiter, who took their drink order.

Once he'd gone, Hermie asked, "How do you define a thief?"

"Oh, I want to hear this," his sister called from the table next to his, where she sat with Poros, Del, Alastair, and Bach.

Hermie's back was to Del. He was glad that, if they weren't going to be at the same table, at least they were close to one another. It gave him pleasure and pain in equal measure.

"We could all stand some clarification," Prometheus said from the table on the opposite side of Hermie, where he sat with Gertie, Taavi, Raimo, and Mahdi.

The other vampires looked at Del and Alastair.

"I will take a stab at this," Alastair said.

Then, instead of speaking aloud, he said to them telepathically: *A thief exploits a weakness in others for his or her own gain. Rather than earn, the thief takes.*

Del's voice soon followed Alastair's: *And while smugglers are not always thieves, if what they are smuggling is a person, or a dangerous weapon, or cultural artifacts stolen or previously stolen by someone else, we consider them thieves, too.*

Then Bach added: *Greedy capitalists are also thieves.*

"Hold on," Gertie said. "The line is getting blurry."

Hermie had been about to say the same thing. Although he admired the vampires' concern for the disenfranchised, he worried they crossed an important ethical line.

"Well, Bach is a bit of a communist," Alastair explained.

Bach put a fist in the air. "Marx was a genius."

Hermie lifted a finger. "Smart, hard-working capitalists who build wealth are not thieves."

Del's voice startled him from behind. "But those who build wealth on the backs of the oppressed are."

Her words seethed through her teeth. Hermie liked what she had to say—in fact, he was impressed by it—but the way she had said it hurt him. He felt as if she were driving a knife into his heart.

"And how can we know the difference?" Hestie asked.

"Research," Gertie answered. She turned to the vampires. "Am I right?"

The waiter returned with their drinks, delivered them, and left.

"This is a very interesting conversation," Prometheus said with a grin. To Poros, he added, "I wonder what your sister would say about building wealth."

Poros shrugged. "Who knows?"

"Athena would support the builders," Hestie said. "And sometimes capitalists are the builders."

"And sometimes the builders are in a sweat shop," Del said curtly.

"Amen," Bach said, lifting his fist into the air again.

Hermie couldn't resist a glance back at Del, for a chance to read her face. Why was she so angry? Was her anger directed at him? If so, what had he done to deserve it?

Alastair's voice came into Hermie's head again as the lessons continued. *Let us begin with a simple scheme. The best way to rob someone is with two parties. One party creates the distraction while the other steals the goods.*

Del added: *The two best distractions are violence and sex.*

Hermie's mouth fell open.

Penny laughed. "The expression on your face, dude."

"Hermie never had sex," Jinsoo said, matter-of-factly.

"Shut up. Neither have you, bro'," Hermie said, fighting the blush crossing his cheeks.

I did not mean actual sex, Del said.

She meant a flirtation, Taavi said, *usually with the target.*

Del, we should demonstrate on the man sitting by himself across the plaza, Mahdi said. *See him?*

Yes.

"I have another question," Gertie said. "You're vampires. Why not use your power of invisibility?"

"Shh," Penny warned. "No need to tell the entire island of Malta."

Gertie lowered her voice. "Sorry."

"We *do* use it," Taavi said.

"Even so," Raimo said, "a distraction makes the target less likely to notice us. Invisibility is not foolproof. We can still be heard and felt."

"And smelled," Bach said with a laugh. "Some of us smell worse than others."

Hermie relished the soft chuckle from Del behind him. It was the first hint of laughter from her all day.

"Do not speak ill of the dead," Sophia chastised.

"Kagan liked to be teased," Bach insisted.

"As you may already know, Gertie," Taavi said, "vampires cannot make their clothes invisible."

Gertie nodded. "The vampires I used to know never wore them. They created an illusion of clothing for mortal eyes. Why don't you do that? Wouldn't it be easier to use your power of invisibility without clothing?"

"Indeed, it would," Alastair said. "But the wind on the sea can be beastly to our skin."

"The cold does not bother us," Taavi said. "But the wind constantly tickles, like flies."

"If there are no more questions," Mahdi said as he climbed to his feet, "Del and I will demonstrate."

Del stood up and walked around the plaza. Along the way, she plucked a few flowers from the raised borders of the cobblestone path. Hermie's breath caught at the graceful yet strong silhouette Del made in the dark night. Her long curly hair begged him to touch it. Her stunning figure made him forget why they were there. But most of all, it was her deep black eyes that haunted him.

Then Mahdi sauntered to the other side of the fountain and sat at a table not far from the target. Like Taavi, Mahdi was charismatic and a bit of a clown. As he sat down, he gave a grin and a thumbs up toward Hermie and their group, causing Penny to roll her eyes. Hermie watched as Del approached the table, where the man was sitting beneath the dim lights of the patio cover.

Del tripped and fell to her knees, dropping the flowers on the ground. Hermie resisted the instinct to help her.

"Oh, no!" she cried, rushing to collect the flowers before the wind could sweep them away.

The target jumped to his feet and scooped as many of the flowers as he could from the ground.

"Thank you, sir!" Del said in a pleasant voice and with a charming smile. "Am I silly to want them so much? They are for my mother's grave. They remind me of her, you see. Do you speak English?"

"No, I mean, yes, I speak English. And no, I don't think you're silly. I think you're sweet."

"Thank you, sir, but it is you who are sweet, for helping me."

Mahdi moved in from behind and bumped against the distracted target.

"Excuse me, sir," Mahdi said before he continued across the plaza.

Once he'd passed the fountain and was returning to their group, Mahdi stuck his front teeth out, grinned, and did a little dance.

Penny rolled her eyes again.

Alastair said telepathically: *Notice how Mahdi made physical contact with the target? If the object to be stolen is* on *the target, firm pressure must be applied to the body so the object can be lifted without being felt by the target.*

Del put one of her lovely hands on the stranger's shoulder. "Thank you again for helping me."

"Would you like to join me for a drink?"

Hermie did not like the way the stranger was looking at Del. Seeing the man's attraction, his earnest desire for Del, made Hermie check himself. He had to control his feelings. He was acting insane.

Then Hermie noticed that Mahdi had left the stranger's wallet behind on the pavement near Del's feet.

"Oh, sir. Is this your wallet?" Del asked.

"Huh? Um, yes! It must have fallen when I stooped to pick up the flowers."

"I think we are even, are we not?"

The target frowned. "I believe I am in your debt, miss. How about a drink?"

"I must go, sir. Thank you, anyway."

When Del returned to her seat, she said to Hermie, "Your turn."

CHAPTER TWO

Fails

When it was Gertie's turn to participate in a practice scheme in the plaza on the island of Malta, she felt at a distinct disadvantage, being a mortal among vampires and gods. She'd been feeling especially self-conscious, ever since Hestie had called her out for being the only one in need of training.

Plus, she was cold, having forgotten her jacket, though she wasn't about to complain. She hadn't eaten dinner, either, but she'd rather starve than appear weak before the others.

If only Taavi could be persuaded to drink from her. The thought of the extreme euphoria that swept through someone who'd been fed upon made Gertie's mouth water—as if she could taste the vampire virus on her tongue. After the euphoria, the strength would follow, along with speed, x-ray vision, and mind powers. Best of all, with the vampire virus, you could fly and make yourself invisible to mortal eyes. Gertie longed for that.

"You and Taavi create the distraction," Alastair said to her. "Fight or kiss—your choice. And Hestie, you be the thief this time."

Gertie clenched her fists. If she screwed this up, it wouldn't help Hestie's opinion of her. No pressure.

She glanced at the captain, who seemed amused by the pirate training as he enjoyed his beer.

He lifted his mug and said, "Good luck."

"When will it be the captain's turn?" Gertie asked Taavi.

"Never," Prometheus said. "Never, ever, ever will I go by the name of pirate, no matter the cause. But cheers to you." He lifted his mug again.

Their group had moved down the plaza from The Black Pearl to The Galley Bar and Restaurant, so they could work on new targets without arousing suspicion. Their newest target was a middle-aged woman sitting alone at a table across the street, where she sipped from a glass of wine and gazed at the dark, shimmering sea.

Follow my lead, Taavi said to Gertie with a wink as he took her by the hand.

For a split second, he reminded her of Jeno.

As they crossed the street together, Gertie said, "I like your new clothes."

"Thanks."

He was wearing a gray t-shirt with a black leather vest and black jeans.

Taavi stopped near the deck, not far from where the target was sitting, and stood close to Gertie. His body was long and lean, and he took Gertie into his arms and gazed down at her with his golden eyes from beneath dark, thick brows. His dark, wavy hair blew in the wind. She had her hair tied in a ponytail at the nape of her neck. When Taavi smiled, a single dimple appeared in his left cheek.

I am going to kiss you, okay? Then you slap me and call me a terrible name. Pretend you do not appreciate my advances. He winked again. *Of course, you and I know otherwise.*

Gertie chuckled. *This should be fun.*

Gingerly, Taavi caressed her bottom lip with his. Then he pressed his mouth firmly against hers as he pulled her into a tighter embrace. Gertie lost herself. She hadn't been kissed like this, with so much longing and so much hunger, in such a long time. Part of her knew that Taavi was acting, but another part of her hoped that he wasn't.

Still dazed moments after the kissing had stopped, Gertie looked up at Taavi, bewildered. Where she had previously been drawn to him by the prospect of his bite, she was finding herself longing for more.

He grinned. *Any moment now, you can slap me.*

"Oh," she whispered, snapping out of it.

Remember to be dramatic, he added.

"Um, okay."

He lunged for her again, his mouth covering hers. Her body shivered with pleasure. She didn't want it to end.

He pulled away, laughing. "Gertie! Concentrate!"

She slapped his cheek so hard that it stung her hand. "Leave me alone!"

Taavi took a step back, looking shocked by the blow.

"How dare you!" Gertie added. "You, you…" she couldn't think of a bad name to call him.

He pulled her toward him, and she tried to fight him off, but when he pressed his lips against hers again and circled his arms around her waist, she kissed back. Before she knew it, she had grabbed fistfuls of his hair.

The others are watching, he said.

Again, she snapped out of it and slapped his cheek. She glanced at the target and noticed the woman was walking away from her table, her purse in hand, and leaving the bar altogether.

"Did Hestie have a chance to…"

"No," Taavi said.

Hestie flung her head back in frustration. It had finally been her turn to be the thief, and Gertie and Taavi had blown it for her.

Earlier in the evening, she had enjoyed playing the distraction with Poros, as Hermie had made the steal. Poros had pretended to propose, and everyone in the plaza had applauded when she'd pretended to accept. Hermie had had no problem slipping the purse from the back of the chair of his target.

It had been fun to pretend that she and Poros were getting married. It had made her wonder if that could be their future.

She'd also laughed with delight when it was Jinsoo and Chidori's chance to distract as Poros stole. The yellow canary had fluttered above Jinsoo and had pegged him with peanuts. Jinsoo had pretended to be annoyed, crying "Stop that, you crazy bird!" The people in the plaza had been in stitches while Poros had lifted the wallet from his laughing target.

Then they'd moved down to another outdoor café, where Hermie and Mahdi had staged a brawl while Jinsoo stole bags from three targets sharing the same table.

After each success, the crew had toasted to the victors, who were high on adrenaline, before the spoils were inconspicuously returned to the targets. Hestie had been itching to play the thief.

Now, she returned to her table, where Poros rubbed her back and said, "There will be other chances."

"I know. I thought I had it. I was so close."

When Gertie and Taavi caught up to them, Hestie asked, "What happened, guys?"

Gertie's face turned as red as a beet. "Sorry."

Taavi, in his usual happy-go-lucky way, said, "That target was ready to leave. We will get the next one."

Hestie nodded and lifted her glass of iced cola. "Cheers to that."

"I say we shake it out," Taavi said with a gleam in his eyes.

"What do you mean?" Hestie asked.

"It is something we do," Alastair said.

"We shake it out," Penny repeated.

"We should not waste time," Del objected.

"Oh, come on," Taavi insisted. "We need to regain our focus."

"I agree," Mahdi said. "This is an important part of our process. They should learn it."

"I want to learn it," Gertie said eagerly. "Please?"

Hestie found herself wanting to learn it, too, out of curiosity, if for no other reason.

Del shrugged.

Taavi's grin widened. "Good. So, this is what we do. All together, we clap twice," he clapped his hands together twice, "snap twice," he snapped his fingers twice, "and then one person in the group sings a word or phrase. Then we clap twice, snap twice, and the next person adds a word or phrase to the song."

"Huh?" Hermie asked.

"We make up a song," Alastair explained. "And if you cannot think of a word or phrase to go with the song when it is your turn, you are eliminated from the game."

"We should keep practicing our techniques," Del said.

"I want to play the game!" Jinsoo cried. "Please?"

"Please?" Gertie said, too.

Del shrugged. "Okay."

Taavi and Mahdi high-fived one another, and then Taavi led the group with two claps, two snaps, after which he sang, "My love."

Penny moaned. "It is always love with you."

Despite her objection, Penny and the group continued with the game. They clapped twice, snapped twice, and then Mahdi sang, "is like."

Hestie laughed as she watched each player struggle to come up with the next word or phrase in their made-up song. They had begun to attract the attention of others. A few people had gathered in the street to watch and to listen.

Hestie laughed gleefully when Jinsoo added a phrase about kimchi to the song. By the time it was her turn, the song had become a little convoluted, but she had known what her part would be from the very beginning. She sang, "Oooh, baby."

That makes no sense, her brother said to her telepathically, but the rest of the group was in near hysterics—even Del, who'd been moody all day.

Once they'd made it all the way around the group, ending with Gertie, they all sang the made-up song, claps and snaps included, in its entirety:

My love
Is like
The ocean
At night
Shimmering
Brightly
Like stars.
But kimchi
Is sour
Oooh, baby
Unlike
Our love
Will forever be.

Then they laughed so hard that Hestie thought she would pee in her pants.

Once they'd recovered, Del said it was time to move on.

Prometheus settled the bill, and then they strolled through the cool, windy night down a cobblestone path.

"That's a good spot," Penny said, pointing to a string of benches in front of Beans Café. "There are a handful of people dining across the street—not too few and not too many."

Porcs took Hestie's hand and led her to one of the benches.

"Hestie, try again," Alastair said as he raked a hand through his sandy-colored hair. Then he turned to Gertie and Taavi. "And you two distract. But this time, try fighting."

Hestie didn't think the mortal's cheeks could grow any redder, but they did.

Laughing, Taavi said, "No worries."

"Don't blow it for me this time," Hestie said to Gertie before she crossed the street.

Hestie lingered near a potted palm, inspecting its leaves, a few yards away from the target. She was startled when Gertie's voice rang out, loud and clear, over the patio.

"Who *was* she? Tell me her name, you cheating douchebag!"

Taavi backed away with his hands in the air. "Please. There is no one else but you."

"Liar!" Gertie cried. "I trusted you! I gave you my heart! And after a year of being together, you kiss the first pretty face that likes you in my absence! How dare you do this to me!"

As the target gawked at the spectacle Gertie was making in the street with Taavi, Hestie strolled through the tables where others were eating and drinking. The adrenaline coursed through her, exhilarating her as she snatched the purse from the chair beside her target and continued toward the street, in the opposite direction of Gertie and Taavi.

She wanted to shout with joy at her victory, but she hadn't gone far when someone approached her.

"Excuse me, miss?"

Hestie turned to see a man in uniform—a security guard.

"Yes, sir?" Hestie asked as her throat tightened.

"Does that bag belong to you?" he asked.

In less than a second, Alastair was at her side.

"May I help you, sir?" Alastair asked the guard.

"No. This is not your concern. I saw this woman take this bag…"

Hestie made the purse disappear. "What bag?"

The security guard gaped.

"Look here, sir." Alastair stared into the eyes of the guard, mesmerizing him. "You are mistaken."

The guard's face slackened. "Pardon me. Good night."

The security guard walked away, but the woman whose purse had been stolen was now approaching them from the restaurant.

Alastair mesmerized her before she could complain. Then Hestie used her powers to place the stolen purse on the chair where the target had been sitting.

The woman returned to her chair and, seeing the bag, glanced around, baffled.

Gertie and Taavi continued to argue, distracting the others seated on the patio. Hestie was grateful that at least their side of things had been a success, or she might have found herself in worse trouble.

A thief must never draw attention to herself, Alastair scolded as they returned to the others. *You should have removed your big hat before going in. Who wears a hat at night, anyway? You could have carried it and used it to conceal the purse.*

"Got it," she said. "I'll do better next time."

The trick is over, Taavi said to Gertie telepathically. *Stomp off angrily, toward the others, and I will meet up with you shortly.*

She was still reeling with anger. Nikita would have been proud of how well Gertie had played her part.

"I never want to see you again!" Gertie shouted before she turned away from Taavi and crossed the street to join the others on the benches in front of Beans Café.

Despite her Academy-award-worthy performance, Gertie was feeling dizzy, cold, and weak. When Taavi rejoined her a few moments later, she asked him, telepathically, *Please, take a drink from me. I hate being the weakest one here.*

I do not think that wise, he replied. *Perhaps you should ask another.*

She was about to ask Taavi what he meant but supposed she already knew: Their relationship was on the verge of becoming toxic. Her body had responded to him against her will, and it had angered her, because she wanted to be faithful to Hector. To make matters worse, she longed for Taavi's bite. Without a doubt, he longed for her blood.

Once they had rejoined the group, Raimo, whose dark stringy hair hung over his dark eyes, said, "We need to feed. We know a place across the sea in Sicily—a bar where the regulars know what we are and what we have to offer."

"Drink from *me*," Gertie said.

"There are eight of us," Del pointed out. "And we need more than a pint between us."

"We'll meet you back at the ship," Prometheus said to the vampires.

Gertie turned to Del. "Take me with you. Just drink enough from me to give me your powers."

"Come on, Gertie," Prometheus said. "You need food and sleep."

Hermie followed the captain and the others back to the ship, wondering where he'd gone wrong. He thought he'd had a connection with Del, but now she wasn't giving him the time of day. Maybe that's how vampires were. Maybe they were incapable of having deep feelings.

The *Marcella II* seemed empty without the vampires there. Jinsoo asked Hermie if he wanted to play *Urban Fighter*, but Hermie wasn't in the mood.

"I think I'll go to bed," Hermie said.

On the way to his cabin, he passed the vampire crates in the laundry room. Still troubled by Del's aloofness, he sat on her crate and decided to wait for her. Only a few minutes had passed, however, when he thought of a better idea: He would look for her in Sicily.

Not wanting to risk the scrutiny of the others, he told no one before god-traveling from the ship to the night sky. He stopped near the peak of Mount Etna, which towered from the east coast of Sicily, near where the Mediterranean reached the Ionian Sea. He scoured the land below, searching for his vampire friends. Compared to Malta, Sicily was an enormous island, its landscape teeming with people, even at night. Where should he begin?

As he hovered there beneath the stars, wondering what to do next, he sensed Selene not far above him, making her rounds in her silver, iridescent chariot. Her long, silver hair blew in the wind, as did her long, luminous robe. Her chariot was pulled by two silver horses with manes as long and iridescent as hers.

"Hello, Hermie!" she called from above.

"Hi, Selene!" He flew toward her and stroked the manes of her horses.

"What are you doing out here, all alone?" she asked him.

"Looking for my friends. They're, er, vampire pirates who work for Hermes."

The moon goddess smiled. "Hecate's friends. Yes, I know them."

"I don't suppose you noticed where they went tonight?" he asked, highly doubting that she had.

He was surprised when she said, "Of course, I did. What else have I to do alone in my chariot but to study the creatures of the night?"

Hermie's mouth dropped open "Really? Wow! Could you point me in their direction?"

"La Luna Rossa," she said. "The Red Moon. It's a pub in Syracuse, on the coast between The Musciara Resort and Hotel Sbarcadero. It's very old. That's why they like it. It's nearly as ancient as they."

"Thanks!" Hermie cried. "Have a nice night!"

"You, too, little god. Be careful."

Hermie flew through the windy night toward the coast of Syracuse, where the streetlights lit up the city, and music could be heard pouring from the bars and cafés and into the streets. The streets were filled with the sounds of people talking and laughing. He spotted La Luna Rossa not far from a marina filled with ships. Two men stepped from the pub and stumbled across a parking lot toward the docks. One of them was singing while the other laughed. They were passed by another man leaving the docks for the pub. La Luna Rossa appeared to be a popular place for sailors.

Hermie followed the sailor into the pub, where it was loud, smoky, and crowded, and scanned the dark room for the vampires. They weren't difficult to spot, because they were the most beautiful people there. Mahdi and Bach played pool with sailors, who, by the appearance of blood on their wrists, seemed to have been fed upon already. Penny and Sophia sat at a table with two men who had blood stains on their necks. Taavi stood near the jukebox with a blonde in his arms swaying to the slow music. His lips pressed against the woman's neck. Alastair sat alone at the bar, staring at Hermie with a quizzical brow. He'd probably noticed Hermie the moment he'd entered the establishment.

Hermie sat on the empty barstool beside Alastair. "Where's Del?"

"How did you find us?" Alastair asked.

"Does it matter?"

Alastair shrugged and pushed his sandy-colored hair from his eyes.

"Where's Del?" Hermie asked again.

"She went to the ladies' room."

"I didn't think vampires…"

"She went for a drink."

"Oh."

Hermie glanced around for the bathrooms and, after seeing a sign, followed it down a long, narrow corridor, where a man was standing against the wall outside of the ladies' room. Del emerged seconds later and immediately noticed Hermie. Instead of greeting him, she went into the arms of the stranger. He kissed her on the mouth. Hermie shuddered as Del kissed the stranger back.

Hermie didn't know what to do. He resisted the urge to pulverize the mortal. Should he return to the ship with his tail between his legs? No. He refused, no matter how awkward he felt.

Approaching them, he said, "Hello, Del."

"Who's this kid?" the man, probably in his mid-thirties, asked. He spoke Italian.

"No one, really," Del said with a laugh before she resumed kissing the stranger.

Hermie fumed. "Can't I have just a moment of your time? I came a long way to talk to you."

"You are interfering with my dinner," she said. "I promised Lorenzo that I would take him flying. Siete pronti, Lorenzo?"

"I'm always ready for you, Del," he said.

So, he wasn't a stranger, Hermie thought.

Go away, Hermie, Del said to him telepathically.

But, I don't understand. I thought we were…friends.

Friends? With, what did you call it? An animal magnetism? A chemistry?

Yes.

To Lorenzo, she said, "Un momento per favore."

She took a few steps toward Hermie, until they were so close that he could reach out and touch her long, curly hair, if he dared.

"You need to understand something," she said. "The sooner you get it, the better."

"I'm listening," Hermie said, feeling lost in her deep, dark eyes. Was she mesmerizing him? No. She had once told him that her powers only affected mortals, not gods.

"We are on a team with an important mission. There is no room for romantic entanglements."

"But, Del…"

"Besides, we both know it could never work. What happened to Mina—what I did to Mina—will always be between us."

Before Hermie could object, Del flew to Lorenzo with lightning speed and vanished from the corridor.

Hermie thought of following her, but, in the end, he returned to the *Marcella II.*

Author's Note

The *Vampires and Gods Series* is a crossover story. Characters from two of my other series—*The Underworld Saga* and *The Vampires of Athens*—join forces to face a common threat.

I tried to write this series so that it could be read before or after the other books. If you started with this book, you might like to read Gertie's origin story in *The Vampires of Athens* and Hermie and Hestie's origin story in *The Underworld Saga*.

The first book in *The Underworld Saga*, called *Thanatos*, can be found for free on my website at www.evapohler.com, when you sign up for my VIP list.

EVA POHLER

Eva Pohler is a *USA Today* bestselling author of over thirty novels in multiple genres, including mysteries, thrillers, and young adult paranormal romance based on Greek mythology. Her books have been described as "addictive" and "sure to thrill"—*Kirkus Reviews*.

To learn more about Eva and her books, and to sign up to hear about new releases, and sales, please visit her website at www.evapohler.com.